# FIRST CONTACT CUBE

# FIRST CONTACT CUBE

David Hiers

For more information on this
or other books by David Hiers,
Go to: **www.dhiers.com**




Copyright © 2015 by David Hiers
All rights reserved.
ISBN: 069240046X
ISBN-13: 978-0692400463

## Acknowledgements

I would like to thank Deborah and Catherine Deborah for their continued assistance, encouragement and patience throughout the creation of these books. Without their kind words, I would never have succeeded.

# PROLOGUE

Two ships winked into existence in the far reaches of the solar system. One-second they were part of two vast alien navies battling across this solar system and the next they were not. Thrown 65 million years into their future, they were alone, the fate of their respective species unknown. The only constant, the only familiar fact, was the other ship - their enemy. So rather than celebrate their survival or marvel that they had just proven their greatest theoretical physicists' theories about worm holes and time/space rifts, they did what they knew best, they continued their war.

Once again aliens visited Earth. But this time it was not by battling alien navies, it was by only two ships, the last two ships. The war continued, as wars do, until both sides were killed. The last survivors of both species died, but Earth survived the encounter. Indeed, most people on Earth never even knew the aliens had arrived, fought and died. Though they all knew about a nuclear explosion in China, mistakenly attributing it to terrorists.

Of the few people who knew the true facts of the encounter, only one person survived who had actually communicated with the aliens. His name was Mark Williams.

# CHAPTER 1

"Mr. Williams, we will be landing in Pensacola in ten minutes," the steward said, waking Mark from his sleep. Mark stretched. He waited a minute before raising his seat. It had been in full recline position, letting him sleep during the long flight in a passable bed. He was the sole passenger in a government owned G-5 jet, the same type used by corporate CEO's and movie stars.

'I could get used to traveling like this,' Mark thought, even though he knew he would never ride in one of these planes again. 'Better enjoy it while you can.' He got up and walked to the small lavatory to splash water in his face. He looked in the mirror. A fiftyish looking man with salt and pepper hair looked back. 'Tired,' he thought. He looked tired. But that was understandable. After all, he had just flown half-way around the world, having taken off from Guam with only one refueling stop somewhere in California. He ran his hand through his short hair, letting that pass for a combing. The steward came back into the cabin.

"We will be landing in just a minute. If you would please be seated and fasten your seatbelt," he said.

Mark complied and looked out the window as the plane descended.

"What time is it?" Mark asked.

"It is three p.m., Pensacola time."

"What day?" Mark was having trouble keeping track of the time changes.

"Thursday."

"Thank you."

Mark looked out the window trying to get his bearings. On his right shone the twinkling blue of the Gulf of Mexico. On his left a green vista spread out, mostly forest with some winding roads and blue rivers. He spotted the Intracoastal Waterway. Where were they? He studied the landscape beneath him. A river headed north from the Intracoastal. Could that be Wolf River? They were getting pretty low, so that would be about right. He would be landing at Naval Air Station Pensacola. The next landmark should be Perdido Bay. Yes. There it was. The plane banked. He spotted the Perdido bridge and looked out the opposite window to see Pensacola in the distance. Now they were coming down to the base. Fort Barrancas, an old civil war fort, passed beneath him. The plane touched down easily and after slowing, turned and headed for one of the hangers. Mark hoped Beth, his wife, would be there waiting for him. He was tired and wanted nothing more than to just go home.

"Welcome to Pensacola, Mr. Williams," the steward said as they taxied to a stop in front of one of the hangers.

"Thank you."

"Watch your head," the steward said as Mark walked up to the open door.

Mark did not have any luggage. He had left Pensacola a little over three weeks ago with little more than the clothes on his back and his passport and now was returning the same way.

But what an amazing three weeks! A clandestine trip to China with the CIA searching for alien artifacts, he had been caught up in an alien war and nearly killed. The aliens had killed three CIA agents in his team. The other two agents made it out of China just in time. Sergeant

Jeffreys, the Marine Sergeant who had accompanied Mark from the very beginning, was lying in a hospital with burns from an alien weapon. Fortunately, he would survive. Mark was the only civilian in the group.

Mark walked down the steps of the plane and stepped onto the tarmac. The familiar hot, humid, Florida air washed over him like a moist blanket. A sailor was waiting for him.

"Do you have any luggage, Sir?" he asked.

"No," Mark answered.

"Then come with me, please, Sir," the sailor said as he escorted Mark across the tarmac to the nearby building. He made it halfway to the building before a side door opened and a woman came running out. Mark was never so glad to see his wife. He ran to greet her. They embraced on the tarmac, while the sailor waited silently nearby.

"I was so worried," Beth said after a long hug. "And then when I heard about the explosion, I just knew you were dead."

"I made it," Mark said as Beth hugged him again.

This time when she finally let him go, she asked, "What happened?"

"Let's get to the car first," Mark said. Turning to the sailor, he asked, "Is there anything else you need before I leave?"

"No, Sir."

"Great." Turning back to Beth he said. "Let's go home."

Once they got to the car, Beth bombarded Mark with questions. "What happened? Were you right? Was it the blue-grays? Were you near the explosion?"

"One at a time," Mark said. "I'm sorry I couldn't give you any information when I called from Guam earlier, but they were pretty strict about censoring. But to answer your questions, I'm fine. It was the blue-grays.

And they are now gone. But start driving. All I want to do is go home. And tell me something first. I've been sequestered for the last couple days. What is the news reporting? What's the official version? Then I can tell you what really happened."

"The official word is that some terrorists tried to steal a nuclear bomb from the Chinese. The Chinese thwarted the plot, but in the process the bomb went off."

"Any word of U.S. involvement?"

"No, although the U.S. and the rest of the world are offering to help treat the fall-out. They say all the terrorists were killed in the explosion."

"How about aliens? Any mention of aliens?"

"Not a whisper. Not even the Enquirer."

"So they managed to keep that part secret again," Mark said.

"So there were no terrorists," Beth said.

"No. Not unless you call an alien a terrorist," Mark said. "Here's the condensed version of what happened. I was right. The call that I heard, the vision if you will, was sent by the blue-grays. It turned out to be a cube, a control cube, although we did not figure that out for a while."

"We?" Beth asked.

"I was set up with a team of CIA agents, who took me into China, which is where we thought the signal was coming from. We posed as tourists. Sergeant Jeffreys, the Marine who I met last year on the *U.S.S. Ronald Reagan*, he was there, too. Which was a good thing because he saved my butt a couple of times." Mark managed to avoid saying "life", no need to upset Beth anymore than he already had.

"I would like to meet this Sergeant Jeffreys and thank him for getting you home safe, again."

"We will have to arrange that," Mark agreed. "Right now he is in a hospital in Guam."

Beth looked over alarmed. "Oh no…"

"He's okay. Or he will be. A cat blasted him. It was a near miss. But he got some burns and banged up a bit. They say he will be fine. I talked with him before I left. He will be fine. He is one tough Marine."

"Thank heavens for that," Beth said.

"Yea. It was pretty scary. But I am getting ahead of myself. Where was I? Oh, yes. The blue-grays and the cats were still fighting their war against each other."

"I thought both alien ships were lost last year then the wormhole collapsed."

"They were," Mark said.

"Then how did they come back?"

"How? Oh, sorry. I forget that you haven't heard any of this yet. I've been debriefed so many times, I forget that you don't know."

"No, I have been stuck here in Pensacola for over three weeks wondering if you were alive or dead," Beth said.

"I know," Mark said. "Let me back up. Last year, two alien ships arrived in our solar system through a collapsing wormhole, one blue-gray and one cat."

"I know that. That was all last year," Beth said.

"Right. But what we did not know last year is that the two ships that came down and battled at the *Ronald Reagan* were not the same two ships."

"So more ships arrived?" Beth asked.

"No. The main blue-gray ship, I call it the mothership, sent down a smaller ship, which I refer to as a tender. That's the ship we saw on the *Ronald Reagan*. And the cat ship, the one that came through the wormhole, could divide into two independent ships. Two halves, if you will. One of those halves attacked the *Ronald Reagan*. Both the tender and the half of the cat ship were lost last year. But that still left the mothership and the other half of the cat ship out there in space and they were continuing their war. Of course the cats outgunned the blue-gray ship, so the blue-grays were trying to get a nuke to use against the cats. That's why they sent down control cubes."

"What is a control cube?" Beth interrupted.

"It looks a lot like the memory cube they sent to me last year. About two inches in diameter, although with more facets than the square memory cube."

"But what does it do?" Beth asked.

"Remember the memory cube gave me visions of past events, the blue-grays' history, their battle with the cats."

"Yes."

"Well, the control cube connects the same way, through your mind. But it takes over. It controls you."

"Controls you? How?"

"I don't know how. It's part of the blue-gray technology. They created control cubes to control species across the universe. They customized it for each species. In this case they sent control cubes down to China. The cubes sent out psychic signals, like a beacon, asking to be found. I guess I heard it because I have the right DNA. But others heard it also, anyone with the right DNA. Anyway, whoever finds it, once they touch it; they are controlled by the blue-grays. Not directly, but the blue-grays use it to plant a mission into the subject's mind.

"In this case the blue-grays wanted a nuke to use against the cats. They sent down the first control cube, which is the one that I heard. But someone beat us to it, a Chinese man. He found it just before we got there. But then a cat arrived and killed him and either took the control cube with him or destroyed it. We were lucky we weren't there, because the cat would have killed us too. As it was, the cat killed three of our group. Sergeant Jeffreys dragged me under a rock ledge and the cat went by without seeing us."

"You almost got killed by a cat? You didn't tell me."

"Sergeant Jeffreys saved me."

"I definitely need to meet him."

"Anyway, we thought that was the end of the mission and we started heading home," Mark continued. "But then the blue-grays sent down several more control cubes. I could hear them, but still did not know what they were. So we tried to find them also. When we found them we discovered they were control cubes."

"How? How did you know?" Beth asked.

"When I got near them, I could feel their power. Their call, if you will. It was almost overpowering. We had to destroy them before I succumbed and touched them."

"What would have happened if you touched them?"

"Then I would have been under the blue-grays' control. To make a long story short, the cats got to a couple of the cubes first and destroyed them. A Chinese Colonel who was in command of a Chinese nuclear artillery unit found the last cube. He came under the blue-gray's control. We did not know that at the time. All we knew was that someone with the cube was near a Chinese nuclear facility. We couldn't get near it, so we talked Washington into getting the Chinese involved. I actually got to speak to the President again. This is getting to be a habit."

"Well, don't let it go to your head," Beth said. "You still have to do the dishes."

Mark chuckled. "Yep. My fifteen minutes of fame are over. Actually, I don't even get fifteen minutes since it is all classified."

"Okay, finish your story. You got the Chinese involved."

"Yes. Before then we were trying to avoid the cats and the Chinese, which was getting pretty complicated." Mark neglected to tell Beth that he had been beat up by a

Chinese patrol when they got too close to a restricted area. "So the President contacted the Chinese and Sergeant Jeffreys and I were sent to liaison with a Colonel Lui. The bad part was that Colonel Lui was the one under the blue-gray's control."

"Oh no! How did you know?"

"We were flown up to an underground bunker where we met him and his staff. When I met him, I could sense that he was under control of the cube."

"Sense? What do you mean, sense?"

"I really can't explain it. It has something to do with my contact with the cube last year. And, I think, my ability to sense the control cubes. Anyway, I could tell that he was in possession of the control cube."

"So the person who was assigned to help you find the control cube is the one who is under its power," Beth said.

"Correct."

"What did you do?"

"I had to do some quick tap-dancing."

"I bet."

"I managed to talk to Colonel Lui alone. I told him that I knew that he had the cube and that I had also been in contact with a cube and that I wanted to help him."

"Did he believe you?"

"No," Mark said. "I thought he did. But then he sent Sergeant Jeffreys and me on a decoy mission while he planned to deliver a nuke to the blue-grays." Mark neglected to mention that the Chinese soldiers on the decoy mission tried to kill him and that he only escaped because Sgt. Jeffreys managed to grab one of the soldier's machine guns and fought their way out. Instead he said, "We managed to evade our guards and headed back to Colonel Lui's position."

"Why did you do that?" Beth asked. "Go back, that is."

"It's hard to explain," Mark answered. "We agonized about that. We kept debating whether we should interfere with the blue-grays' plan or whether we should just leave well enough alone. I thought that if the cats won, which they probably would since they were militarily superior, then they would be really pissed that we had helped the blue-grays, even if it was under duress. And since the cats had the ability to destroy the Earth, as they demonstrated sixty-five million years ago when they crashed two asteroids here, then we had better stop the blue-grays. That was my thought process, anyway."

"How would you stop them?"

"I didn't know. But I felt I should at least go and see what I could do. We ended up climbing this mountain that overlooked a valley where Colonel Lui planned on meeting the blue-grays. We watched as the Colonel pulled a nuclear missile launcher, one of those that sits on a truck, out into the valley and started disassembling the warhead. When the warhead was detached, the blue-grays arrived in a small ship. I call it the pod. I can't describe it because it had some type of cloaking ability that made it invisible. You could only see inside it when the hatch opened. Otherwise it was completely invisible. But it was really small on the inside, like a two-seater.

"Anyway, the blue-gray met with the Colonel and went over to the warhead. That's when the cat attacked, but Colonel was prepared. He had fire teams with missiles and machine guns stationed on both sides of the valley. When the cat ship swooped down, all hell broke loose, missiles, machine guns, and the electrical sound of the cat's weapons. It was over in seconds. And the cat won. When we peeked out from our hiding place, everything was a smoking ruin. It looked like everyone was dead, every human that is. The cat was trotting the blue-gray. But some Chinese soldier managed to survive, hiding in the tunnel to the bunker. He opened fire on the cat with a heavy machine gun. That was a mistake. He missed. And it really pissed off the cat.

"The cat ran into the bunker and all we could hear was the sound of his energy weapon. Now we had a problem. The cat had won, just like I was afraid they would and now humans had independently attacked the cats. I figured that meant we were now on the cat's hit list. That meant when they left they would probably lob a couple of asteroids at the Earth."

"So what did you do?" Beth asked.

Mark hesitated.

"You attacked the cat," Beth said.

"Yes," Mark answered reluctantly. "I had to make a quick decision and that seemed the only way to save the Earth. Remember, I personally watched the cats almost destroy the Earth sixty-five million years ago in one of those visions."

"But that was a vision."

"That vision was an actual event as seen by a blue-gray. And now, thanks to the memory cube, it is one of my memories. So to me it is as if I had lived it. Which in a way I did," Mark said. "So we attacked the cat. Sergeant Jeffreys found one of the portable Chinese missile launchers and I had a machine gun. When the cat exited the bunker, we fired."

"And?" Beth asked when Mark paused.

"We hit it," Mark said quietly. "At least it went down. Jeffreys was knocked out when the cat shot at him. It was a near miss. I checked on Jeffreys and then on the blue-gray. I touched the blue-gray and that's when I realized they communicated by touch. I had a psychic link with it."

"What did it say?"

"It didn't say anything. They don't talk by speech. Or at least he didn't. What I felt was incredible pain. The blue-gray was dying and I felt it, along with anger at the cats, at us, at the whole unfair universe. And then it died. But not before I learned that the blue-gray had set an alien detonator on the nuke. It was the blue-gray that detonated the nuke. Not the Chinese, not the cat, not some terrorist. It was the blue-gray."

"How did you get away?"

"I tried to stop the nuke, but I didn't know how. The blue-gray was dead, so I couldn't communicate with it, assuming I could have if it were alive. There was no way to get away. All the trucks were burning. The cat ship was hovering a hundred feet in the air. Jeffreys was unconscious. I had the impression from the blue-gray that there was only a very short time before the nuke went off, so dragging Jeffreys down into the bunker did not seem like a viable option. Not with a nuke about to go off on its doorstep."

"You obviously made it," Beth said. "Stop holding me in suspense. How did you get away?"

"You are as impatient as the interrogators from Washington."

"I'm going to be worse than them if you don't answer my question. I may make you walk home."

"The blue-gray's ship," Mark said.

"The blue-gray ship? What made you think they would take you?"

"It was the only option left," Mark said. "I carried Jeffreys to the blue-gray ship and climbed in. It was a tight fit since it was so small. It flew out seconds before the nuke exploded and dropped us off on the *Ronald Reagan*."

"Why?"

"I'll tell you the same thing I told Washington. The only plausible explanation is that since I was trying to help the blue-grays by attacking the cats, they returned the favor."

"That does not make much sense," Beth said. "Why would they care?"

"That's the best I have," Mark said.

"What did the blue-grays tell you?"

"They never told me anything. The only contact I had was with the dying blue-gray, and I already told you about that."

"But why would they take you out of there?"

"Why do you stop on the side of a road and save a turtle that is about to cross the highway?" Mark asked.

"You're comparing us to that turtle?"

"Like I said. That's the best I can do."

"What happened then?"

"Nothing. That's it. We were literally dropped off on the deck of the *Ronald Reagan* and the blue-gray ship disappeared. Actually, it never did appear. Remember, the ship was cloaked. It's invisible. The only thing the folks on the *Ronald Reagan* saw is when we suddenly materialized on their deck."

"Bet that caused a bit of a stir," Beth said.

"Particularly since we were dressed in Chinese clothing and covered in dirt and blood. Jeffreys was still unconscious and was taken to sick bay. I was interrogated several times. The first time was by the President since the nuke had just gone off and he had to figure out what was going on before he called the Chinese premier, or who ever controls over there. Then I was taken to Guam where I was interrogated some more and then finally brought back here."

"What happens now?" Beth asked.

"Nothing. The aliens are gone and I'm back to being a lawyer."

"No more alien interpreter?" Beth asked.

"Nope. Just meek, mild-mannered lawyer, Mark Williams."

"I like that better," Beth said. "Every time you run off on these alien adventures of yours you almost get yourself killed."

"Well, the blue-grays and the cats are gone," Mark said. "So those adventures are over."

They drove a few blocks while Beth considered Mark's comments. "That's kind of a let down, though," Beth broke the silence.

"What is?"

"Aliens visit the Earth. Actually two alien species visit the Earth and then leave and we have nothing to show for it. Only a few people ever actually see them and we have no new knowledge from them."

Mark was quiet for a moment. Fortunately, Beth was driving so she did not notice. "But isn't that better?" Mark finally said. "Remember, we debated this last year. Their technology is so far superior to ours. They have space ships, travel through wormholes, do DNA splicing, can do mind control and who knows what else. Mankind is not ready for that type of technology. We can barely handle what we have and even then we often seem on the brink of some disaster. I shudder to think what would happen if we got hold of that mind control knowledge."

"You're probably right there," Beth said. "But space travel? That is pretty exotic."

"Would you want to go into space?" Mark asked.

"Probably not," Beth said. "But the idea is fascinating."

"Ideas are," Mark agreed. "It's the actual practice that is not always what it is cracked up to be."

"Well, I'm glad you're home," Beth said.

"Me, too. And if I have my way, I am never leaving again."

# CHAPTER 2

Dark clouds scudded across the night sky as Mark walked across a back pasture of his small farm. It was a week since he had arrived home. Having returned to work, he was slowly adjusting to being back. He spent a lot of time walking around the back pastures of his farm, particularly at night when he couldn't sleep. He told Beth it was therapy. That was partly true.

'Not long now before the rain hits,' Mark thought as he looked at the dark clouds racing overhead, blotting out the moon. He made it to the barn as the first drops hit the tin roof. Before long the downpour deafened Mark. He slowly walked between the rows of round hay bales to the back of the barn, finding his way by touch as the rain blotted out all ambient light. He brushed his hand past the last round bale and then held it out in the open space in the corner of the barn. He advanced slowly, arms out like a blind man until his fingers brushed against something. A hatch spiraled open out of nothing, revealing the interior of a small craft bathed in a soft, iridescent glow.

Mark climbed into the craft. He leaned against the wall and it slowly molded around him, forming a seat. The sound of the rain disappeared as the hatch spiraled close. Displays materialized above him as the craft awaited his commands. Mark was not planning on going anywhere, he was just getting out of the rain.

He had not told the entire truth to Washington or to his wife. The part he had omitted was that the dying blue-gray was the last blue-gray. There were no more. The cats had killed the others last year. So when Mark had carried Jeffreys to the blue-gray's ship, it was empty. Mark had climbed in and tried to fly the ship, relying on his past experience with the visions to control the craft. Mark had the dead blue-gray's personal cube, a cube that acted as a combination computer, smart phone, telepathic link and who knew what else. He had taken it right before he ran back to help Jeffreys. Mark could access the cube, just like he had accessed the blue-gray's cube a year before on the *Ronald Reagan*, but he did not know how to control it. It had been agonizing trying to access the controls of the blue-gray's ship as he watched the detonator countdown to zero. At the last possible second the ship had obeyed his command and flown him and Jeffreys to safety as the nuke exploded.

Hovering safely over the Pacific Ocean, Mark had to decide what to do next. Jeffreys was lying unconscious at Mark's feet, probably bleeding to death. He needed urgent medical attention. Mark could see the *Ronald Reagan* in the distance on the alien sensors. But what would he do with the ship? He could not turn it over to the government. He did not trust the government with the blue-gray technology. They would exploit it and the result would be catastrophic, of that he was certain. But Jeffreys needed medical care and the *Ronald Reagan* was the answer.

Mark considered dropping Jeffreys off on the deck and then flying off. But that would not work. If he then flew home, how would he explain how he got there? It would be hard enough explaining how Jeffreys got back to the ship. And he could not just dump Jeffreys off and run. Not after all they had been through together. He would have to stay with him to make sure he was taken care of properly. So he had flown them both to the *Ronald Reagan* and landed them on the deck. Then he had sent the ship, along with the cube, to fly off by itself so the government would not have it. That had been hard, sending the ship away. But as he lay on the flight deck of the *Ronald Reagan* with Sgt. Jeffreys lying unconscious in his arms, he knew he had no other option.

So the ship disappeared, leaving him and Jeffreys behind. To the people on the flight deck it was as if they had materialized out of thin air as the cloaking capability of the small ship hid them until it departed. If Jeffreys had not been hurt, Mark would have had some fun with that entrance. But his sole concern was getting Jeffreys down to sickbay.

When Mark arrived home, he held his breath when he went out to the barn to see if the ship was there, if it had indeed followed his command. As he walked out to the barn he kept telling himself that even if it was not there, he had made the right decision. He had saved Jeffreys and kept the alien ship and the cube out of the hands of the government. He could still remember vividly how his stomach tied up in knots as he stepped into the barn and looked around. He saw the round hay bales stacked in rows, the tractor parked next to them, but no sign of the ship. Of course the ship was invisible, he had told himself. So he walked slowly through the barn with his hands held out in front of him, searching for the ship like a blind man. When he got to the back of the barn his hand had hit something in mid-air. The ship was there! His excitement was muted when he realized he did not know how to open the hatch. But as he slid his palms over the ship, the hatch materialized out of thin air. So now he had an alien ship and the alien's personal cube, a cube that contained all the knowledge of the blue-grays literally at his fingertips. The question was, what should he do with it?

That was a week ago. Every night he had gone for a walk and ended up in the barn. Each night he had gone to the pod. Sometimes just making sure it was still there. Other times he would climb in and sit in it. But he never touched the cube.

Truth be told, the cube scared him. It was, after all, alien technology, very powerful alien technology. He had been exposed to the memory cube last year, a cube that allowed him to experience first hand the selected memories of his blue-gray "host," as Mark referred to them. These visions were vivid, real, containing everything except for the blue-grays' thoughts and feelings. But even then the visions were powerful enough to kill Mark when a cat shot his blue-gray host. The shock or pain had stopped Mark's heart. If he had not already been in sickbay, he would have died.

Then there was the control cube, the cube that commanded Colonel Lui to turn over a nuclear bomb to the blue-grays. Mark had never touched that cube, but he had gotten close enough to feel its power. It was designed by the blue-grays to control humans and they had certainly gotten the programming right.

Now Mark had a personal cube, the same cube held by each blue-gray. It recorded the blue-gray's life, what it saw, did and felt, as well as its thoughts and feelings. But the cube did more than just record memories. It was the blue-gray's method of communication. It was their cell phone, personal computer and who knew what else. From his brief contact with a personal cube last year on the *Ronald Reagan*, Mark believed the cube contained all the knowledge of the blue-grays. That was what kept Mark from telling the government about its existence. It contained the blue-grays' scientific knowledge. Knowledge way too advanced, in Mark's opinion, for mankind to receive at this time. Mark remembered growing up during the Cold War with the threat of nuclear obliteration and mutually assured destruction being common household topics. That was not that long ago. Mark could only imagine how much worse it would be with the technology available from the blue-grays.

But Mark was torn. Although he was convinced he could not turn the technology over to the government, he could not just send the ship and the cube away. Its possibilities haunted him. It was like a drug. He knew he should not touch it, but he could not resist. And so each night he would come out and just look, he would not touch.

But tonight he thought he would just give it a slight touch. Just for a minute. There were so many unanswered questions from last year and from China. What harm could there be in just getting those answered? And then he could decide what to do with the cube and the ship.

Tentatively, Mark reached down and let his fingers touch the cube.

*Images filled Mark's brain. They floated around, overlapping, some close, others distant. The images swirled, steadied, new ones taking the place of old. There were hundreds, maybe thousands of these images floating in no apparent order.*

*Mark had experienced this once before, when he had touched the dead blue-gray's cube back on the Ronald Reagan. He had only been in contact with it for a couple minutes, but he would never forget the experience, infinite knowledge at his fingertips, just waiting for him to explore. He never got the chance to explore last time. But now he had time, plenty of time.*

*He stared at the swirling images. Each image was like a postcard floating in space. Inside the postcards were images, some static, others moving. He mentally touched one of the postcards or images and suddenly he was in a spaceship. Before the vision encompassed him, he mentally stepped back and touched another. He was standing in a field of short-stemmed purple plants that came up to his knees. Overhead, orange clouds skidded across the sky, hi-lighted by flashes of lightening. An acrid wind blew across his face. He pulled out of the vision and touched another. He was in a lab, working with a microscope.*

*'This is like channel surfing or surfing the web,' he thought. He flipped through some more visions.*

*Standing in another lab, lying in sleeping quarters, eating, walking down a corridor. He flipped through the cube, not staying anywhere long enough for a vision to take over. Another corridor. Another room. A cafeteria? A workstation.*

*'These blue-grays spend a lot of time indoors,' Mark thought. There was so much information here. He could be here forever. He would have to figure out how it was organized. What did he want to know? What did he want to see? Mark thought for a minute while the postcard visions swirled around him. Maybe he should start with the cube's owner. How about his last minutes? Mark knew what had happened since he had been there. Perhaps that would help him find the vision in this vast array. Mark concentrated on the final minutes in China before the nuclear bomb detonated.*

*Pain filled Mark's consciousness. He lay on the ground, his legs burning with pain. A cat stood over him.*

*Mark remembered this. The cat had attacked. The blue-gray was lying on the ground, legs missing, while the cat tortured it.*

*The cat pointed to the nuclear warhead next to him and then pressed his weapon against the blue-gray's side. The blue-gray laughed, not out loud, but in his mind. 'You will die,' the blue-gray thought. 'I have won. I will avenge my species. You will die in a nuclear blast.' Mark pushed deeper into the vision and realized what the blue-gray was talking about. The blue-gray had known the cat would find him, so the first thing he had done was set the detonator on the warhead so he could vaporize the cat.*

*Mark had thought the blue-gray had set the detonator after the cat's attack. As it turned out, the blue-gray was just checking on it* while Mark and Jeffreys battled the cat. And the detonator was much more complicated and more sadistic than simply a timer. The blue-gray wanted the cat to die, but he also wanted the cat to know that he was going to die and could do nothing about it. The detonator had a timer with a countdown so the cat would know when he would die. It was also programmed to explode immediately if anyone tried to tamper with it. And finally, it had a proximity detector, so if the cat attempted to go back to its ship, the bomb would explode. And the blue-gray's ship would not allow the cat to operate it. So the cat could only stay there and watch as the seconds ticked by before it died.

Mark pulled away from the vision. He did not want to stay connected while the blue-gray died. Mark was back in the area of swirling images. 'Ok,' he thought. 'I can access specific visions by concentrating on them. Now what? Another world? Most of my visions have been of Earth. I would like to see another world, an alien world. Perhaps the one he had just seen with the orange clouds.' With the thought of the dying blue-gray stuck in his mind, Mark tried to concentrate on the orange cloud planet.

A sun blazed against a black sky. Mark paused. 'This is not the orange sky planet,' Mark thought. But it looked alien. He went deeper into the vision. A blue-gray monitored the displays. He was pleased. The production units were working fine as they slowly crawled across the asteroid's surface, mining the heavy metal. He had three more rotations left to his shift, before he could take a break. He was so bored. The process was completely automated. Two hundred mining units crawled tirelessly in formation across the surface of this asteroid. The blue-grays had moved the asteroid close to this system's star and set it on a slow rotation. The sun melted the surface of the asteroid, which then solidified when the rotation took it to the dark side. After several years this process had refined the metal and given the asteroid a perfectly smooth, spherical shape. That's when the blue-grays moved in with their mining equipment. The mining units were positioned just behind the terminator line, the line denoting the suns rays, so they were in the shade, while large slender poles, hundreds of feet high, held solar arrays in the sun, *maintaining their power supply. The units rode on large flat tracks on semi-solid, cooling metal, which was easily mined. The cooling metal was pumped to large holding frames where it solidified into octagonal tubes that were launched into space, where they would stay in low orbit, shielded from the star by the asteroid until a freighter came to collect them.*

*The blue-gray had arrived on one of the freighters to collect the tubes. He stayed to reprogram the mining units since the asteroid was now half its original size due to the mining operation. He had repositioned and reprogramed the units to ensure optimal performance and was staying for twenty additional rotations to ensure that the operation ran smoothly. After that, the asteroid would remain unmanned as the units were fully automated. Now he had only three rotations left and the tedium was weighing on him as he begrudged the twenty-rotation rule.*

*An alarm beeped. He looked at it in disbelief. Alarms never beeped. Blue-gray technology made alarms unnecessary. Machines always took care of themselves. The alarm beeped nonetheless.*

*He walked over to the offending console, convinced that the alarm was an error. What he saw, took him aback. Mining unit 137 was reporting a transmission error. That was not possible. He had checked all the units and they were working properly. Yet unit 137 was not reporting in. He pulled up a satellite view and checked on it. There it was, in line with the other units. He ran telemetry checks and still came up negative. The unit was not reporting in. Well, he thought. At least I won't be bored. With that he went to the locker. He would don a suit and skate over to the offending unit and fix the telemetry.*

*Mark watched as his host donned a protective suit and stepped out of the airlock. Outside there was some gravity due to the heavy nature of this asteroid. The blue-gray stepped into two skateboard looking devices, which Mark recalled using in one of his past visions. The anti-grav skateboards were surprisingly fast and Mark was soon zooming across the featureless, smooth surface of this asteroid, heading for the horizon. There were no landmarks to guide him, but an artificial blue line appeared in front of him, which the blue-gray was following.*

*As the distant horizon began to brighten, Mark spotted their destination, a bump in the distance. As they neared, Mark could make out the mining unit. He was not ready for its size. Only about two stories high, it stretched back out of sight. Mark did not understand the blue-gray's units of measurement and there were no familiar landmarks to judge it by. Nonetheless, Mark guessed that the unit must be over a half mile long. He wondered what was wrong with it. Then he remembered that he did not have to guess, he could access the blue-gray's thoughts, although he had to concentrate more to do so. During the trip over, he had been so enamored by the view, he had lost his concentration and was now only picking up sight and sound. Mark sharpened his concentration and the rest of the vision filled his mind.*

*The unit looked fine, the blue-gray thought. What could be wrong with it? He skated over to the airlock and securing the travel sticks on the side, he stepped in and cycled the unit. The system was slow and he wondered if it would open at all. At length the entryway opened. He noted that his sensors had not cleared, meaning the environment was not safe without a suit. That was fine. Blue-gray suits were not bulky, rather they were almost skin-tight with a rigid bubble-type helmet, so moving around would not be a problem. Besides, he did not think he would have to be here long. Just long enough to check the telemetry circuits and get the communications back on line. He walked down the hallway, irritated with the gravity that kept him from simply floating down the hall. Most of his time was spent in space and he had grown to enjoy the effortless flying through tunnels. Walking, and directions like up and down were unwelcome distractions.*

*He arrived at the control station, which appeared to Mark as a solid blank, black wall. The blue-gray pressed his gloved hand against the wall and its finger pods sunk in ever so slightly. Symbols glowed from the wall above his fingers, which Mark could now easily understand. The main transmitter relay was malfunctioning and the backup had not properly come on line. The blue-gray ran a quick systems check and entered another diagnostic code. Nothing happened. Stupid, the blue-gray thought. If that worked, the system would have done it by itself. He paused and considered. Then he entered a more complicated series of codes, complete with bypasses and system-skipping instructions. This time new symbols materialized. Success!*

*He watched, satisfied, as the telemetry found the orbiting satellite and began transmitting its data, starting with error and restart messages. When the two systems had finished integrating a new error message flashed on the wall. The blue-gray stared at it in disbelief. The mining unit was not moving. It was already behind its programmed position. Now that was a problem. The units had to be exactly positioned. Too close to the terminator line and the unit would sink into molten metal. Too far and they would not be able to mine the metal.*

*The blue-gray ran through the systems, trying to isolate the malfunction. Finally he located a control circuit that was not responding. When his attempt to reprogram it remotely failed, he decided he would have to replace the circuit. That was simple enough. The circuit was a modular unit that could simply be plugged in. Checking the schematics, he was relieved to see that the unit was easily accessible. It was outside, but not too far from the access hatch. The problem was that there was not a replacement on this unit, but there was one on his ship. He went out the hatch and retrieved his travel sticks. Donning them, he skated back to his ship.*

*Mark wondered if he could fast forward through this vision without losing it. However, the sheer novelty of skating ten feet above this round asteroid, with black space and more stars than he had ever seen hanging over him, kept him from doing so.*

*The blue-gray arrived back at his ship, which looked to Mark to be very similar to the transport he had seen over the Ronald Reagan. He cycled through the airlock and then proceeded to a storage area. Rather than rummaging through crates and boxes, which is what Mark expected, the blue-gray simple placed his hand against the wall near the hatch and waited. A moment later a container rose through the metal of the floor, which then solidified underneath it. The blue-gray placed his hand against the container. When satisfied that it contained what he needed, he scooped it up and took it to another room where he went to work programming it. Mark skipped ahead in the vision until the blue-gray finished programing it and headed back to the mining unit.*

*Once again Mark enjoyed skating over the asteroid. The blue-gray seemed to be on autopilot as he skated back to the mining unit, absently thinking about working on other projects. Mark used the time to gaze at his surroundings. It was dark as they were on the night side of the asteroid. But that did not bother the blue-gray. It was the sky that held Mark's attention. Solid black with an infinite number of the brightest stars Mark had ever seen. As they neared the mining unit, Mark thought that the distant horizon was lighting up. The blue-gray ignored it and headed to the side of the unit, leaving the flying sticks hovering one foot above the ground. He crawled up on an extension of the mining unit, a kind of platform jutting out about 10 feet and accessed some controls on the floor. Here he had to physically open an access panel, rather than having the metal melt open for him. He found the old unit and disconnected it. He closed the access panel and went around the unit to the airlock, which was about 100 feet away and around a corner. It took forever to cycle through the airlock. He went to the control room to reboot the system. More time passed as the system rebooted and his replaced unit came on-line. But the mining unit still did not respond to the command to move.*

*What was going on? The blue-gray thought. The blue-gray picked up the old control circuit that was sitting on a nearby bench and examined it. Surely it just needed replacing. Then he noticed it, a small hole about an inch wide at the top of the unit. Turning it over, he noticed a matching hole, although a bit bigger, on the opposite side. A micrometeorite had pierced the unit. And since it had an exit, it would have damaged anything below the unit as well. He pulled up the diagrams and searched for the next thing the meteorite would have hit before it expended all its energy. There it was, a control relay, a very simple part. He would have to replace it* as well. Fortunately, there were replacement relays on this unit. He obtained one and went back to the airlock, which once again took forever to cycle.

When the outside hatch opened, he stepped out and caught himself right before he stepped off the platform. The ground beneath him shimmered. Only then did he realize how light it was getting. He could not see the terminator line from his vantage point, but his suit told him the temperature had climbed significantly. He had not paid any attention to the time and now the terminator line was approaching from behind. It was then that he remembered that he left the flying sticks over by the replaced part. That was only 100 feet away, but 100 feet that he could not walk on the ground. To test his theory, he took the relay out of its container and placed it for safe keeping on the platform. He lay down and reached down to the ground and pushed the now empty container against the ground, watching in dismay as it sank into the melting rock. As if to confirm this, he felt the mining unit start to shift. If the production and storage portions of this mining unit were past the terminator, they would be already sinking into molten metal and would soon drag the rest of the unit with them.

Starting the unit was no longer an option. He had to get off. There was no one else on this asteroid and no ship near. He would have to save himself. He had to get to his flying sticks and skate back to the safety of his ship. He looked around. The platform was fully enclosed except for the portion facing out. That way led to the molten ground. He would have to climb up the outside of the unit. But there were no handholds. He could jump. But the only way to jump was out, and that would land him on the molten rock. His suit did not have maneuvering ability, so he could not change his trajectory once he jumped. No, this way was a dead end. Literally. He would have to go back into the ship and use another access point, where he could get to his flying sticks.

He cycled back through the lock, willing it to speed up. His hearts beating faster as he felt the mining unit tilt further forward. This time he was actually running uphill when he ran through the corridor. Thinking frantically, he opted for the top hatch, the one *that serviced the solar array. He jumped up access tubes as he felt the unit sink some more. He reached the top access and hit the emergency override, allowing the hatch to open without the time-wasting cycling. Once on the roof he quickly climbed, jumped and ran over to the side where he had worked. When he got to the edge, he looked down to the small ledge where he had replaced the component. He would have to jump, but that was not a problem, particularly in this gravity. The problem was that his flying sticks were nowhere to be seen. He walked the edge of the roof, using it as a vantage point to scan his surroundings. Only then did he realize that the entire mining unit must have shifted and was now floating, or really, starting to sink in molten metal. He must have drifted away from the flying sticks, which should have stayed stationary where he left them. That would explain why he could not see them. As he searched, the unit tilted at a thirty-degree angle and starting to slide down, like a ship slowly sinking at sea. Only this ship was slowly sinking into molten metal. There would be no surviving this. The blue-gray looked around one more time and then resigned himself to his fate.*

*Mark prepared to pull away from the vision. But before he disengaged, he saw the blue-gray go back to the solar mast. There the blue-gray took out his personal cube with the intent to transfer his being, his memories, his life, to the orbiting satellite, so it could be found by the others and his life remembered. The last thing Mark saw before the blue-gray detached the cube and sent its contents into space was the sight of molten metal climbing up the side of the mining unit as it sank into the melting asteroid.*

Mark let go of the cube and the pod materialized around him. He sat there breathing heavy, a feeling of loss weighing him down. He had died. No, his host had died. How could the blue-grays watch these visions? He looked at his watch. The whole vision had taken less than ten minutes. He was emotionally drained. But if it were not for the last vision, Mark thought he would have been fine. This cube was a lot easier to use than the memory cube he had used on the *Ronald Reagan.* That made sense, Mark thought. Since the blue-grays were constantly in contact with the cube, it would not do for it to be an energy drain on them.

Mark smiled. Exploring the cube was going to be fascinating. But for now he would head back to the house. There would be plenty of time to explore the cube later. And he would have to tell Beth about the pod and the cube. He could not keep this secret from her. The only reason he had kept it a secret for the past week was that he was afraid the NSA was bugging their house. He had developed a paranoia against the government. A well-founded paranoia, he believed. He would have to get somewhere safe so he could tell Beth what was going on. He was afraid to take her to the barn unprepared in case she freaked out. If the NSA were listening, that would be hard to explain. He would tell her out on the boat. Miles offshore should be safe. And this weekend it looked like the weather would clear. He would tell her Saturday during a fishing trip.

# CHAPTER 3

The next night, Mark went for a walk. He would be able to tell Beth about the pod and the cube this weekend. In the meantime, he wanted to explore the cube a little more. This time he would concentrate on one of last year's visions. When Mark sat in the pod, he thought of the velociraptors when he touched the cube.

*Mark swooped several hundred feet above the treetops. He was skating through the air over the jungle, the wind blowing across his face, as he studied the jungle below.*

*'This is it,' Mark thought, as he recognized the vision. 'I did it. This is the vision on board the Ronald Reagan.'*

*Mark's host glanced down into the jungle canopy below, giving Mark a glimpse of his alien feet resting on the anti-grav skateboards. 'This is where they tested the velocirapters after doing the DNA modification,' Mark thought, remembering how a year ago he had struggled to make sense of the vision, wondering whether he was missing a channel, the thoughts and emotions of his host. Mark mentally pushed deeper into the vision and the missing channel came on.*

*'They should be just ahead,' the blue-gray thought. 'This better work.' He had been stuck on this backwater planet far too long with nothing to show for his time. His team had seeded this planet with genetic markers, attaching them to viruses so they would infiltrate a wide spectrum of the planet's inhabitants, modifying their DNA as the virus spread, allowing his team the mental access they*

needed to control their targets. The results had been disappointing. The virus had spread across numerous species, but the DNA changes had been erratic. Some had taken, but others had mutated beyond useful parameters. And even those that had taken, many of these species were too primitive for their use. They required constant monitoring. The goal of this program was to create independent units which could be dropped on the cat's worlds and attack the cats without any further control or prompting from the blue-grays. That goal was remaining elusive.

He was focusing on these lizards. They were natural predators and already worked as a primitive pack while hunting. Standing a little over a meter in height, they would be ideal if he could properly program them. He had already bred in a vicious claw to their back feet, which greatly increased their lethality. Now he just had to increase their teamwork and ensure they could adapt to changing situations, while maintaining their mission. His earlier attempt with these lizards had been disastrous. At first they had failed to even utilize their new killing claw. Once that was resolved, they merely used it to indiscriminately slash at their prey. That would never work against the cats. They would have to move in fast and disable them before the cats knew what was happening. Otherwise the cats' counter-attack would wipe them out. So he programmed them to look for weak points, tendons, and arteries. Not wasting a move on non-vital areas. He had to get that down in the more instinctive areas of the brain, as these creatures did not have much cognitive ability.

He triggered his display. Symbols materialized in the air in front of him, showing him the location of his targets. Mentally he toggled the display and infrared images of two of the creatures appeared. He slowed his flight above the jungle canopy and then deftly angled down between giant tree branches, stopping about 100 feet above the ground. Two of his target lizards were in the clearing below him. He activated his display again and watched as two more creatures entered the clearing, snarling at the others. Ignoring the newcomers, he searched for a suitable test. 'There,' he thought. Three lumbering herbivores in the distance would make for an *interesting test. The herbivores were large, but stupid. They were too big for any one of his lizards to successfully attack. Could the lizards work as a team?*

*Beneath him seven of the lizards were now in the clearing, circling and snapping at each other as they played their dominance games. He did not have time for this nonsense. Irritated, he snapped out a mental command and the lizards settled down. Another command and they headed out, single file, in the direction of the target creatures. Chastising himself for the control he exerted, he justified it as he did not have time for distractions. The teamwork modifications he had written into their DNA had to be tested. If it did not work, he would have to abandon this species and try another. He was loath to do so after he had spent so much time with these lizards.*

*He followed as his lizards headed out. Soon they caught scent of their prey. They hesitated, probably realizing that this prey was beyond their individual capabilities. He stayed back, studiously avoiding any input now that the test had begun. His lizards hesitated a moment longer, seemingly confused, and he feared that his experiment had failed. The lizards split off in different directions in the tall undergrowth. Had they given up? He followed their progress on the infrared display that hovered in the air before him. AS the herbivores grazed, one of them moved farther away from the other two. Would his lizards pick up on this change? They did! They stealthily changed their approach to box in the lone prey. This was excellent, he thought. Just what he had been striving for? He held his breath and watched.*

*Before the predators completed their encircling maneuver, one of the prey rose up and bellowed a warning. All three prey looked up, startled. 'Damn, not after all this work,' he thought. He assumed his lizards would either give up or blindly rush their intended target in hopes of overcoming it by sheer numbers. Neither approach would be helpful against the cats. Surprisingly, the predators started hooting to each other. Then two veered off to attack the two larger prey while one rushed at the separated prey from the other direction. The two groups of prey began backing up in panic, which further separated them from each other. The predators jumped and roared and made a fearsome display at their targets, but never actually made contact, the intent clearly being separate them. The prey were confused and scared, hollering and roaring, but still backing away from the threatening predators. When they were separated by about 100 yards, the remaining predators, who had stayed hidden during this attack, suddenly leaped out onto the unsuspecting lone prey.*

*The attack was vicious and incredibly swift. One moment the prey was backing, standing twenty or thirty feet tall and the next there was a blur of bodies and it lay on the ground with huge gashes across it. The velociraptors had first taken out the back tendons, effectively crippling the creature and then attacked the throat, mortally wounding it. The whole attack was over in seconds and the creature was dead before its two companions could decide to help.*

*That was encouraging, he thought. This attack far surpassed the rudimentary teamwork this species had demonstrated earlier. Maybe there was hope for his project yet. Then he could get off this planet and do some real good by mounting an attack against the cats on one of their own planets.*

*As he considered these events, he continued to watch. Now, instead of stopping to eat the downed creature as they had in the past, his lizards disappeared into the undergrowth. This caused even further consternation with the remaining prey, as they no longer knew where their enemies were located. A moment later a lizard jumped up in front of the prey causing them to step back in alarm, only to be cut down from behind by the rest of lizard pack, which once again attacked the hindquarters first and then attacked their heads and throats with killing blows. Once again the attack was over in seconds. Only then did the lizards converge on the carcasses to feed.*

*He watched a few moments to confirm his findings. This was excellent. Exactly what he had been looking for. He would have to make a few minor adjustments and do some more testing, but this test was very promising. Pleased with his progress, he skated up over the jungle canopy, back towards his habitat. He could not wait to let the others know about his breakthrough.*

Mark let go of the cube. Five minutes, the whole vision had only taken about five minutes. The original vision had taken 30 or 40 minutes on the *Ronald Reagan* and he had been exhausted afterwards. This cube was a vast improvement over the memory cube.

Mark smiled. Last year he had figured this vision out, though he had never guessed that the blue-gray's had seeded the entire planet with modified DNA. Glancing at his watch, he decided he better head back to the house. He could not wait to tell Beth.

# CHAPTER 4

The anchor hit the clear blue Gulf water with a splash as the chain ran out of the locker. Mark let the anchor line run until he was comfortable that the anchor had set on the sandy bottom eighty feet below. He scanned the horizon with his binoculars, ensuring that no other boats were in sight. He had anchored eight miles south of the Pensacola Pass on this cloudless Saturday morning. The seas were calm with a light breeze blowing from the East. He picked up a fishing pole and let the weight take the hook down about twenty feet before he stopped the line and set the pole in the starboard pole caddy.

"Aren't you going to put any bait on it first?" Beth asked.

Mark shook his head as he stepped into the cabin, motioning Beth to join him.

"You going to leave the engine running?" Beth asked as she followed.

"Yes, until I'm sure the anchor is set," Mark replied as he pulled out a pen and started to waive it slowly around the small cuddy cabin while staring at a light at its tip. Beth started to say something, but Mark held his finger up to his lips so she just watched and waited. When he had finished, he turned to her. "Now we can talk."

"What is that?" Beth asked as she sat on the cushion near the hatch.

"It detects bugs, the electronic type," Mark explained.

"Where did you get that?"

"There's a shop here in Pensacola that sells all this type of stuff. A paranoid's dream come true. I got it there."

"So now you are paranoid. You think the NSA is spying on us?"

"They did last year. Which is why I insisted we go out so far to go fishing and why I'm leaving the engine running, for the background noise."

"Why would they spy on us now?"

"Think about it. I am the only human who has had direct contact with aliens and their technology. And I am anti-government."

"You are not anti-government," Beth said.

"But I am wary of the government's power. That can be interpreted as anti-government."

"But why spy on you now? It's over."

"To see if there is anything I haven't told them."

"Judging by all this cloak and dagger stuff, I suppose they are right. So what is your secret? What haven't you told them?"

"The blue-grays are dead. All of them."

"All of them?"

"Yes, all of them."

"When did they die?" Beth asked, leaning slightly forward.

"That day in China. The last one died detonating the nuke."

Beth paused. "Then who flew you to the *Ronald Reagan*?"

"I did," Mark said, a smile on his face.

Beth stared at Mark. "You did?" she asked incredulously. "You flew the blue-gray ship?"

Mark smiled and nodded. "I learned it from the blue-gray's personal cube."

"Then where is it now?"

Mark's smile was threatening to break his face. "It's in the barn."

"The barn? Our barn? You are hiding an alien spaceship in our barn?" Beth said, her voice rising.

"Yes. That's what I have been dying to tell you."

Beth just sat and stared. "And you haven't told the government, why?"

"Because mankind is not ready for this type of technology," Mark finished.

Beth paused to consider again. "I have to agree with you there."

"I admit the spaceflight is tempting," Mark said. "But all the advances in that ship, the cloaking technology, everything, you just know it would be used for military purposes. And that's before we even get to the cube and all its possibilities."

"You have a cube? A control cube?"

"No. I have the last blue-gray's personal cube. The same type I got to use briefly on the *Ronald Reagan* right before the cat opened the wormhole. But now I get to explore it at my leisure."

"When have you been doing that?" Beth asked.

"I've only done it twice so far. Thursday and Friday night, when I went for a walk at night."

"I thought you were having nightmares."

"I was. So I would go for a walk and then sometimes I would swing by the barn."

"Why didn't you tell me sooner?"

"We had to come out here. I had to be sure no one was listening. And with the weather lately, I had to wait until we had a calm day. You remember the NSA last year. I was afraid they might still be watching us."

"So you put it in the barn? How obvious is that?"

"It's cloaked. It's invisible." Mark said.

"What do you plan on doing with it? You're not planning on keeping it in the barn forever, are you?"

"Why not?" Mark answered.

"It's an alien spaceship."

"Yes. And it will hold two people," Mark said. "Think about all the traveling we could do. Free. We could have dinner in Paris, go diving in the Caymans, go shopping in Tokyo, all in the same day. Well, maybe not the same day. But we could go wherever we wanted, whenever we wanted. The ultimate retirement."

"We could go to Paris?"

"See. I knew you would understand."

"This sounds too good to be true. What if we are seen?"

"The ship has a cloaking device. We would have to plan our trips. We wouldn't want to materialize in front of the Arc de Triomphe for all to see. We would have to land in some alley. And we would have to use cash. No credit cards to track us. And no cell phones. Or we could use burner phones. I've seen them in the movies. We would have to research them. But with a little planning, the world is at our fingertips."

"And you can fly this thing?"

"Yes," Mark said. "I flew it from China to the *Ronald Reagan*."

"You hesitated. How can you fly it?"

"With the blue-gray's personal cube. It's the interface for me. Their technology is so advanced I am not flying it. I merely think where I want to go and the ship does it all by itself. I can't tell you how it does it. When I'm in the ship and connected to the cube I know how it works and what to do. But once I am no longer connected I can't tell you any of the details, its all Greek then."

"So how did you get it here in the barn?"

"When we got to the *Ronald Reagan*, I gave it a command to go to the barn. I really didn't know if it would work. But I couldn't give the ship to the government. So I pictured our farm and the barn and told the ship to come and hide here. And it did!"

Beth paused as she considered what Mark had told her. "You're saying that the blue-gray's spaceship is now our play toy?"

"Something like that," Mark said hesitantly.

"The concept is fascinating," Beth agreed. "Although it seems a bit selfish."

"It does when you put it that way," Mark agreed. "But I don't know what else to do."

Mark paused, watching Beth as she considered this information.

"I thought we could just keep it here and explore it," Mark continued. "Perhaps I could share some of the discoveries without letting anyone know where they came from. You know, do it slowly. The things we thought were safe to share."

"That is certainly a better concept than us just playing with it."

"I think so. Although a little playing with it, the pod that is, could be our perk. But I don't intend to go flying around now," Mark said. "I would want to explore it first. Get much more comfortable with it. I just mention the travel as a possibility down the road, kind of a fantasy."

"It is an interesting premise."

"I've been thinking about it a lot," Mark continued. "But we do have to be careful. We can't tell anyone. And we can't talk about it at home."

"Have you tried that pencil wand thingy in the house," Beth asked.

"I have. But according to the shop owner, there are all sorts of different methods, like lasers on windows and other real hi-tech stuff. This doesn't pick up all of them."

"So we might be bugged here on the boat?"

"I don't think so. The wand came up clear and I searched the boat pretty carefully when I loaded it this morning, looking for anything out of place. And this far out, I figure we are as safe as we can get."

"And we will never turn the ship over to the Feds?" Beth asked.

"Do you really think we ever could?"

Beth thought for a minute. "Probably not. I agree that we are not ready for this technology. Not as a society anyway. But what do we do when we die? What happens to the ship then?"

"Man, you are the planner, aren't you."

"Well, you have to have a plan."

"We could give it to the kids, assuming they could access it, or we could program it so that it returns to the Mothership. Then no one can get it," Mark said.

"The mothership. I forgot about the mothership. Where is it?"

"It's out in space. I'm sure the pod knows where the mothership is. We could go there if you want."

"Go into space?"

"Why not? It is a spaceship. We could go to the Moon, or Mars. Or visit the rings of Saturn."

"You can do that?"

Mark hesitated. "The ship can, certainly. I would want to get a bit more familiar with it before I made that type of trip."

"But you haven't done it, yet?"

"No. I just flew it to the *Ronald Reagan*."

"Then what have you been doing at night when you said you were going for a walk?"

"Actually, I have been going for a walk. I walk around the pond or the back pasture. And then I end up in the barn on the way back. Sometimes I just look at the pod or sit in it and think."

"What about the cube?" Beth asked. "What are you doing with that?"

"The possibilities are endless," Mark said. "Right now I'm taking it real slow. Like I said, I only accessed it twice so far. First I just scanned it, like looking for the table of contents. Then I thought I would try to fill in some of the gaps from last year. I watched one of the past visions, one with the dinosaurs. But this time I could hear what the blue-gray was thinking. It was fascinating. And what we figured out last year was correct, they were doing genetic modifications on the velocirapters to make them more vicious. To have them fight the cats for them."

"Wow."

"Yes. And I also learned that they seeded the whole planet with modified DNA genes. The ones they use to communicate. I'm wondering if some of those DNA sequences might have survived and that is how they communicated with me?"

"Survived 65 million years and across several species?" Beth asked skeptically.

"It's just a thought," Mark said. "They attached them to some virus so they would be widespread. It's just a theory as to how I can communicate with them."

"That is a lot to think about," Beth said.

"Yes. It's been keeping me up at night."

"What else have you discovered?"

"Not much yet," Mark said. "I skimmed around, trying to figure out how to control the cube. How to search it."

"How do you?"

"It's all in your mind. It was like being in a giant room with visions swirling around."

"Visions?"

"Picture yourself floating in a giant, black void. And all around you there is a blizzard of postcards, some near, some far, all spinning around you. If you mentally reach out and touch a postcard, you see or live whatever vision or event that postcard contains."

"And what do they contain?"

"As near as I can tell, everything."

"Everything?"

"Yes, all the knowledge and events of the blue-grays. All there for the asking."

"That is incredible," Beth said.

"I know. It's mind-boggling."

"I need to think this through," Beth said. "Is there anything else you haven't told me?"

"No," Mark said sheepishly. "That was it."

"You can turn off the engine. Let's do some fishing while I digest this. And when we get back I want to see this ship of yours."

## CHAPTER 5

When they got home, they barely took time to put the fish in the refrigerator before Beth insisted they go out to the barn to check on the horses.

"You lead," Beth said when they got down to the barn, so Mark led her between the hay bales to the back.

"I don't see anything," Beth said when they got to an empty space behind the hay. Mark reached his hand into the empty air. "Aaaah," Beth exclaimed as the hatch spiraled open. Mark held his finger to his lips in a silent "shush." He climbed into the pod and motioned for Beth to follow. Beth hesitated a moment before stepping in. It was cramped with the two of them.

"Lean against that wall," Mark said as the hatch spiraled close. Beth complied and yelled as the wall started to mold around her. "It's okay, it does that," Mark said.

"So this is the pod," Beth whispered in awe as they sat across from each other, bathed in an iridescent glow, their knees almost touching.

"You told me about the blue-grays and their technology. But to actually see it, to feel it. It's hard to believe." Mark just sat there in silence, giving Beth time to absorb what she was seeing. "How do you control it?" Beth asked after a long silence.

"With this," Mark said as he moved his hand to the side. The wall rippled and a cube emerged. Beth stared at it. It was about two inches in diameter and multi-faceted. Each facet had different colors that appeared to originate from the very center of the cube.

"So that's the cube," Beth said.

"The blue-gray's personal cube, yes."

"How does it work?"

"You just touch it. Like this." He reached down and brushed the cube with his fingertips. Mark's eyes seemed to unfocus.

"Mark," Beth said sharply. "Are you okay?"

Mark let go of the cube. "Yes, I'm fine. Why?"

"You looked, odd," Beth stammered.

Mark laughed. "Jeffreys told me that I get a faraway look in my eyes when I touched the cube."

"You could say that," Beth said. "Or possessed. It's kind of creepy."

"It's because of the information I am receiving. Like trying to watch TV at the same time you are holding a conversation."

"You were never very good at that," Beth said.

"Fortunately, I am better with the cube. I had no control with the memory cube. I would be unconscious until the vision it sent ended. With this cube I have control. I can scan the visions, but am still aware of my surroundings. I can also stop the visions or jump around at will."

"What is it like?"

"The memory cube was like being in a movie as one of the actors. You were living the vision from his viewpoint. The personal cube is that and more. I've only accessed it a couple of times so far, once on the *Ronald Reagan*, once in China and then this week. It was very brief on the *Ronald Reagan* and even briefer in China. So I am not an expert yet. This week I entered a vision, like with the memory cube, but this time I could receive the blue-gray's thoughts and feelings. When I skate over the surface, it's like walking in a museum and seeing all the displays. No. A better example would be walking through a library, looking at all the books. And then you could pick up any book and open it, immerse yourself in it. But instead of just reading the book, you live it. You knew it, instantly. It would have made law school so much easier. No agonizing over *Marbury v. Madison*."

"Could I do it?" Beth asked.

"Sure."

"How?"

"Just touch it. Remember, it doesn't work for most people. But maybe it will for you."

Beth leaned forward and the wall around her flowed to adjust to her changed posture. "I could get used to this chair," Beth said after her initial surprise. She reached forward and hesitantly touched the cube. Her brow furrowed in a look Mark recognized.

"You're not getting it, are you?" Mark said.

"No."

"Jeffreys did not either. Nor did anyone else on the *Ronald Reagan*. Not at least the people who tried it. I was really hoping to share this with you."

Beth let go of the cube. "It just proves what I have always said."

"What's that?"

"That your DNA is pre-historic."

"I don't know that for sure," Mark objected. "I was just guessing."

"Show me how this works," Beth said.

"You already saw," Mark said. "You said it makes me look like a zombie."

"I said possessed."

"Ok, possessed. Is that better than a zombie?"

Beth ignored the comment. "Show me how you get the visions."

"There is not much to see from your seat," Mark said.

"I know. But I have heard so much about this. I want to see for myself what you do."

"Ok. But with this cube I can choose where to go."

Beth thought for a moment. "See if you can replay how the blue-gray's arrived here in our time."

"Good a place as any," Mark said as he reached for the cube. "This may take a little while," he warned.

"I'm not going anywhere."

Mark concentrated on the vision he received last year showing the blue-grays traveling through the wormhole and then touched the cube.

*The inside of the pod faded, replaced by a view of the inside of a much larger ship. The mothership, Mark realized as he allowed himself to drift down into the vision. 'But when? I want to see when the blue-grays first got here,' Mark thought.*

*The scene shifted. Mark was sitting in a command chair in the blue-gray mothership.*

*The black hole filled the forward-looking view, while the rear view danced with energy. Two ships were locked together by pulsing energy, which peeled off to the sides of the black hole. The view danced with colors, pulsing like a living creature, brighter and brighter.*

*'I remember this vision,' Mark thought. 'The blue-grays sent it to me last year. It's when they came through the wormhole.'*

*A flash knocked out the views and Mark was in the bare control room. The ship lurched and the room stretched and bent.*

*'I need to go deeper. I need to hear their thoughts,' Mark thought as he concentrated on the vision. The scene repeated.*

*The black hole filled the forward-looking view, while the rear view danced with energy. "We cannot survive this," the blue-gray warned his companion. "Our ships are locked together by the energy weapons."*

*"We need to enter the wormhole," his companion said.*

*"We can't enter while we are firing. There is to much random energy,"* another blue-gray responded. *"It is already interacting with the sides of the wormhole"*

*"We enter now or we die,"* Mark's host said.

*The view danced with colors, pulsing like a living creature, brighter and brighter.* *"We are getting dangerous readings,"* a blue-gray reported. *"The worm hole is becoming unstable."*

*A flash knocked out the views and Mark's host and two other blue-grays were sitting in their command chairs staring at bare walls. The ship lurched and the room stretched and bent like a Salvador Dali painting. Mark's blue-gray screamed. Time stood still.*

*It seemed like an eternity, but could have just as easily been merely a second. The room snapped back to normal proportions. The three blue-grays stared at each other from their command chairs. Were they really still alive? A view materialized above Mark's chair as the ship's systems came back on line. The blue-gray stared uncomprehendingly at the view. Stars slid crazily across the view as if the ship were spinning.*

*"Control the ship!"* *the command filled his brain from his companion.* *"Control the ship!"*

*He tried to enter mental commands to control the ship. When the ship did not respond, he resorted to manually entering the commands. The stars slowed and stabilized. Another view materialized and Mark glimpsed the cat ship tumbling through space far behind them.*

*"The cats made it through!"* *a blue-gray exclaimed.*

*"Attack it,"* *his companion said.*

*"We can't attack,"* *Mark's host responded.* *"We barely escaped it already. We have to run. The fleet can protect us."* *With that he entered commands to the ship and the cat ship quickly disappeared in the distance.*

*"Where is the fleet?"* *he asked.* *"I'm not raising anyone."* *Symbols danced in the air above him, symbols that Mark now could read. They gave the coordinates of all nearby objects. Only asteroids registered. He expanded the scope and the symbols*

*changed. Asteroids and now three planets, but no ships, except the cat ship spinning in the distance.*

*"We don't have much time," his companion said. "We have to jump before the cats regain control of their ship and attack."*

*"We can't jump," another said. "The wormhole generator is damaged."*

*"Find an asteroid and hide," the first said. A view materialized depicting the asteroid field with symbols superimposed. "That one," the blue-gray said. "It has some heavy metals in it. Enough to confuse scans."*

*"The cats will search it," Mark's host objected.*

*"We have to start somewhere. We can leapfrog from there. But now we have to get out of sight."*

*"Where is the fleet?" the third blue-gray repeated. "I am not reading anything. I can't find anyone in this whole system."*

*"Your scanner is probably damaged," the second said. "We will hide on that asteroid and make repairs."*

*Mark fast-forwarded through the vision as the blue-grays hid their ship on an asteroid. Mark slowed the vision down when it appeared that the blue-grays were getting agitated again. He backed it up and replayed the scene.*

*Mark's host sat and stared at the displays. He re-ran the diagnostics and then checked the display again. The systems were working fine. "The fleet is gone," he told the others.*

*"They jumped already? All of them? How is that possible," his companion replied. "We have not been out of touch that long. Your system is wrong."*

*The blue-gray bristled at the rebuke. His system was not wrong, although he wished it were.*

*"I will fix your system for you," the companion said, contempt dripping from his statement.*

*Mark's host's temper flared. To attack his competency like that. He would show him. He reached over and touched the other blue-gray, dumping his thoughts into the other's mind without any warning or preamble. A shocking breach of etiquette for his position, but he did not care. He would not be insulted and he knew his explanation would otherwise take too long. He watched with satisfaction as the companion looked up startled and then just stared as the import of the message sunk in.*

*"We are alone," the companion said, rather than asked.*

*"Yes."*

*"The sensors could be mistaken," he said without conviction.*

*"The sensors could be wrong. But the stars do not lie."*

*The companion pulled up the navigational star field chart and compared it to the stars now showing on the display. "How long?"*

*"Twenty to the tenth to the tenth rotations," Mark's host responded.*

*Even with the cube, Mark did not understand the blue-gray's sense of time or distance, although he sensed that this was a long time. Mark watched as the blue-grays grappled with the answer he had discovered last year. 65 million years. The end of the age of dinosaurs. The two asteroids that the cats crashed into the Earth caused the extinction of the dinosaurs and created the KT line, the line of sediment geologists carbon dated back 65 million years ago. Professor Benson, a paleontologist with the University of California, Berkeley, had used that event last year to confirm Mark's visions and provide them with a timeframe of what Mark had seen in the memory cube.*

*They were alone, except for a cat fighter that had traveled with them and whose mission was to destroy them. They had no misgivings about what the cats would do. They had studied the cats, a surprisingly primitive species with singular hatred against the blue-grays. They would have to destroy the cats or be destroyed by them. Their respective species may be extinct, but their war would continue until one or both ships were destroyed.*

*Mark fast-forwarded through the vision as the blue-grays sat in sorrow, trying to comprehend what had happened to them. When they finally came out of their stupor, Mark slowed down the vision.*

*"What do we know about this system now?" one of the blue-grays asked. "Did the third planet from the star survive the cat's attack?"*

*"I am sending probes out now," the other blue-gray said.*

*Mark watched as tiny probes shot out from the mothership and then winked out of existence. Mark knew they had microgenerators on them that allowed them to make spatial jumps within this system. The probes winked back into existence above the various planets and started sending back their data. In minutes the blue-grays had more information about the entire system than mankind had yet obtained despite hundreds of years of study and countless satellites.*

"*The fifth and six planets from the star have excellent mining opportunities and would also make good places to hide the ship,*" *one of the blue-grays reported.*

"*The third planet has urtendon,*" *one blue-gray reported, which Mark somehow understood to mean non-natural background radiation.*

"*Study that planet more closely,*" *the first blue-gray commanded.*

*Mark fast-forwarded the vision to the report.*

"*More advanced than when we left, but still very primitive,*" *one blue-gray was saying. "I have atomic residue readings, so they have split the atom. There is a lot of space junk around their planet in low orbit. It does not appear that they have any functioning space flight capabilities. At least not beyond their planet.*"

"*I did not think the lizards had that evolutionary capability,*" *the other said.*

"*They have had a millennium of rotations.*"

"*Still. I am surprised that they evolved any further.*"

"*There is a lot of background noise coming from this planet in these frequency ranges,*" *the third reported as symbols filled the air above their seats.*

"*Follow the radiation findings. We may find a weapon yet.*"

"*Fusion weapons are primitive,*" *one blue-gray objected.*

"*Primitive they may be, but you can still kill with a club.*"

"*You would have to get pretty close to club the cats with a fusion weapon.*"

"*Right now a club is better than nothing. Follow the radiation.*"

*Mark watched as their sensors scoured the Earth, searching for radiation hot spots. Mark recognized nuclear power plants from their distinctive outlines, even when seen from the orbiting blue-gray probe as its optics made it appear that he was viewing from a low-flying plane. The probe orbited over the Pacific. A reading came up over a barren set of islands. 'Could that be Bikini Atoll, the sight of many nuclear tests?' Mark wondered. Then they were over open ocean and the readings decreased. Suddenly a hot spot showed up and the probe zoomed in on it. Mark made out a ship. As the view zoomed in closer, Mark recognized it as an aircraft carrier. 'That must be the Ronald Reagan,' Mark thought.*

*"They have nuclear powered vessels," the blue-gray reported, disappointed.*

*"They must have weaponized it. There is too much background radiation for it simply to be from power."*

*"Unless they had a lot of accidents."*

*"Keep looking. Look for weapons grade readings."*

*The probe zoomed in on the Ronald Reagan, symbols flowing above the display as the probe analyzed different readings.*

*"I think I found it," Mark's host reported. "I have 25 concentrated readings inside the nuclear powered vessel. They appear to be contained and do not appear to be associated with the power of the ship. And they are the wrong type for power. They could, however, be utilized as a crude weapon. Under the right circumstance they would produce an explosion of the seventh magnitude."*

*"Only a seventh?"*

*"I said they were crude."*

*"A seventh would be sufficient if the cats were close enough," the third blue-gray said.*

*"You don't have to worry about them being close enough," the second said. "If we show ourselves, they will be right on top of us. The trick would be to have enough time to ready the weapon and then get away while it detonates, but while the cats are still there."*

*"Then we have your lizards set it up for us," the first said. "You said your experiment was proceeding well. How about it?"*

Mark's host was concerned. His lizards did not have this type of ability. And that was eons ago. He sent a bio-probe down to the vessel. As it neared the vessel, he started obtaining more detailed readings.

"There is a new dominant life-form on the third planet," Mark's host reported. "These are not the lizards. Or if they are, they have evolved beyond recognition."

"Can you work with them?" the second asked.

Mark's host continued his scans. While he did, the third blue-gray reported. "These appear to be warships," he said. "Look at their formation and their structure. They don't appear to be useful for anything else. And theses structures appear to be weapons. Perhaps a projectile weapon or a primitive missile."

"I'm not finding any genetic markers," Mark's host complained.

"I thought you seeded this planet with your DNA sequence before we left."

"I did. And we should be able to pick up the marker tags. They are designed to transmit at this range."

"Perhaps they did not survive the eons."

"They are designed to be hardier than the original sequencing. They should be dominant."

"Maybe your lizards did not survive," the second said.

"The markers were designed to cross species. They should have survived."

"Then just create a new set," the second said.

"No. That will take time. I will have to start all over. This new species bears very little similarity to the lizards. I will need time to rework the studies."

"We do not have time. Once the cats see us, they will be on us."

"There is a deep fissure in the ocean near that vessel," the second reported. "We could hide down there while you worked with this species."

"But the time," Mark's host protested, thinking back to how many turns he had labored before the lizards showed even a hint of promise. "I need to find a marker. They can't all be gone."

"Then find one," the first said. "But stay with this group of vessels. They have the material we need for our club," he smirked as he used the phrase.

Mark fast-forwarded the vision again as the blue-grays sent down probes to study the Ronald Reagan and the surrounding task force. The probes scanned the floating vessels and then the flying vessels. When Mark noticed the probes were flying over Hawaii, he slowed down the vision to catch the blue-gray's thoughts.

'I have got to find a marker,' Mark's blue-gray host thought. 'They think it is easy to start from scratch and create the right genetic coding. What do they know about coding? It will take forever. I need to find a marker. If it stayed in their evolutionary matrix, then all I will have to do is adjust it, not recreate it.'

Mark watched as the blue-gray expanded his search. He had been told to stay with this group of vessels because they had the nukes. When his search of the task force came up negative, the blue-gray followed some of the aircraft as they flew to an island, which Mark recognized as Guam. The blue-gray's searched for the marker on Guam, but again came up empty. A number of aircraft flew from Guam, but most of them were large passenger planes. The blue-gray chose to follow another group of fighters, reasoning that they must be related to the military vessels carrying the nuclear weapons. His assumption paid off when they landed at a base on a small group of islands. 'Hawaii,' Mark thought.

The blue-gray sent his bio-probe to scan the base and then the islands, searching for the genetic marker, but he kept coming up negative. Could it be that the genetic marker died out over time? That just did not seem possible. The DNA sequence should have been dominant. It should have survived over all natural sequencing.

Scores of aircraft flew to and from these islands, but most of them were the large passenger planes. The probe scanned them, but no markers were found. Would he have to set up a brand new gene sequence? If so, he would not be able to use any research from the *lizards, this species was too far removed from them. But the time it would take. He did not have the time. A formation of six fighters took off, heading towards a larger landmass. The bio-probe's scan of these pilots came up negative, but he followed them nonetheless, hoping that the larger landmass would give him better results. In the meantime, he sent another bio-drone down to the original floating vessels to obtain more detailed information about this new species.*

Mark chuckled as he skipped ahead in the vision. Although the blue-grays had followed military aircraft to Guam, Hawaii and now towards the United States, the planes they were following now were the Blue Angels, which although they military, they were not assigned to the Ronald Reagan task force. But, of course, the blue-grays would not know that. Mark considered disconnecting from the cube. What he had watched was fascinating, but he was taking time and Beth would be waiting. He wondered how long he had been immersed in the cube in real time. He hesitated as he watched the vision fast forward. The probe had followed the Blue Angels all the way to NAS Pensacola, where it now hovered, waiting for further instructions.

As Mark started pulling away from the vision, he noticed the Blue Angels taking off again. A day had already passed in the fast-forward play of the vision and now the Blues were going on a practice run. Mark slowed down the vision. Maybe he would get to ride with the Blues if the probe followed them. Sure enough, the bio-probe started following the Blue Angels, picking one jet and then another as it completed its scan.

Mark smiled. He had always wanted to fly with the Blue Angels. It was a low practice, since heavy clouds kept the Blues from going too high. The probe followed the last jet and then discontinued as it came up negative. The probe slowed and dropped, waiting for further instructions. A blip registered on its scanner and then was gone.

The blue-gray spotted the blip and immediately took control of the probe. 'What was that?' the blue-gray thought. He re-ran the probe's history. The blip was clearly not coming from the fighter. He had the probe re-trace its route, sensors on maximum, looking *for the blip. He slowed the probe and dropped its altitude while repeating the survey. There it was, a faint blip coming from the ground. The probe followed the blip until it was hovering over a wooden structure common in this area. The blue-gray had the probe send a signal that should activate the marker, letting him know if the gene sequence was still intact.*

*Mark stared in disbelief as the blue-gray ran his tests.*

"I know how they found me!" Mark said excitedly as he let go of the cube.

Beth jumped at the sudden outburst. "Who found you?" she asked.

"The blue-grays."

"The blue-grays? What?" Beth asked.

"Last year," Mark explained. "The reason the blue-grays sent the message to the Navy, my website with my picture on it. I always wondered why they chose me. Now I know."

Beth waited a moment, then said, "Are you going to tell me, or do I have to ask?"

"Sorry," Mark said. "I had actually guessed half of it," Mark said. "But now I have confirmed it."

"You still aren't starting from the beginning."

"Right. By the way, how long was I in there?"

"About five minutes," Beth said, checking her watch.

"Wow. I will never get used to that."

"How long did you think it was?"

"I'm not sure. A long time certainly. I fast-forwarded a lot so I can't be sure. I think I scanned several weeks, maybe a month or two."

"Weeks? Months? How does this work? Aren't you supposed to be exhausted?"

"No, that was the memory cube," Mark explained. "And an earlier version at that. This is the blue-gray's personal cube. It works differently. Remember, I accessed one of these very briefly on the *Ronald Reagan* after the first blue-gray was killed. But then it stopped working when the blue-gray's ship disappeared."

"But how does it work?"

"I don't know? I just touch the cube."

"No. I mean, what do you see when you are in the cube. How do you choose what you are seeing if you are in a blizzard of visions?"

"Oh, I just concentrate on what I want to see," Mark said.

"And it just shows up?"

"Well, yes, sometimes. The problem is I do not know what to look for. I can find the visions they showed me, but after that it is hit or miss. When I was skipping through the cube last night, or was it the night before? Anyway, I watched a vision I had seen before. But then I wanted to see something new. I thought it would be neat to see an alien planet. I had briefly seen one by accident when I was surfing through the cube. So I tried to go back to it."

"Did it work?"

"Yes and no. I didn't find the vision I was looking for. But I did find another vision of an alien planet. I ended up being a blue-gray on a mining asteroid orbiting a star somewhere. He was tending to the automated machinery that was mining molten metal from the asteroid."

"Wow. Did you understand it all?"

"At the time I did," Mark said. "Although now I could only tell you what I saw. I couldn't give you the technological details, like how they did it or even what type of metal they were mining."

"That is too cool."

"Yes. But it was scary too. The blue-gray died when there was an accident and the mining equipment he was on sank into molten metal."

"He died?"

"He was about to," Mark explained. "He uploaded his thoughts before he sank. I only saw up to the point he uploaded his cube. That may explain why I found that vision. I had just watched the blue-gray die in China and my thoughts may have triggered the vision of another blue-gray dying. Like I said, I am new to this."

"That was yesterday, right? What did you find out just now?" Beth asked.

"Oh, right. This is just like being in the cube. It is so easy to get sidetracked."

"What did you find?" Beth repeated.

Mark told her about the vision, ending with the fact that he had the genetic marker the blue-grays were searching for.

"You have a 65 million year old DNA marker?" Beth asked.

"You have often accused me of acting like a caveman."

"I said you had the manners of a Neanderthal," Beth corrected.

"Well, it turns out you were correct," Mark said.

"May I have that in writing?"

Mark ignored her last comment as he continued. "65 million years ago the blue-grays were genetically modifying the velociraptors in an attempt to use them in their war against the cats. I saw that in one of the visions. But what I did not know then is that the blue-grays did not focus entirely on the velociraptors. Remember, I said they seeded the entire planet with a DNA sequence."

"So what does that have to do with finding you?" Beth asked.

"I have that DNA sequencing."

Beth looked confused. "How? Humans were not even around 65 million years ago."

"No, we weren't. But the blue-grays seeded the planet with this sequence. It went into the plants, the animals, even the algae. It was in our food. Then when it got eaten, the DNA sequence would go into the new creature. This particular DNA sequence has a marker on it which the blue-grays can receive and I've got it."

"Let me get this straight, the blue-grays planted a DNA sequence on Earth 65 million years ago, which has traveled from species to species and finally ended up in your DNA?"

"Yes."

"How is that even possible?"

"I can't tell you the science behind it," Mark said. "I understand it when I am in contact with the cube, because I am thinking like a blue-gray and understand what a blue-gray understands. But as soon as I let go of the cube, I only understand things in human terms, and this blue-gray technology is far too advanced for me to comprehend in human terms. However, the concept is not that bizarre."

"You think?" Beth said.

"We have it today."

"We implant DNA sequencing for telepathy today? I don't think so." Beth said.

"N, not that. But we do have genetically modified crops. In fact, I think I read somewhere that they are taking DNA from a salmon and inserting it into tomatoes to make them more cold resistant."

"We put fish DNA in a tomato?" Beth asked. "Where did you read that?"

"I don't recall. But that is what the environmentalists are getting all upset about. That we're messing with the DNA of plants and they have concerns about the effect it will have on humans. Certainly you have read that they are blaming the hormones in chicken and beef for why kids are hitting puberty so early now."

"I have heard that," Beth admitted.

"Anyway, the fact remains that the blue-grays planted a DNA sequence on earth 65 million years ago and for whatever reason of the genetic lottery, I have it."

"Are you saying that you are telepathic?"

"No. Remember, it is a DNA strand that remains dormant until the blue-grays activate it."

"So you are telepathic now?"

"No. I'm not telepathic at all. I wish I were. But it allows the blue-grays to communicate with me. They use it for control."

"When did they activate it?"

"I don't know. Probably sometime after the drone found me. It could have…" Mark paused, lost in thought. "I know exactly when they activated it, or at least when they found me," Mark said.

"You do?"

"Remember a little over a year ago when I got that migraine at work. You had to come get me and drive me home because the migraine was so bad I couldn't function."

"I remember," Beth said. "It was odd because you never get migraines."

"Right. And I remember the Blue Angels were practicing over Pensacola. They were so loud we had to stop every time they flew by."

"The Blue Angels fly over Pensacola all the time. How do you remember it was that day?"

"Because I remember joking about suing the Blue Angels for causing my headache. Obviously, that was when the drone was following them and found me. It had to be the blue-grays."

"Are you going to tell the government any of this?" Beth asked.

Mark hesitated. "No, I don't think so. They already know all of this anyway. Not in this detail. But it is what we had guessed, or I had guessed, and told them before.

This is just confirmation that I was right. I'm now getting it directly from the blue-gray's perspective. I don't know how I can tell them without them asking a lot of questions that I don't want to answer. And as the feds love to say, they don't have a need to know this anyway," Mark concluded. "Remember, we can't talk about this in the house."

"Does that cube of yours come with a paranoid channel?" Beth asked.

"You disagree? You're the one who held an NSA agent at gunpoint here in the barn last year."

"No, I agree," Beth said. "It's just too bad we can't share this. Imagine what advances we could make."

"Yes. It is a Pandora's box," Mark said. "And I am afraid of what it holds. Let's explore it for a while before we decide whether or not to open it for the rest of the world."

## CHAPTER 6

Monday found Mark at work, bored to tears. At eleven o'clock he called Beth and invited her to lunch. "I can't seem to focus," Mark complained as they sat down at a corner table in Portabello Market.

"You brought me to lunch to tell me you're bored?" Beth asked.

"Yes. No." Mark quickly added. "Of course I wanted to have lunch with you."

Beth laughed. "Got you."

Mark smiled.

"So what's the problem?" Beth asked.

"I feel like I am wasting my time. All I do is shuffle paper. It is so meaningless."

"Mid-life crisis," Beth said. "Bound to happen. Next you will want a red sport's car, which is perfectly understandable. But you already have the trophy wife. I draw the line at another."

"No, I'm serious. What good am I really doing?"

"How about putting food on the table and getting the kids through college?"

"We could do that on your income."

"Oh, you do have it bad."

"What?"

"Don't you get it? Look at what you have been through." Beth lowered her voice. "You have made contact with aliens. You have flown in spaceships and watched the Earth struck by asteroids. You made a clandestine trip to China, were almost killed several times and watched a nuclear bomb go off from a front row seat. Of course what you are doing now seems dull and boring."

"Well, when you put it like that," Mark said. "But what do I do about it?"

"You just get over it," Beth said.

"Just like that?"

"Yep. You aren't going to repeat any of it. The aliens are gone. You can reminisce if you want, but only from the safety of our farm. I, for one, have no interest in repeating any of it. Sitting around waiting to see if you survived was not my idea of fun."

"I can't imagine…"

"No, you can't. But don't worry. I'm not going to have to do that again because I'm not letting you out of my sight."

"I can't say I blame you."

"Maybe you should write a book," Beth said.

"A book? About what?"

"What you went through."

"You know I can't publish that. It's all classified."

"Just write it," Beth said. "Get it out of your system and maybe add any observations or discoveries you make while thinking about it and then give it to the government. Who knows, when it is finally declassified, you might have a best-seller on your hands."

Mark laughed. "Sure, I could call it *Meeting Aliens*."

"Too boring," Beth said. "Something snappier. How about, *First Contact*."

"That sounds better."

"Good. Now if your midlife crises is over, I need to get back to the office."

"I'm going to go take my nightly walk," Mark said to Beth. "Don't wait up."

"Okay. Just don't stay up too late."

Mark went into the backyard and stared upward. Stars filled the sky, as the moon had not come up yet. He opened the gate and walked out into a back field, heading for the barn. His eyes started to adjust to the dark as he walked into the barn and down the path between the hay bales. He paused before getting to the pod, trying to decide whether he should continue or not. Finally, curiosity won out and he stepped over and reached out with his hand. The pod hatch spiraled open. He climbed in and sank into the seat as the hatch spiraled closed. Mark pressed his hand against the side of the chair and the blue-gray's cube emerged from the wall.

'What do I want to know?' Mark asked himself. He thought for a moment. 'I want to know what the blue-grays were doing the year between the *Ronald Reagan* incident and China.' With that goal in mind, Mark reached over and wrapped his fingers around the cube.

*Mark was floating down a long gray tube. There was no sensation of up or down. At the end of the tube he twisted 90° and propelled himself through another tube, now going straight up from the original tube. A hatch spiraled open at the end and he emerged into a large circular room. 'This looks similar to the science room in my earlier visions,' Mark thought. But now he was weightless. Was he in the mothership? And who was his blue-gray host? Was this the blue-gray from China or another blue-gray? Mark could not tell. How did he get the blue-gray's thoughts last time? He tried to imagine what the blue-gray was thinking, even as he realized how ridiculous that proposition was.*

*Blue-gray thoughts and feelings welled up, like a giant tsunami, anger, loneliness, the need for revenge. All these thoughts swirled around in Mark's consciousness, threatening to overwhelm him.*

*'This is a vision, it's not real,' Mark told himself. The host's thoughts clarified.*

*"I have to perfect the control cube technology," the blue-gray thought. "The last version was too strong. We were too hasty putting it together and could not make good contact. I have to refine it" Despite their primitive nature, this species had the capacity to form and implement their own plans. He should only have to provide a goal and a timeframe. This species social structure was still a mystery. The initial assumption had been that anyone with the blue-gray's planted DNA markers would be dominant as that would provide rudimentary telepathy capability. But after observing the last failed attempt, he questioned that assumption. The airwaves on this planet were cluttered with all sorts of transmissions and he wondered if that was this species' substitute for their inability to telepathically communicate. No matter, he thought. He would not stoop to verbal communication. It was too primitive and unreliable. He would rely upon his species' tried-and-true method of controlling their subjects through their minds. He would have to develop the right combination to interact with the leftover DNA fragment that some of them still possessed.*

*As the blue gray immersed himself in the technology needed to refine the control cube, Mark pulled his consciousness away.*

Sitting in the pod, the cube sitting just below his open hand, Mark glanced at his watch and realized he had only been in contact with the cube for less than a minute. Thinking about his last vision, Mark touched the cube again.

*Mark was back in space, floating in what he considered the science room, while the blue-gray worked diligently on the control cube technology. This vision was similar to one he had sat through last year, one he had no interest in repeating. Using mental muscles he did not know he had, Mark consciously pulled himself away from the vision.*

*The sudden change caught Mark by surprise. He was standing on the flight deck of the Ronald Reagan, or actually his blue gray host was, while Mark was 50 feet away approaching slowly. Mark experienced a profound sense of déjà vu as he watched the scene from the previous year on the flight deck of the Ronald Reagan unfold from the perspective of the blue-gray. The subject human was slowly approaching. The human reached for the control cube, only to be thrown back by the contact. 'The settings must be too high,' the blue-gray thought. The human reached for the cube again, only to be knocked down again. Frustration welled up in the blue-gray. He did not have time to fix the control cube technology. Before the human could get up again, a bright light filled the sky above them.*

*Mark knew what would happen next. He had lived this event from the other side. The cats were attacking. They would neutralize the Ronald Reagan with their weapons and then a cat would jump out of its ship and shoot the blue-gray. Last year when Mark had a vision where a blue-gray was killed, he had gone into cardiac arrest. Mark not want to repeat that event, especially since he was not in a sick bay where a doctor could resuscitate him. When the cat leaped out of its ship, Mark pulled out of the vision, leaving the blue-gray staring at the cat, frozen in place as if it knew its fate.*

*Mentally trying to jump ahead to the next scene, Mark found himself viewing Earth from outer space. Looking down at the ocean, the view zoomed in until the Ronald Reagan filled the scene with the cat's ship and blue-gray's ship hovering nearby. The vision was detailed enough for Mark to see the cat jump out of the blue-gray ship and run across the flight deck, taking a second random shot at the dead blue-gray, while Mark and Sgt. Jeffreys huddled in a catwalk just off the flight deck. Concentrating more on the vision, Mark became the blue-gray onboard the mothership, watching the events on Earth play out through a remote pickup orbiting the Earth. 'No, no, no,' he mentally screamed as anger, dread and hopelessness filled him. Unable to do anything, he watched the hated cat shoot his comrade. 'We just needed a little more time. Just a little more time.'*

*The blue-gray watched as the cat engaged the wormhole generator and the humans started shooting at the cat ship. 'Right, like that would have any impact.' The cat did not even bother shooting back. 'We just needed a little more time.' And then the wormhole wavered and disappeared.*

*'Hah!' the blue-gray thought. 'You were so smart, so arrogant. You let the wormhole get out of sync. Serves you right.' But the victory was short-lived. He knew that was only half of the cat's attack ship. The other half was still hiding, waiting for him. Waiting to kill him.*

*Now it was just the two of them, one blue-gray and one cat, the last survivors of both of their races, marooned in this time as they continued their war. Determination welled up. He would not allow the cats to survive the destruction of his species. He would continue their mission. He would use the species on this planet to help him destroy the cats. He would kill the last cat even if he had to kill himself to do so. The cat species would not survive his. But first he would have to perfect the control cube technology. And he would have to perfect the plan.*

*The humans were not capable of doing it themselves. That much was clear. But he would need their help to prepare the device. He would not have the time to go down and get one and arm it before the cats arrived. First, he had to perfect the control cube technology. As the blue-gray formed its plan, Mark pulled away from the cube.*

He had been right. The wormhole had wavered and collapsed, taking the cat with it. Mark was tempted to stay and explore some more, but he knew he had to get some sleep. He climbed out of the pod and watched as the hatch closed and the ship disappeared, leaving him standing alone in the barn.

## CHAPTER 7

"Claire is coming home this weekend," Beth said over dinner.

"Really?" Mark said. "I thought she was going to wait for Thanksgiving before she came home."

"She was, but one of her classes cancelled, so she decided to come home for the weekend."

"Probably needs to do her laundry," Mark said. "It's amazing. A university as large as Florida State and they don't have any washing machines."

"She is coming home to see us," Beth said.

"I will bet you anything she brings home her laundry," Mark said. "And we better get some steaks. That's another thing that Tallahassee doesn't have, steaks. I don't know how she survives. Always comes home starving to death."

"You are just making that up," Beth said.

"How much?"

"How much what?" Beth asked.

"The bet. She will bring home her laundry and want a steak."

"I am not going to bet. She is coming home to be with us," Beth said.

"That's because you know I am right."

"You are not," Beth said, irritation clear in her voice.

Mark let it drop. It would be good to see Claire. She was in her sophomore year at FSU and by all accounts enjoying it. Beth was actually having more trouble dealing with the separation. Empty nest syndrome, they called it. It did not bother Mark. FSU was only three hours away and he could text or call her anytime. He actually thought he talked with Claire more now, texted actually, than he did when she lived at home. And he often had business in Tallahassee and would call her and treat her to a steak at the Outback. It was their older boy, Michael, whom they did not see much anymore. He had graduated last year and was now working for a company in Virginia designing Eco-friendly housing. Mark was not really sure what that meant, but Michael was really excited about it. Mark was looking forward to Thanksgiving when both kids were coming home.

Later than night, after the dishes were done and Beth had curled up with a book, Mark stated that he was going for a walk.

"Ok," Beth said. "Let me know what happens."

"I will."

As Mark walked out to the barn he considered how to explore the cube. He needed to actively search it, rather than accessing it randomly. What did he want to know? 'Everything,' he thought. He had been reviewing some of his past visions, watching them with the missing channel. Maybe he should continue doing that. He thought back to his visions from a year ago. Which ones would he like to relive? Which ones did he still have questions about? Then the answer hit him, the cats. He had never figured out why the blue-grays sent the cat visions. What did they have to gain by sending those? When Mark climbed into the pod, he concentrated on the cats and touched the cube.

*An elongated blue-gray finger reached out and touched the third cube on the console. His vision changed...*

*A cold, blue-gray alien looked down as he lay vulnerable on his back. Restraints held him.*

*Mark recognized this vision. This was the brief cat vision he experienced in sickbay when the corpsman tried to restrain him. It had been the first time the cat vision had controlled him, filling him with rage, and resulting in him beating up three corpsmen. That had really scared him as he thought the visions were starting to control him and he was afraid that if discovered, he would be locked up. Or that he would accidentally hurt someone. He had always wondered why the blue-grays sent that particular vision. He focused back on the vision.*

*Overhead lights glared painfully in his eyes. The blue-gray was reaching towards him with a short rod, clearly some type of weapon. Rage welled up within him and he felt his lithe, muscular body tense in anticipation. He flexed his body, letting his claws slide out, thin, sharp and deadly. He summoned the energy in his core, let it coil, and grow, until in a focused burst his arms and legs whipped out with his deadly claws. The blue-gray alien jumped back in shock as the restraints parted and he was free…*

*Mark tried to focus on the cat vision, tried to receive the rest of the cat's thoughts, but to no avail. It was gone. He tried to repeat the vision and found the blue-gray's portion.*

*An elongated blue-gray finger reached out towards the third cube on the console. "This had better work," the blue-gray thought. It was rare to capture a cat alive. Either they died in battle or they died shortly after being taken captive. This cat was still alive, although for how long he did not know. So he had a very short window of opportunity to study it. He needed to find a way to control the cats. To conquer them the same way his kind had conquered numerous species in the past. But the cats were resistant so far. He had finally managed to conduct a scan on a living cat and now was about to access it to see what it contained. He touched the third cube on the console.*

*Confusing, primitive, visions swirled through the blue-gray's mind. He focused his attention, trying to identify them. Anger, mindless anger. Unfocused, blind rage. The blue-gray wondered how such a primitive species could master space flight. There wasn't enough self-consciousness here to maintain a tribal unit, let alone build a technologically advanced society. He wondered if the cats were the recipients of another species' technology. Perhaps they were the tool of another race. Much like the blue-grays sent out other species to battle for them. That was a troubling thought. What if there was another, more advanced species that was sending the cats out against them? He would have to find out. As the blue-gray pondered these thoughts, he suddenly realized that the anger was rising in the cat at an alarming rate. Suddenly the cat flexed his body and the restraints parted, the cat was free. The blue-gray jumped back in alarm. He reached for his weapon, but was too slow. The cat leaped and the blue-gray felt the cat's claws in his neck...*

The vision ended. Mark sat in the pod, sweat soaked and gasping, a sharp pain in his throat that slowly receded as the vision cleared. That was close, Mark thought. He would have to be more careful. It would not do to die in the pod. Beth would know where he was, but could not access the pod.

"I think I figured out why the blue-grays sent me the cat visions," Mark said to Beth the next day. They had met for lunch at the Portabello Market in the Pensacola Cultural Center.

"You have?" Beth dug into her salmon salad. "Is that what you were thinking about last night?" That was their code for his times with the cube. They really did not think that the NSA would be monitoring them here, but they still tried to be a bit circumspect about what they said. Just in case.

"Yes. I was pondering why they sent me the cat visions. After all, the cats hate the blue-grays. You would think they would not send that to me."

"That does not make much sense," Beth agreed.

"Well, as it turns out, that was not their intent," Mark continued. "The blue-grays captured a cat, actually a couple of cats. Based upon what I saw in the visions last year," Mark added quickly. "Anyway, they tried to scan them so they could use their control technology over them, like they did with the dinosaurs and countless other species. But they could not get a good read on them. Or they could not understand them. I don't know which. What the blue-grays received in their scans was unfocused, confused anger. Not something you would expect from an advanced race. The blue-gray did not question that, possibly because they considered the cats their enemy and there is a natural tendency to dehumanize your enemy."

"That's our natural tendency," Beth interjected.

"True."

"And I don't think 'dehumanize' is really the right word," Beth said.

"But you get my point," Mark said. "Anyway, as I was saying. The blue-grays considered them primitive and unfocused. And their general anger would make us hate or fear them. The blue-grays did not realize that what I received in the cat visions were the cat's actual thoughts and fears. Under a different set of circumstances, I think we would have sided with the cats, not the blue-grays, if we had a choice."

"Assuming that either one of them would have sided with us," Beth said.

"True. Neither species would have paid much attention to us. Actually," Mark said after a pause. "If they came here today, I think the blue-grays would have just taken over with their mind control."

"What would the cats have done?" Beth asked.

"That's a good question," Mark said as he took another bite of his chicken-walnut salad sandwich. "I'll see if I can figure that out during my walk tonight."

That night, Mark concentrated on the cats again as he accessed the cube. His fingers brushed the cube and the visions rose in his mind.

*Trapped, he watched helplessly as five blue-gray aliens encircled his mate and advanced, weapons ready.*

*Mark had witnessed this scene before. 'Take it back farther,' he thought, as he tried to concentrate on backing up the vision. The scene shifted.*

*He was a cat locked in a cage. He paced the small cage on all fours as frustration welled up inside him. He and his mate had been captured when their ship was hit, knocking them out. The blue-grays had them before they awoke, otherwise they would never have been taken alive. Cats did not do well in captivity. They required open spaces. The only way they survived space was by pairing. Historically, paired cats would spend a lot of time in caves caring for their young. This trait had remained despite all their technological advances, so their civilization had grown with open spaces, balanced by small enclosures for the pairs. Their space exploration mirrored this biological necessity. The ships were designed as small living spaces and only paired cats could operate the spaceships. Unpaired cats, even the most highly trained, could not survive long voyages in the cramped ships. They had tried holograms that gave the illusion of giant vistas, but this only served for short trips. For long trips the unpaired cats had to be sedated, only awakened when they were near their destination or actually on the ground.*

*Now he and his mate were captives of the blue-grays and he paced when the blue-grays took his mate from the adjoining cage. He knew they were trying their mind control on him and he focused all his energy on his hatred of the blue-grays, trying to block out all other thoughts. It was exhausting, but it gave him a purpose, a focus. It kept him sane while he waited for an opportunity to break free.*

*Mark mentally fast-forwarded through the vision.*

*A hologram display materialized in front of the cats cage. He watched as the image clarified. There was his mate, crouched, ready to spring, her claws already extended and fur bristling. She snarled and barred her fangs, her body tensed as she gazed at a blue-gray at the door of her cell. A blue-gray alien behind her aimed at her and a bolt of lightning shot out, striking her in the back.*

*The cat screamed and threw himself against the bars, scratching at them with his extended claws. Rage filled his being as the sight of his dead mate hovered in the air outside his cell. Blind fury filled him as he threw himself repeatedly at the cell bars until he finally collapsed in a stupor.*

Matt paused the vision. He did not know if he could watch anymore. The emotions of the cat filled him, strong and overpowering. Mark did not know how the cat could survive this loss. Obviously, he could not. And Mark wondered whether he, Mark, could survive the cat's loss. A hatred of the blue-grays welled up in Mark and he wondered how much of that was his own hatred and how much was the cats'. Unable to resist, Mark fast-forwarded through the vision to see what happened next. He was afraid of what he would find. But like someone passing a wreck on the highway, he could not resist looking.

*An indeterminable time passed, with the cat laying lethargic on the floor. When all attempts to rouse him failed a blue-gray entered, weapon held ready. The cat ignored him. The blue-gray approached warily and pressed a wand-type device against the cat. The cat felt a sharp prick and the blue-gray stepped back, weapon still held ready. "A biopsy," the cat thought. The blue-grays were known for collecting DNA samples from the species they tried to subjugate. The cat remained immobile, not even its tail twitching. The blue-gray stepped back to the door and then turned to step through.*

*That's when the cat made its move. He dove through the door, driving the blue-gray to the ground. His claws ripped the blue-gray apart before the blue-gray had a chance to react. Then the cat ran down the corridor. Alarms went off. The airlock door at the end of the corridor began to close. Leaping through the closing airlock, he broke free of the trap, landing lightly on all four padded feet as he broke into a run, his claws making scratching noises on the metal deck. He rounded a corner, only to be confronted by two more armed blue-grays. He leaped sideways as they fired, the arcing energy of their weapons singeing his fur, but otherwise missing him. Twisting, he bounced off the wall directly at the two, his claws extended. The first alien dove to the ground, just out of reach. The second was not quick enough. He felt his front claws dig into the alien's scalp, jerking the blue-gray backwards off his feet, while his hind claws reached for his neck. This blue-gray was going to die. They had not hit the floor before the cat twisted, searching for the second blue-gray. He was not fast enough. The second blue-gray was lying on the floor, his weapon pointed at the cat. The cat dove as the weapon fired. White light filled his eyes.*

The vision ended. Mark sat in the pod, heart pounding. He started to cry uncontrollably, crying for his mate. His mate? Mark shook his head. 'This is just too intense.' He tried to shake the depression that was enveloping him over the loss of the cat's mate, but could not. As a distraction, he decided to watch another vision. 'It will need to be a blue-gray vision,' he reasoned. 'They are not so emotional. Perhaps, something from the jungle 65 million years ago.' With that thought in mind, Mark touched the cube.

*Mark was standing in the middle of a large green field. Or actually, his host was. The plants, a grass-like fern, came up to his knees. He looked around, listening to the strange animal sounds. The air smelled fresh and shrieks and hoots came from the distance. Mark mentally screamed when a giant lizard jumped out of the undergrowth and leapt at him. The blue-gray merely raised the metal rod in his right hand and fired a bolt of lightening at the creature, dropping it in its tracks. The blue-gray walked over to the creature and studied it. It was about three feet tall and covered with iridescent green scales. It had sharp teeth and sharp claws. Mark could have stared at the creature all day, but the blue-gray did not appear interested in its beauty. He pressed a small tube against the creature's side. 'What is he doing?' Mark wondered and then he remembered that he could access the blue-gray's thoughts.*

*The blue-gray looked at the tube. 'DNA sequence registered,' the tube read. The blue-gray climbed onto his flying discs and skated back to base where he would analyze the new DNA sequence.*

Mark let go of the cube. He would have liked to have skated across the jungle and perhaps see more dinosaurs, but it was late and the cube was like the internet, full of video clips that could keep your attention until you realized that you had spent all night staring at the computer without accomplishing anything. He climbed out of the pod and walked into the field. He stared up at the cold, white stars that filled the sky, pondering the unfairness of life. When Mark went back to the house, Beth was still in the den reading a book.

"Are you all right?" she asked when she saw the look on his face.

"Yea," Mark said without conviction.

"What happened? Are the horses okay?"

"They are fine," Mark said. "I was just," he paused, "...thinking about some of those past visions."

"Anything you want to talk about?"

Mark hesitated. "Would you like to go for a walk?" he asked tentatively.

"Sure, let me just get my jacket."

They walked in silence down to the barn and then to the pod.

"So what happened?" Beth asked as the pod hatch spiraled close.

"I accessed the cube," Mark said. "I wanted to know why the blue-grays sent the cat visions, so I concentrated on the cats. The visions I received were from the cats, scenes of their captivity that the blue-grays somehow recorded. I was the cat. Cats pair or bond and the blue-grays had captured a pair. I watched as they killed its mate."

"That is horrible," Beth said.

"Its worse than that," Mark said. "I was the cat, the one watching. So I felt his pain and anguish when they killed his mate. It was unbearable. It was like watching you being killed. And I couldn't do anything about it."

Beth was silent. "Why did they do it?" she finally asked.

"I don't know. They were enemies. They hated each other." Mark paused before he continued. "The blue-grays never did understand the cat's thoughts and feelings. Although they recorded them, the only part they accessed was the cat's rage and hatred. They never got the rest. I don't know why. So they just regarded the cats as primitive beings."

"It sounds like the cats are the better of the two," Beth said.

"Of the two, I would agree. Although I don't know if the cats would have paid much attention to us if they met us without the blue-grays being involved."

"Two alien species, extinct. It's a lot to think about."

"But they lived 65 million years ago," Mark said. "Speaking of which, you wouldn't believe how beautiful the Earth was back then. It's like walking in a scene from Jurassic Park. I wish there were some way I could record it and show it to you. Paleontologists would go crazy for this type of opportunity. I am actually seeing the dinosaurs interact 65 million years ago. The frustrating thing is that my blue-gray host doesn't care and I can only watch what he did and can't go exploring on my own. And the blue-grays, they are completely amoral. And I'm not just referring to their treatment of the cats. They do not care about any of the creatures here on Earth. They are simply here looking for a weapon to use against the cats. They kill indiscriminately during their research, even when just knocking a creature out would be sufficient for their needs.

"Of course, in all fairness, mankind did the same thing not long ago. And some would say we still do. Just look at the history from our settlers in the expansion out west. We slaughtered Buffalo just for the sport of it. And reports from Africa today on ivory poaching. So I guess we are not any better than the blue-grays," Mark ended morosely.

"Well, at least we aspire to be better," Beth said.

"There is that."

"So what are your plans with the cube?" Beth asked.

"What you mean?"

"You are spending every night with it."

"I guess I am," Mark conceded. "It's just that this is the ultimate history channel. And the sci-fi channel as well. And it is real. It is incredible the amount of information that is here," Mark said as he gestured to the cube sitting inches away from him. "I'm only skimming the surface."

"Anything you can share?" Beth asked.

"I don't know. I guess I could write it down or filter it and give it to people who could use it, like paleontologists. But I'm not sure how I could do that. I certainly couldn't tell them I had the cube."

"What about for medicines or medical research?" Beth asked.

"I've thought about that," Mark said. "But I don't know how to do that. I understand the technology when I am touching the cube. But once I let go of the cube, it's gone. History, I retain because I see it and understand it. I can tell you what the dinosaurs did. What I can't tell you is what their DNA does or how the blue-grays are manipulating it. I wish I could show it to you though."

"I wish you could too. I get kind of lonely sitting here in the house while you're out in the pod."

"I'm sorry, you're right. I have been ignoring you. I'll do better."

"I know you have a new toy," Beth said with a smile.

"It is quite a toy," Mark said with a laugh. "But I will try to control the time that I spend playing with it."

"But you still haven't answered what you intend to do with it in the long run," Beth said.

"We've had this discussion before."

"I know. But we really can't just leave it here forever, now can we?"

"You always were the long-term planner."

"And you never do plan."

"That's true. But for now, how about we just leave it here while I explore it. We can make a decision when I know more."

"That sounds like no plan," Beth said.

"No, that is a plan. We will decide later when we have more information. That's the plan."

"I guess for now that's the best we can do," Beth said.

There was a silence.

"What?" Mark asked.

"I'm losing you to the cube," Beth said. "You are spending more and more time here."

Mark leaned forward in the cramped pod and awkwardly gave his wife a hug. "You won't lose me, I promise. And I will find a way to involve you with all this," he gestured to the pod.

"As long as I don't lose you," Beth said.

# CHAPTER 8

The next time Mark climbed into the pod he hesitated before grasping the cube. How could he make good on his promise to Beth? She could not access the cube. He absently stared at the smooth contours of the inside of the pod, wondering how he could share his experience with Beth. She had been awed by the pod, but could not see what he could while connected to the cube. If he could not share the cube, maybe he could share the pod.

Mark let his hands sink into the sides of his chair. A holographic display filled the pod, showing him the inside of the barn and the row of hay bales. Another display showed alien symbols. He had seen that display before in the memory cube visions, but never understood them. Now that he was connected to the cube, he understood everything, including how to fly. Mark's blue-gray connection wanted to soar the pod out into space, to visit the moon or head back to the mothership. Mark's human side, which had a nagging fear of heights, was afraid of going higher than the barn's roof. The human side won.

Mark gingerly moved the pod down the aisle between the round bales and maneuvered it out the open barn doors and stopped. It was a black night, the moon and stars obscured by low flying clouds. But Mark did not need light. The holographic display showed Mark's surroundings as if it were daylight. Mark could shift the display to show different frequencies. Infrared hi-lighted the birds and small animals in the woods. Mark watched as a fox hunted in the nearby woods, moving cautiously from tree to tree as it tried to sniff out a rabbit, which Mark could see hiding in a pile of branches.

Steeling his courage, Mark maneuvered the pod behind the barn. One of their horses was standing next to the gate to an adjoining field. It whinnied at the pod before turning and galloping away. 'Could he see the pod?' Mark wondered. His blue-gray connection said no. Mark continued maneuvering the pod away from the barn towards a back field, keeping the pod just a foot off the ground, as he was afraid to go higher in case he lost control. He knew his fear was irrational, but he remained cautious nonetheless.

He piloted the pod down a path, across a stream and then up into a field he called the 'back forty.' It was a large, ten-acre hay field surrounded by trees that blocked the view from the road or any neighbors, a perfect field for a practice flight. Once in the field, he experimented with the controls, moving the pod around the field, slowly at first and then faster as his confidence grew. After several laps of zigzagging around, he stopped in the center of the field and studied the displays.

A jet flew in the distance, probably heading for the Pensacola Airport. Seeing nothing else, Mark commanded the pod to rise. Twenty, thirty, forty feet, he climbed. He stopped and hovered at fifty feet, looking at the view. He scanned the sky again. Although the farm had a lot of helicopter traffic from Whiting Field, the Navy's helicopter training field, there were no flights tonight. "Poor weather," Mark thought. He climbed a hundred feet. The pod responded perfectly, seemingly unaffected by the gusting wind. Floating over the treetops around the farm, Mark looked down and realized that his low level practice had flattened some of the hay.

He had made crop circles. He started to worry, but then decided the approaching storm would hide the evidence.

Feeling that this was a successful first flight, Mark maneuvered the pod back to the barn. He had two weeks to build his confidence. This weekend his daughter would be home. There would be no talk of the cube or the pod. The next weekend Beth would be visiting her mother in Gulfport. He would be ready when she returned.

It seemed like an eternity before Friday finally arrived. Beth had left hours ago to visit her mother for the weekend and Mark had finished up the myriad chores on the farm. Thought most people would now lie on the sofa with a beer and watch TV, Mark had much better things to do. He headed out to the barn. Mark left the barn doors open and walked the familiar path between the hay bales to the back of the barn until his hand hit the invisible side of the pod. The hatch spiraled open and he climbed in, sinking into the command seat. Tonight he would fly.

His hand sunk into the controls and the holographic display of his surroundings filled the pod, giving the illusion that he was sitting outside in the open. That was a bit too much for Mark so he adjusted the display so that it showed the confines of the pod. He needed that boundary; otherwise it felt like he was floating free. He scanned his surroundings, looking for anything out of place, any watchers. Finding none, he expanded the view, searching the sky above him. Confident that it was safe, he maneuvered the pod out of the barn and brought it to a hover over the field. He slowly rose, watching the view expand beneath him.

Once again his human side was nervous, while the blue-gray connection was almost bored. "This is so easy," Mark reassured himself. "Just let the cube do it."

Relaxing, he rose a thousand feet up and stopped. His displays showed him aircraft in the distance. A jet headed for the Pensacola airport. A helicopter flew a training mission near Milton. But none were close to him or even headed his way. "Where to go?" Mark wondered. He had not really planned this out. He headed north. North was rural. Not much there, only woods and small towns. Montgomery was several hours away, by car anyway.

He rose to five thousand feet and shot over the countryside. The optics of the pod allowed him to see clearly as if it were noon and overlays allowed him to hi-light possible hazards like aircraft, cell towers or power lines. As he adjusted to the controls, he dropped lower, so he could really navigate. He found I-65 and shot north over the center median, dropping lower and lower until the trees on either side rose above him. He approached a bridge crossing over the highway and easily popped over it before dropping the pod so it sped just fifty feet over the median. Additional bridges and occasional wires crossing the interstate were quickly identified and easily avoided. It was odd to be flying next to the traffic unseen. It was exhilarating. How many times had he fantasized about flying over traffic jams on his way to work? Mark could not translate his speed into human terms, one of the paradoxes of using the cube. But he could compare it to the traffic he shot past, which as he gained confidence seemed to stand still. 'Two hundred, maybe three hundred miles an hour,' he guessed.

He pulled up into the sky and hovered. What to do next? He headed back to the coast. He altered course to avoid an airplane. He thought of following it, but did not want to risk a close encounter. It might interfere with the airplane's controls. He passed Pensacola and shot out over the Gulf. Dropping down, he skimmed over the waves, increasing speed until the waves were a blur beneath him, even with the enhanced optics of the pod.

He shot across the open ocean and then pulled up until he rose straight up towards the stars.

'This must be what the Blue Angels feel like when they are maneuvering,' Mark thought. 'Except that I don't have any G-forces on me.' He slowed his ascent, suddenly realizing that the pod could go into space. He was not ready for that. Not yet anyway. He leveled off and slowed, then stopped. He wondered how high he was, again unable to translate the Blue-gray's measurement system. He spotted an airline traveling far below in the distance. 'If they cruise at 30,000 feet,' Mark reasoned. 'I must be around 40 or 50,000 feet.' This was like diving the Caymans where the water was so clear, you had to be careful not to dive too deep. Here he had to be careful not to fly too high. He glanced up at the dazzling stars and then quickly angled the pod back down towards the sea.

He set course back to Pensacola, cruising low and fast over the water. He changed the display to encompass the entire pod and removed the enhancements. Now the night stars shown down on him as the dark water rushed beneath his feet. It was as if he were flying free. He swooped and swerved, feeling like Superman. The lights of Pensacola appeared in the distance as he sped towards the shore. He shot over Fort Pickens on its sand spur near the Pensacola Pass and then skimmed across Escambia Bay towards the Bay Bridge. Picking of speed, he shot under the bridge and then soared back into the sky where he stopped once again and hovered.

The lack of solidity around him made him nervous and he readjusted the display so that he could once again see the inside of the pod. His fear of heights started reasserting itself. Reluctantly, he angled the pod back to his farm. 'Another good test run. This will work,' he thought. 'Beth will enjoy this. I just have to keep the display showing the pod and not completely clear. That was a bit unnerving.' The farm appeared in the distance and Mark slowly flew the pod back into the barn.

# CHAPTER 9

Beth walked into the house, dropped her bag on the table and collapsed on the sofa. "That is a long drive," she complained.

"Did you run into traffic?" Mark asked.

"No. It's just two hours of driving on I-10."

"Good thing your mother lives near Gulfport, that's only two states away, not three."

"She had talked about moving to New Orleans. The traffic there is much worse than Mississippi."

"How would you like to go out for dinner? My treat. We can go out somewhere special, just you and me."

"My, are you asking me out on a date?" Beth asked.

"Yes, and I have just the place," Mark answered, a smile on his face. "I was thinking steak," Mark said as he handed a handwritten note to Beth. It read: *Good for Dinner for two at Bern's Steak House, Tampa.* "I already made reservations, one for today and one for tomorrow. I did not know if you might be too tired today or if the thought of a nice meal would be a welcome one. We can cancel whichever reservation we don't want."

Beth raised her eyebrows. "You don't want to go to McGuires, or Global Grill?" she said, naming two popular Pensacola restaurants.

"I thought this would be a treat," Mark said. "We could just bop down, have dinner and bop back. Won't take any time at all." Beth noticed Mark had that smile on his face again. He was up to something.

"Just bop down and back," Beth repeated.

"Yep. Take no time at all," Mark said, his smile threatening to break his face.

"It looks like you have this all planned out."

"Yep. I thought it would be a nice treat for you."

Beth looked at the note again.

"Would you mind tomorrow after work? I'm just too tired to dress up and go out tonight."

"Sure. You got yourself a date."

"Right now all I want to do is sit on the sofa and have a glass of wine," Beth said as she uncorked a bottle. "Did you keep the papers?"

"Yes. They are on the coffee table."

Beth poured herself a glass of wine while Mark sat in his chair and opened up his laptop.

"You still have work to do?" Beth asked.

"No. I'm scanning some scientific journals, trying to see if there is something I can apply the blue-gray technology to."

"Find anything so far?"

"No. I don't understand any of it. Ours or the blue-gray's." They settled into a comfortable silence as each read.

"Did you read this?" Beth broke the silence a little while later. "The Navy is denying that one of their jets flew under the three-mile bridge."

"The Pensacola three-mile bridge?"

"Yes. Some local fishermen claim to have seen something fly under the bridge last weekend."

Mark looked over sharply as his stomach tightened. "Last weekend? When?"

"Let's see." Beth started to read aloud, "John Thomas and Bubba Winters report that they were fishing at the end of the pier around midnight, Saturday night, when an object streaked under the center span of the three-mile bridge. They were unable to identify the aircraft, but reported that it left a rooster tail down the bay consistent with a low, fast flying jet. The Navy denies that any Navy aircraft were in the vicinity and both the Navy and Pensacola airport report no unusual radar traffic that night. There was some early speculation that it might be a cruise missile headed to the Eglin Air Force test range. Eglin officials refused to discuss details of their missile tests, but did say that no tests would be conducted near Pensacola and certainly not under the three-mile bridge. Pensacola Police Officer Wilson, who responded to the first report noted that Bubba's pickup was filled with empty beer cans and he warned both fishermen not to drive."

"Now that's an article you don't read everyday," Beth concluded.

"Yea," Mark responded with a slight edge to his voice. "Got to love Pensacola. Never a dull moment."

Beth continued to read the paper, but Mark could not concentrate. He would have to be more careful flying the pod. He had never considered atmospheric or water disturbances.

The next night they got home from work about six p.m. "You look wonderful," Mark said as Beth walked down the hall. She was wearing a business outfit, which could easily double as casual dining wear. Mark was still wearing his suit. "Before we go," Mark said, winking at Beth, "Would you mind coming down to the barn and checking on one of the horses. I think she may be getting a bit thin. I need to know if I should increase her feed."

"Sure," Beth said. She felt silly when she slipped on some farm shoes and carried her pumps in her hand down to the barn. Once in the barn, Mark made a dramatic show of pointing out the horse and asking how she looked. "She looks fine," Beth said.

"Since we are here, we might as well check on the others," Mark said, but then led Beth to the empty space in the back of the barn. Mark reached out and the pod hatch spiraled open. Mark helped Beth in and the hatch spiraled close.

"This is a pretty elaborate ruse," Beth said after the hatch closed. "Do you really think anyone is watching or listening?"

"I haven't spotted anyone," Mark said. "But better safe than sorry." Mark moved his hand and Beth watched it sink into the armrest of the chair. Immediately, holographic displays materialized between them, the largest showing the inside of the barn.

"You are sure about this, right?" Beth asked a bit uneasily.

"Yes," Mark replied.

"You know I don't like to fly."

"You will like this. It is quite safe. I've been flying it all weekend while you were gone. It is simple. I even did a test run to Tampa."

"Okay," Beth said. "But take it slow."

There was no sensation of movement. The only way Beth knew the pod was moving was by the changing holographic display floating between them. She watched as they moved down the aisle between the hay bales and then out the open barn doors. They rose slowly over the farm until they hovered about two hundred feet above the barn.

"We are really flying?" Beth asked. "This is what we are doing?"

"Sure is," Mark said with a grin.

"How are you doing it?"

"I'm just telling the ship what I want to do. It's doing the rest." Beth stared in wonder at the display. "Let me show you how this works," Mark said. "Now we are not going to move at all. We are still hovering. Watch." The holographic display spun and expanded. Dots appeared here and there, with alien symbols hovering next to them. "These are all the planes in the area," Mark explained. One of the dots expanded until it was easily recognizable as a passenger plane, possible a 737. Beth gasped as they zoomed closer. "We haven't moved," Mark said. This is just a zoom view of the plane. We are still over the farm."

"How do you know?" Beth asked. "It looks like we are moving."

"The pod is telling me where we are," Mark said. "Through the cube. I am in contact with the cube. Here, look." The display reverted back to the view of the farm from about a hundred feet or so in the air.

"This is confusing," Beth said.

"Not when you are connected to the cube," Mark said. "I just wanted to show you what was around. If you are ready, we can go."

"You sure it is safe?"

"Safer than flying commercial."

"Okay, let's go."

The view of the farm suddenly shrank beneath them until it was lost in the distance. The lights of Pensacola came and then fell behind as they shot out over the Gulf of Mexico. The dark ocean below suddenly was easily visible, as if looking at it at noon. "I've adjusted the display so you can see," Mark explained. Clouds shot past underneath and the moon came up overhead. The space between her and Mark acted as a giant 3-D display. "Here comes Tampa," Mark said and Beth noticed lights on the horizon in the distance. Their speed slowed as the city spread out below them.

"How does it know where to go?" Beth asked, still marveling that there was no sense of movement.

"I uploaded GPS maps into it. We can go anywhere we want."

"How did you do that?"

"I didn't. I wanted to know the coordinates and the pod automatically accessed the information and assimilated it. I really don't know how it did it. Now if you would please return your seat backs and tray tables to the upright position, we are ready to land."

The display adjusted as they descended so it appeared to be daylight. A building and parking lot centered in the display.

"Is that it?" Beth asked.

"Yes. We are going to land right behind that stand of palm trees. There are no cameras and we will be out of sight when we step out of the pod."

"And no one can see us now," Beth asked as they hovered fifty feet over the parking lot.

"No, right now we are cloaked." They descended until they were parked just behind a palm tree in the corner of the parking lot. "Here we are," Mark said. "Now when I open the hatch, I would like to exit quickly, so we minimize the transition time."

"Okay."

"Ready?"

"Ready," Beth said.

The hatch opened and Beth quickly stepped out into the warm night air. Mark followed and the hatch spiraled shut behind them. Beth looked around. They were standing behind some palm trees in the corner of a parking lot. The pod was nowhere to be seen. She had half expected to still be in the barn. Mark took her hand

and guided her across the parking lot to the front entrance.

"This is unbelievable," Beth whispered.

"Isn't it?" Mark agreed. "Reservation for two," Mark said when they entered the restaurant.

"What name, Sir?" the receptionist asked.

"John Smith," Mark replied, prompting Beth to glance at him.

Once they were seated, Beth turned to Mark. "John Smith?"

"Well, I couldn't reserve it under our real names," Mark said.

"But John Smith? You might as well say, John Doe."

"Believe me, I was tempted. The good part is that here we can talk openly. We don't have to worry about the NSA spying on us."

"Is that why you said not to bring our phones?"

"Right. I've seen too many movies where they tracked people down by their cell phones. I have this phone which we can use if we want," Mark lay a phone on the table. "It's a burner phone. Or that's what they call it on the TV shows. It's a pre-paid I got in Pensacola for cash so it can't be tracked to us and the GPS is turned off."

"This is very cloak and dagger."

"Just basic, really. And we pay with cash so there is no credit card receipt from Tampa. Otherwise, it is just a quiet, normal, date for two."

"Normal? We flew here in a spaceship." Beth said the last part in a hushed whisper, glancing furtively around. The restaurant was crowded and loud. No one was paying them any attention.

"The new normal," Mark said with a wink.

The waitress came and took their drink orders. "Another benefit," Mark said. "No worries about DUI. The ship flies itself."

Beth looked dubious. "Just the same, you probably should limit yourself to one or two glasses of wine."

"Wouldn't due to take a wrong turn and end up on Mars," Mark said with a laugh.

"So where is the pod now?" Beth had to wait for the answer as their drinks arrived and their waitress described the night's specials. After they ordered, she repeated her question.

"It's in the same spot, but hovering about twenty feet up," Mark said. "That way I don't have to worry about anyone bumping into it."

"How do we get back to it?"

"I've got the cube in my pocket. With the cube this close, I'm in constant contact with the pod."

"Are you having visions now?" Beth asked.

"No. I'm not holding the cube. I can just sense the pod in the background. Like sitting at a window seat and watching your car in the parking lot."

"This is so weird," Beth said.

"You get used to it."

"I suppose." Beth paused to sip her wine. "So tell me about this weekend. What were you doing while I was visiting Mother?"

"I spent a lot of time in the pod. I had flown it once before around the fields. This time I started ranging farther, getting used to how it works. I flew around the countryside and then to the beach, out over the Gulf, and then finally did the test run to Tampa."

"And no one saw you."

"No. The pod is cloaked. Not only visually, but radar. When I was on the *Ronald Reagan*, they couldn't track either alien ship. They could get a visual, but no radar. So as long as I don't create a heat signature, like the cat ship did when it entered the atmosphere, or create noise, like the blue-grays did in the Mariana Trench, then I am invisible."

"And the ship flies itself?"

"Basically. I tell it what I want it to do and it does it. I don't have to think about rudders or anything else, just what I want it to do. Not how to do it."

"How does the ship fly? What is its power source?"

"I have no idea."

Beth looked up surprised.

"No idea? What if you run out of gas?"

"It doesn't use gas."

"You know what I mean."

"It's not going to run out."

"How do you know?"

"When I am a blue-gray, or connected to the cube, I know exactly how to fly it and I can access the cube to learn how it works. But I can't translate any of that into English or even a concept that humans could understand. That is the paradox with the cube. I don't know how to translate the technology so we can understand it. I can translate visions because I see them, live them. But technology, physics, chemistry, there is no translation."

Beth waited while their meal was served before continuing the conversation. "If you can't translate it, perhaps the cube is not dangerous. Perhaps you could turn it over to the government."

"Perhaps," Mark said. "Let's stick with our plan and let me explore it some more before we decide what to do with it."

"You mean, stick with our no-plan, plan," Beth said.

"Right. Our no-plan, plan."

"What else have you found?"

"I found the mothership."

"The blue-gray's mothership?" Beth's voice rose in disbelief.

"Yes. I found it."

"Where is it?"

"It's hiding on an asteroid waiting for the pod to return."

Beth glanced closely at Mark. "You didn't fly the pod to the mothership?"

"No, although, that is not a bad idea. It is a spaceship after all."

"But you don't know how to pilot a spaceship," Beth objected.

"I don't, but the blue-grays do. I keep telling you, it's all done by their computers. It's just like flying here. It's easier than using my MacBook Air."

"So how did you find it?"

"I just sat in the pod and basically asked it to show me where the mothership was located. And it did. I actually could fly there right now. We could."

"Don't get any ideas," Beth said. "I think I'm doing good just agreeing to fly to Tampa."

Mark nodded his head in agreement. "Oh, I agree. I would want to get very familiar with the pod first. I'm just saying that it is very doable."

"But space flight is so complicated. First, of course, is the fact it is space. No atmosphere. Radiation. All the things NASA has to contend with every time they send something up to the International Space Station. And then there is docking. It is incredible complicated."

"For us it is," Mark said. "For the blue-grays it is nothing, routine."

"What about the atmosphere," Beth said. "Suppose you went to the mothership. How would you breathe?"

"I researched that already," Mark said. "The blue-grays keep the atmosphere of the mothership the same as the planet they are investigating. That is, if that planet's atmosphere is compatible with them. That way, they don't have to adjust when down on planet. I checked all of this on the cube. The mothership's atmosphere is the same as Earth's sixty-five million years ago. I imagine that is a little different from ours today, but should be easily compatible, probably healthier. No pollution. Anyway," Mark continued. "The mothership is intact. The damage done in the battle sixty-five million years ago has been repaired and the ship is fine, waiting for instructions. I think I could fly the mothership. I could even jump it."

"Jump it?"

"Yes, jump it. I could jump it through a wormhole. I could fly that ship anywhere in the universe."

Beth put down her fork, her meal forgotten. "You're serious."

"Yes," Mark said, barely able to contain his excitement. "Think about it. When I told you I had the pod, I said we could travel anywhere. I didn't consider the mothership. With it we can really go anywhere. And I mean anywhere. We can visit the planets. We can jump to another solar system."

"And that's something you want to do?"

"It's tempting," Mark said. "We would have to take it one step at a time. Get comfortable with the idea. But when I'm connected to the cube, I'm a blue-gray. It's as common to them as it is for us to get on a plane and fly to Europe. Although a bit quicker."

"I don't like to fly," Beth said.

"You would if you were connected to the cube," Mark said. "It takes all the mystery and fear out of it. It all seems second nature. Like driving a car."

Beth resumed eating in silence. Mark concentrated on his meal, giving Beth time to absorb what he had told her. By the time they ordered dessert, Beth was ready to talk again. "So what are you going to do with the mothership?"

"We can do anything we want with it," Mark said.

"But is that fair, using it just for us?" Beth asked.

"Oh, I know what you are getting at. We had the same conversation about the pod, whether we should turn it over to the government," Mark said.

"I know that I agreed with you that we should not," Beth said, cutting Mark off. "But that was just the pod and this is the mothership. A spaceship."

"The pod is a spaceship," Mark said.

"The mothership," Beth repeated. "You said it was a science vessel. It could probably cure cancer and AIDS and everything else. Do we have the right to withhold that knowledge from the human race?"

"Don't you think I haven't agonized over that question," Mark said. "But I think the answer is the same as before. The mothership does contain marvelous knowledge. I know it can gene-splice a dinosaur's DNA. I did it. Or at least my host did it while I watched. And suppose that I could learn, or possible describe it sufficiently so some scientist could learn to do it. But this is a Pandora's box.

"We know the blue-grays have already perfected the control cube technology. It works. The person who controls that could take over the world. And I mean that literally. Some people would be immune, I suppose, but the majority of people would be influenced if not completely controlled by that technology. How do you disclose one without disclosing the other? The blue-gray's society evolved with the ability to have mind control. They learned and adapted with it. We would gain that knowledge overnight. There is no way we would be ready to handle that evolutionary leap. That path leads to mind wars and a series of dictators. Add to that nuclear and biological weapons, not to mention DNA manipulation, and I wouldn't give the human race a snowball's chance in hell of surviving."

"You paint a very rosy picture," Beth said.

"Tell me if you think I'm wrong."

Beth took a bite of her crème brûlée. Then another. "Do you think you could disclose some of the positive advances without letting anyone know their source?"

"I wonder the same thing," Mark said. "The problem is that I need to be connected to the cube to understand the advances. So I would have to be connected while I was explaining it to some scientist, so I could translate the blue-gray information into terms that humans could understand. That would be hard to keep hidden. And the NSA may still be monitoring us, although perhaps not as tightly as before. Which is why we don't talk about these things while at home or at work. And if the NSA ever got wind of this they would swoop in and grab up the pod and the cube, and probably me. That would be the beginning of the end. I think we would both agree that they are the last people who should get their hands on this technology."

"No argument from me there," Beth said.

As they finished their meal, Beth said. "This is just a thought. We have several friends who are doctors, Benjamin, for instance. I wonder if there is some way that you could give him some of this information and let him run with it."

"That is an idea," Mark said. "I'll start exploring the cube and see if I can locate some of that information and then figure out how to translate it. We would have to be very careful. I don't even want to think about the possibilities if it ever leaked out what was really happening."

With that, they paid their bill in cash and walked out into the parking lot. They casually strolled behind a stand of palm trees where Mark called down the pod and they quickly stepped inside.

# CHAPTER 10

A week later, Beth and Mark were once again out on their boat fishing.

"So how goes the exploration?" Beth asked as she cast her line out.

"This week was pretty much a bust," Mark said. "I never got any time to explore," Mark said. "Monday we flew to Tampa for dinner. Which was wonderful," Mark added quickly.

"Nice save," Beth said with a smile.

"Tuesday and Wednesday I worked late," Mark continued. "And Friday we went out to dinner with John and Dorothy. So that left Thursday."

"It rained buckets Thursday," Beth said. "You stayed in."

" I was just too tired to go out. However, what I saw before was fascinating," Mark said. "I told you about the vision on the mining planet. Their technology is absolutely phenomenal. They are living our science fiction."

"They are space aliens," Beth said, obviously unimpressed.

"Yes, but to see it, to live it. That is incredible."

"Have you found anything useful, yet?" Beth asked.

"By useful, you mean the cure for cancer or something like that?"

"Something like that."

"No. I really haven't learned how to search it yet."

"I thought you said you found their visual table of contents. That area with thousands of floating visions," Beth said.

"Oh, I did. But the visions are just floating there randomly. They are in no particular order. Or no order I understand, anyway. I don't know how to search them intelligently. I just stumbled across the asteroid vision. And although that was interesting, it has no bearing on us at all."

Beth considered for a moment as she reeled in her line. "My bait was stolen," Beth eyed her empty hook.

"Nice of you to feed the fish."

"The fish better enjoy it while they can," Beth said. "With the weather changing, we won't be able to come out here much longer. It is already too cold to dive comfortably."

"You can always wear a wet suit."

"I'm a southern girl, I want warm water. I'm not use to the cold." She baited her hook and cast the line. As it sank, she turned to Mark. "Have you tried searching specifically for something in the cube?"

Mark paused before answering. "Maybe I should search for weapons and see what I find. That is after all what my concerns are, that the government will use the cube to make weapons. Weapons so advanced that we won't survive them."

"You could search for the control cube," Beth suggested. "You said earlier that you were really concerned about that."

"I could," Mark said, although he was reluctant to voluntarily search for control cubes while touching a cube. What if the control cube information he found took over? "But I think I'll get more familiar with the cube before I go looking for that."

"You think it's dangerous?" Beth looked up from the hook she was baiting.

Mark caught the concern in her voice. "Not dangerous per se," Mark back-pedaled. "It's just such a powerful tool, I don't want to go blundering around it until I am much more familiar with how this cube works."

"If it is dangerous, maybe you shouldn't be playing with it," Beth said, undeterred.

Mark realized he was like an addict with the cube. He could not stand the thought of losing it. Not with all the knowledge it contained. Truth be told, he could easily lose himself in it for days or weeks if he were not careful. The experience was so overwhelming. "It's a library," Mark said, trying to ease Beth's concerns. "The only thing dangerous in a library is the knowledge in the books, not the books themselves."

"Unless it's the books in the restricted section," Beth said.

"Restricted section?"

"At Hogwarts, you idiot. Remember the books were chained to the shelves."

"Oh, right. I'll make a point of staying away from any visions that are chained to the shelves."

"You do that. Remember, Professor Dumbledore is not here to save you."

"I will make sure to stay out of the restricted section," Mark said with a laugh as he cast his line. 'If only it were that easy,' Mark thought. He had not figured out any organization to the visions so he did not even know where the figurative restricted section would be. And he accessed the cube while enclosed in the pod where no one could see him. If he got into any trouble, he was on his own. Only Beth knew where the pod was and she could not open it. What that meant was that he was on his own when it came to exploring the cube. He would have to be very careful handling it. Perhaps he should explore it in the house with Beth around. That way if he got into trouble, at least she could help him. Assuming that the government did not have a camera in their house. He would have to consider that option.

## CHAPTER 11

"This has been a long week," Mark complained as he chopped onions for an omelet.

"It was," Beth agreed as she read the Saturday morning paper. "And the weather was terrible. At least it looks like it will be a nice weekend."

"Want to go diving?" Mark asked.

"I don't know. Last time the visibility was pretty bad."

"That's because we caught an outgoing tide. And with that rainstorm, the river runoff ruined the viz. But I really want to go diving."

"What's the marine forecast?" Beth asked.

"The Gulf is iffy, four to six foot seas."

"We could wait and see how Sunday looks," Beth suggested.

Mark studied the weather app on his iPad. "Doesn't look much better," he said with a sigh.

"Just another bad day in paradise," Beth said. "I guess we'll have to mow the yard. The good news is that it will probably be the last time we have to mow this season, after all, it is mid-October."

"Wait a minute," Mark said. "Another bad day in paradise. That reminds me. The dive master said that on the Cayman Island dive that we took."

"I remember."

"Lets do that."

"What?"

"Lets dive the Caymans," Mark said.

"When do you want to do that?" Beth asked.

"I would really like to dive them right now."

"We can't dive the Caymans now."

Mark caught himself. "But wouldn't it be nice to be able to? Just hop down there, take a dive, and come back."

"It would be nice," Beth said noncommittally.

"It would actually be easier than diving here. We don't have to take the boat out."

"We need a boat there," Beth said.

"No, we don't. Remember Little Cayman. The wall is only about one hundred yards off the beach. You can do a beach dive."

Beth looked over at Mark. "You're serious."

"It would be fun," Mark said.

Beth pondered Mark's suggestion for a minute. "Would you plan on renting gear or taking it?"

"Taking it," Mark said.

"Wouldn't it be a bit cramped?"

"Not that much. We just need skins, fins, mask, snorkel, and the aluminum sixty-fives. It wouldn't be too bad."

Beth laughed. "I'll think about it."

"I'll check the weather down there. See what the extended forecast looks like." Mark pulled up the weather on his iPad and showed it to Beth. "Want me to see if I can plan this?" Mark asked.

Beth looked at the iPad. "Sure," she said.

"Deal. You have breakfast. I have to do some stuff in the barn. When I get back, we'll see about planning this trip." Mark placed an omelet and orange juice on the table and headed outside. He came back an hour later. "When you get the chance," Mark said. "I need you to come down to the barn and check something out. I've been organizing down there."

"Ok," Beth agreed. She went into the bedroom and saw Mark putting some pants over his bathing suit.

"Good idea," she said and did the same thing. They then walked out to the barn and to the pod. The hatch spiraled open and Beth saw it was already loaded with their dive gear. She climbed in and leaned against the wall, which conformed to her body contours.

"Let's hope the NSA or the neighbors didn't see you walking out to the barn with all the dive gear."

"That would be hard to explain," Mark said. "Fortunately, we don't have any neighbors living close enough to see. Besides, we could just say we are putting it up for the season. I hope the NSA is not watching too closely."

"You are paranoid," Beth said.

"Well?"

"I didn't say it was a bad idea, I just said it was paranoid."

"And just because I'm paranoid…"

"…Doesn't mean someone is not out to get you," Beth finished.

"See, a bit cramped, but it all fits," Mark said as he piloted the craft out of the barn. After checking that there were no nearby planes or helicopters, he shot straight up before heading due south. They made the trip in minutes.

"Do you remember where we dove last time?" Beth asked as they circled Little Cayman, the smallest of the three islands.

"No. But it should be easy to choose," Mark said. "Look how the water suddenly turns dark blue. That has to be the ledge."

"There's a nice little beach over there," Beth said, pointing to the display floating in front of them. "It is not near the road that circles the island. And the dark patch of water is really close there."

"Ok. We will land there," Mark agreed. As he piloted the craft down to the beach, they stared at the displays. "Look, you can see all the way to the bottom in the shallow area."

"I love how clear the water is down here," Beth said.

"Remember when I refused to roll off the back of the dive boat on our fist dive because I was afraid I would land on the coral head?" Mark asked.

"Yes. And the dive master looked at you like you were crazy."

"Then he told me it was sixty feet deep. I thought it was about ten."

Mark landed the pod and they climbed out, taking their tanks and the bags holding their fins, masks and snorkels. "Let's leave our dive bags here," Mark said. "That way we can find the pod after I close the door."

"What are you going to do with the cube?"

"I don't think I'll take it with me. Would not do to drop it in a thousand feet of water."

"That would be hard to explain," Beth said. "How we got stranded on a beach in the Caymans wearing only dive skins. No passports or credit cards." Beth paused as she considered her statement. "Maybe we should start carrying passports and credit cards, just in case something does happen. We wouldn't be as stranded."

"That is a thought," Mark conceded. "Although it would still be hard to explain how we got here."

"Yes. But it would make it a lot easier getting home," Beth said. "The option right now is swimming. And that is a long swim."

"Even a commercial flight would be a bit odd since all we are wearing are wet suits," Mark added with a laugh.

"Well," Beth said. "Times a' wasting. Let's dive."

They waded out into the warm Caribbean water, slipped on their fins and masks, and sunk into the tropical paradise. A couple kicks of his fins and Mark was in twenty feet of crystal clear water. The white, sandy bottom gently angled down while giant coral heads dotted the seafloor. Large fans waved in the current and schools of fish flashed everywhere. Mark glanced over to Beth before swimming down to the bottom, weaving between giant boulders. Schools of Yellowtails swam past him while two-foot parrotfish gnawed on the corral, seemingly oblivious to him. They floated through the clear water, admiring the multitude of fish that hovered around them. They came across the Cayman wall, a sheer 3,000-foot drop for which the Caymans were renowned.

Although he was swimming, Mark stopped at the edge of the wall, afraid to swim out over the sheer drop. Logic told him he wasn't going to fall 3,000 feet, but the sudden absence of a visible bottom unnerved him. Laughing at himself, he kicked out over the edge and hung over the abyss. He then focused on the wall and slowly dropped down, admiring the fans and coral while keeping an eye on his depth finder to avoid going too deep.

"That was great," Beth said as they surfaced in waist deep water and started walking up to the beach, fins in hands. "I had forgotten how beautiful the water is down here."

"I could have stayed down there forever," Mark replied. They stripped off their wet suits and lay them on the beach while they dried off. "That was incredible," Mark said. "Did you see the baby puffer fish?"

"Yes. And that spotted eagle ray that came gliding up from the depths."

"I kept looking for an octopus."

"They don't usually come out in the daytime," Beth said.

They continued to compare observations from the dive as they dried off and walked around their tiny private beach. "I wish we could have gone deeper," Mark said. "I wonder what is down there? Imagine, a three thousand foot drop. I can't even visualize that. Can you imagine the sea monsters that are down there."

"Blind, pale creatures," Beth said.

After drying off and sunning themselves for about an hour, they loaded their tanks and dive bags into the pod and climbed in, the hatch spiraling close behind them. The pod lifted off and Mark angled it over the area they had just dived. "You know," Mark said. "We don't have to leave just yet."

"We are out of air," Beth said. "And even if we weren't, we are too close on the tables to dive right away."

"To dive, yes," Mark agreed. "But we can dive with the pod."

Beth looked at Mark. "You think?"

"The blue-gray's transport ship went to the bottom of the Mariana Trench. I don't see why we can't take this down a bit. It's the same technology."

"Okay, but slowly," Beth said.

Mark angled the pod over the water and then slowly descended. He first entered the water in 40 feet of water, just in case. He did not want to sink 3,000 feet if something went wrong. He piloted the pod underwater, getting used to the controls. "It really handles no differently here than in the air," he said. "Let's take it a little deeper." He angled towards the ledge and then drifted over the edge. Staying about twenty feet away from the wall for clearance, he started the descent. The display showed the outside as if they had a 3-D window in the side of the pod. As they sank deeper, Mark adjusted the display to compensate for the lack of light. Mark's blue-gray side was fine with this, but he took it slow nonetheless.

"The most interesting sights are in the shallower depths," Beth commented as they gazed at the more barren wall.

They travelled a few minutes longer before Mark interrupted the silence. "Mind if we go back up? Not much more to see." He was also getting a little nervous traveling down in the depths.

"Not at all. We've seen it," Beth said.

With that, Mark angled the craft back up. He kept his speed slow until he broke the surface. Once back in the air he set course for home. "Quick run over Cuba and then across the Gulf to Pensacola," Mark said, in his best 'this is your pilot' voice. "I'm sorry, but due to the short flight, we will not have meal service." A little while later he added, "Ladies and Gentlemen, we are coming up to Pensacola. Please return your seat backs and tray tables to their upright position as we prepare to land."

Beth rolled her eyes. "You are such a big kid."

"Might as well have some fun," Mark said as the pod zoomed down towards the open doors of their barn.

Another week passed and Sunday afternoon found Beth going through photos from their last vacation in Europe. "Why did you take this picture?" Beth asked as she held out a Parisian street picture with a restaurant in the foreground.

"That's a classic picture," Mark said. "Proves that translation is everything. Who would want to eat in a restaurant called the two maggots?"

"That's Les Deux Magots, the 'g' is soft, and I would. It is a very famous restaurant. Known to the literary crowd. Hemingway used to frequent it. We didn't get to stop there on our last visit."

"Couldn't they come up with a better name?"

"It's not maggots. It's, wait, let me think. It has something to do with statues."

"What about dinner there tonight?" Mark asked Beth. Mark had lightened up about eavesdroppers as he had searched the house with several different devices he had purchased from the Pensacola store where he had bought the special pen. He still assumed their cell phones were monitored, but felt relatively secure in his house.

"Are you serious?"

"Sure. Why not? Actually, it would be a late lunch for us, say three or four p.m. our time." Mark pulled up a weather app on his cellphone. "It's cold in Paris. Forty degrees. But clear. We would not get rained on."

Beth thought for a moment. "That is very tempting. Why not? It would be fun. I suppose we would need Euros."

"Already have them," Mark said. "I exchanged some last week."

"You planned this?"

"Not this exactly. But I figured it was probably only a matter of time before we went to Europe."

"I suppose a quick trip wouldn't matter," Beth said. "Now what should I wear?"

While Beth looked for something to wear, Mark pulled up Street View on Google Earth, looking for a place to land. He seemed to recall a park near the restaurant. That would be a good place to leave the pod where it would not be observed or disturbed. By the time Beth had put together an outfit, Mark had located the park, which was actually a church courtyard only a short walk from the restaurant. Mark quickly changed, and then he and Beth walked out to the barn. They climbed into the pod and Mark sealed the door. The pod cleared the barn and then hovered 100 feet over the farm while Mark scanned the neighborhood, looking for anything out of the ordinary. "I keep looking for eavesdroppers," Mark explained. "Haven't found anyone yet, which makes me think they are probably only tapping our phones."

They flew south out over the Gulf before Mark accelerated. He changed course for Paris and crossed the Florida peninsula around Tampa. Mark waited until they had cleared Florida and were well over the Atlantic before he picked up any significant speed.

"How long will this take?" Beth asked.

"I don't know," Mark said, a bit embarrassed. "I still cannot translate blue-gray time. My guess is around an hour or so."

"This is the way to travel," Mark said fifty-five minutes later as the craft slowly settled into the park.

"Sure is," Beth agreed. "And the best part is that you don't have to go through Atlanta."

After ensuring they were not being observed, Beth and Mark exited the pod. Mark gave it a command to hover at fifteen feet, then he and Beth strolled arm in arm down the Boulevard Saint-Germain to Les Deux Magots. They arrived at 9:40 p.m. local time.

"I am sorry, Sir, but without a reservation, we do not have any tables available," the maitre d' said.

"I didn't think to call for a reservation," Beth said.

"Not that we could have made that call anyway," Mark said.

"Any table would do," Mark said to the maitre d'.

The waiter responded in French, which Mark did not understand.

"Darn, I had been looking forward to this," Beth said.

Mark had been looking forward to a special night and was also a little put off by the maitre d's attitude, who had now turned away to talk to someone else. Mark reached over and touched the maitre d's shoulder to get his attention. "Vous nous donned use table main tenant,"

Mark said. "Il set très important. We have flown all the way from the United States just to come here to eat," Mark added in English. The maitre d' turned back to Mark with a blank look, then immediately became animated.

"But of course, Monsieur et Madame. If you give me just a moment, I will have a table for you." With that he hurried away, while Beth and Mark looked at each other in surprise.

"Why did he change his mind suddenly?" Beth asked.

"I don't know?"

Their speculation was cut short as the maitre d' returned and escorted them to a table with a Reserve sign, which he deftly set aside.

"This is odd," Mark said as the maitre d' informed them that their waiter would be with them shortly and wished them a pleasant dinner.

"What did you say?" Beth asked. "Did you slip him a bribe?"

"No. I just told him we would like a table. I explained that we had flown in from the U.S. just to have dinner here and it was real important to us."

"No. What did you say in French?" Beth asked. "What words?"

Mark repeated what he had said.

"Oh, you ugly American," Beth said.

"What?"

"You said you 'will' give me a table. It was a command. 'Would like' is 'voudre' in French, not 'donnez.'"

"So much for my High School French," Mark said.

"I'm surprised he did not call the gendarmes."

The waiters brought some hot French bread along with a bottle of champagne and two champagne glasses.

"We didn't order champagne," Mark said in English now that he had lost confidence in his French.

"Not yet, anyway," Beth added.

"Compliments of the house," the waiter replied in English as he poured the cold champagne and placed the bottle in an ice stand next to the table.

"I could get used to this," Beth said.

"Try some of this," Beth said. "This is excellent champagne."

"I wonder if they mistook us for someone else?" Mark asked as he sipped the champagne. It was excellent.

"If they did, I hope they don't show up until after we have finished."

"Me to."

They spent the rest of the time enjoying an exquisite dinner, complete with creme brûlée for dessert. "That will certainly blow my diet," Mark said when they had finished eating.

"Yes, but it is worth it. Just do an extra lap at the gym."

They paid their bill with Euros, leaving a generous tip and then wandered down the street arm in arm toward the park.

"That was a wonderful idea," Beth said. "We should do that more often."

"We can. As often as we want, in what ever country we want."

"I suppose we should feel guilty about this," Beth said. "But you were almost killed twice."

"The beauty of the human mind," Mark replied. "We can rationalize anything."

"Now I do feel guilty."

"Don't. Why shouldn't we play a little? What's the harm in that?"

They walked down the street arm in arm. After walking a couple blocks in silence, Beth asked, "So how is your search of the cube going?"

"Very frustrating. It's fascinating, but I haven't figured out how to share any of it."

"You were thinking about medicine."

"Yes. But the blue-grays were only interested in the control technology in our time and I am certainly not going to share any of that. I don't even want to explore that area. And of course the old visions involve dinosaurs, humans had not even evolved then."

"Have you talked with Benjamin?"

"I talked with him about what he does and some of the science over lunch the other day."

"And?"

"And I didn't understand a word he said. I went back to the cube and tried to think about our conversation while I had the cube, but it still did not translate. I'm thinking I might talk to him while I have the cube, maybe I would understand him then."

"You're not going to show him the cube, are you?"

"No. I thought I would just have it in my pocket. Maybe surreptitiously access it to see if it would translate for me."

"That's an idea," Beth said.

"Best I have right now. It's frustrating, we are sitting on all this knowledge, but don't know how to share it."

They walked on in silence. After awhile, Mark said, "Do you want to go anywhere else while we are here?

"What time is it here?" Beth asked.

Mark looked at his watch and did some mental calculations. "About 11:30 p.m."

"I suppose we should get back. Perhaps next time we can walk down the Champs Elysees and do some window shopping."

"That sounds dangerous," Mark said with a laugh.

"So how do you get this pod back down," Beth asked as they walked back to the park.

"When I get within a certain range, I can contact it telepathically. As long as I have this," Mark said as he pulled the cube out of his pocket.

"Works for me," Beth said, the champagne working wonders for her mood.

After glancing around to make sure they were alone, Mark 'called' the pod and they climbed in. "How about a quick loop around the Eiffel Tower before we head home?" Mark suggested as the craft slowly lifted into the Parisian night.

# CHAPTER 12

A week had gone by and Beth was sitting on the couch with her feet propped on the coffee table. She had spent the weekend visiting her mother in Gulfport and had just returned home. "I know the drive is only two hours, but I swear it feels a lot longer than that."

"That's I-10 for you," Mark said. "Straight and boring."

"So what did you do while I was away? Anything interesting?"

"Friday night I had dinner with Mike."

"Mike?"

"Mike Timmons, the criminal lawyer."

"Oh, that Mike. Is he still dating that girl, the one with the insurance agency?" Beth asked.

"I don't know. We didn't talk about that."

"Men! What did you all talk about?"

"This and that," Mark said. "We looked at the harvest moon with his telescope," Mark said. "Remember, he is an amateur astronomer. It seemed so close, you could clearly see the craters."

"You can see the craters with your eye," Beth said, unimpressed.

"But this was as if you were there."

Something about Mark's tone caught Beth's attention. She glanced around the room. Everything was just as it had been when she left, right down to the paper. She picked up the paper, it was Friday's. "Where is today's paper?" Beth asked.

"It must still be in the box on the street," Mark answered a bit sheepishly.

Beth got up and walked into the kitchen. Some dishes were in the drying rack, but otherwise the kitchen was clean. She looked at the dishes and thought they were the same ones when she left. She opened the refrigerator and looked inside. Nothing was changed. "What did you do this weekend?" she asked Mark suspiciously.

Mark glanced furtively around the room before answering. "Nothing much," he said.

Beth realized something was going on. That would explain why she had not talked with Mark on the phone while she was visiting her mother. Mark had said he was real tired and was turning off his cellphone so he could relax. Beth thought there was another explanation and was starting to suspect what it was. "How are the horses?" she asked.

Mark appeared surprised by the sudden change of topic. "Uh, they are fine."

"You haven't been feeding them too much? Have you?" Beth asked. "Last time I thought Dot was getting too fat."

"No. Half a scoop, just like we talked about."

"I want to check on them."

"Right now?" Mark asked.

"Before we forget."

With that, Beth headed for the door. "You coming?" Beth asked as she opened the kitchen door.

"Right, sure."

Beth walked down to the barn with Mark in tow. She walked between the hay bales, a horse whinnied at her from one of the stalls. She ignored him. Walking to the end of the row, she pointed to an empty space and mouthed the words, "Open it."

Mark reached out and pressed his hand against what looked like empty space. The door of the pod spiraled open. She climbed into the pod and Mark followed her. When the door spiraled shut, she turned to Mark, who was now seated inches away from her.

"What did you do?" Beth demanded.

Mark smiled sheepishly. "It was so beautiful and so close. I thought I would just go and look at it."

"At the moon?" Beth asked.

"Yes."

"In this?"

"Yes."

"The moon?" Beth repeated.

"It is a spaceship," Mark said defensively.

"It's a blue-gray spaceship," Beth said. "You are not a blue-gray."

"I am when I have the cube," Mark said.

The way Mark said that gave Beth a cold chill.

"You are a human," Beth said.

"Yes," Mark corrected. "But the ship thinks I am a blue-gray when I have the cube."

"So you flew this ship to the moon while I was gone?"

"Yes," Mark said. "It was incredible," Mark continued, unable to contain his excitement. "You should have seen it! And the view. The Earth coming up over the horizon, pictures do not do it justice."

Beth opened her mouth to speak.

"And the craters. They are huge!" Mark continued. "Like a giant desert. You should have seen it. Wait. You can. I'll show you," Mark said as he sunk his hand into his chair.

"Don't you dare fly this thing right now," Beth said.

"No, I'm not going to fly it," Mark said. "I'm going to show you what it was like." As he said that the space between them filled with a vision of the moon that was so detailed and realistic that Beth almost reached out to touch it. "Isn't it awesome," Mark said. "Now, watch this," the view rotated, giving her the illusion that she was skimming across the face of the moon, just above the surface. "Watch the horizon," Mark said.

Beth looked at the horizon, watching the white emptiness of the moon contrast with the black of space, dotted by millions of stars. She had never seen so many stars. And then a giant blue orb rose up on the horizon. Beth gasped as the Earth appeared, blue and white.

"We aren't there, right?" Beth asked. "We haven't flown anywhere."

"No," Mark said. "This is like a tape from my trip. We are still in the barn. See, look." The pod's hatch spiraled open showing a line of hay bales.

"Ok, good. Just checking," Beth said.

The hatch spiraled close.

"It's beautiful," Beth whispered as the Earth rose up, much larger than the moon ever looked as it came up.

"Isn't it?" Mark agreed.

Beth just stared at the sight.

"The view is breathtaking," Mark added after Beth had stared a while longer.

"It is," Beth said. "Pictures do not do it justice."

They sat and stared at the hologram before them. Mark finally broke the silence. "But other than the view, what does it have to offer?"

"What do you mean?" Beth asked.

"It's airless. Just dirt. No water. No grass. No trees. Nothing living. Why would anyone want to come here?

After the initial fascination over the fact that it is the moon, that is," Mark said.

"I guess to explore. Why climb Mount Everest?"

"Okay. I've never understood that either."

"Actually, we haven't gone back to the moon," Beth said.

"And now I know why," Mark said. "After I came here and the initial awe wore off. Look around. There is nothing here. All the beauty is really there," Mark said as he pointed to the Earth hanging over the horizon.

"The grass is always greener…" Beth said.

"Right. Here there is no grass," Mark said with a laugh.

"I'm still not happy with the fact that you went to the moon," Beth said. "Actually flew to the moon. You didn't tell me."

"Would you have let me come if I had?" Mark asked.

"No, but…"

"Better to ask forgiveness, than permission."

"But what if something went wrong?" Beth said. "This is an alien ship and the moon is, the moon."

"It is an alien ship, an alien space ship," Mark said. "It's like driving a car."

"Cars don't drive to the moon."

"Blue-gray cars do," Mark said. "It really is that simple."

"How do you know what to do?"

"I keep telling you, when I have the cube, I just know," Mark said. "I can't tell you how, I just know."

"So you are saying that for a blue-gray, going to the moon is like driving to town?"

"Something like that," Mark agreed. "Their technology is that far ahead of us."

Beth was silent for a while. "Well, I don't like it. I don't want you flying off to the moon. And without telling me."

"So you can worry?"

"Yes, so I can worry."

Mark laughed. "Okay. I will let you know next time so you can worry."

"I'm serious. This whole thing is," Beth paused.

"Alien."

"Yes, alien. And I don't understand it and it scares me."

Mark leaned over and gave Beth a hug. "I wish I could share the cube with you."

"I know."

"I promise from now on I won't take the pod anywhere without telling you first."

"Thank you," Beth said. "It's just so strange."

"It is that," Mark said.

"Okay, Beth said. "Now you can let us out. I'm exhausted and need to take a bath and go to bed."

# Part II

# CHAPTER 13

It was Wednesday afternoon and Mark was at the office unsuccessfully trying to concentrate on work. Flying the pod around was fun and it had allowed him to include Beth. The trips to Paris and the Caymans had been great. But those were really just diversions. The trip to the moon was what the pod was all about. How could he share that with someone who could really benefit from the trip? How could he take a scientist with him without tipping off the government that he had the pod?

Mark glanced over at the cube, which was sitting on the mantle over the unused fireplace. He had placed it with several other knickknacks, including a rubric's cube, which was about the same diameter. 'Hide it in plain sight,' Mark laughed. Mark was planning on taking the cube to dinner with Benjamin that night. Maybe that way he could translate some of the blue-gray's knowledge into something he could share.

"Mr. Johnson with the State Department is on line two," Mark's secretary's voice on the intercom interrupted his train of thought. "Would you like to take the call?"

Mark had a moment of panic. The State Department, they had found him out. He quickly dismissed the idea. If they had caught him the FBI or NSA would be raiding his office, not calling him on the phone. "Sure," Mark said, wondering what this was about.

"This is Mark Williams."

"Mr. Williams, this is Bill Johnson with the State Department."

"What can I do for you?"

"I have a last minute request for you," Mr. Johnson said. "We have four Chinese lawyers visiting Pensacola on a cultural exchange visit and their schedule for tonight has been cancelled. The host suddenly got sick. We were wondering if you had time to attend dinner with them tonight. Nothing formal, just chat with them about Pensacola or the law. Answer whatever questions they have."

"I've done this before," Mark said. "Although last time it was lunch. Would other people be attending?"

There was a slight pause. "This would just be you and the Chinese lawyers since our local representative took suddenly ill. We can have someone else cover for tomorrow if he does not feel better, but we are scrambling to cover tonight's dinner."

"Last time we had an interpreter. She was State Department, I think from Hawaii."

"You won't need an interpreter. You would meet them at the restaurant. I know this is last minute, but I wonder if you would be able to do this?"

"Sure. Sounds like fun."

"Good. Can you meet them tonight at McGuires at seven?"

"Okay."

"Great. Thanks. They will meet you at the front door of McGuires at seven. Let me give you my cell phone number." They exchanged numbers and then hung up. Mark called his wife next.

"Hey Honey, it's me," Mark said when Beth picked up the phone. "Guess what?"

"You always say that," Beth responded. "What?"

"Remember that luncheon I had last year with the three Chinese lawyers who were visiting the States?"

"Yes."

"Well, they are doing it again. Only this time the host got sick and they asked me to cover a dinner with four Chinese lawyers at McGuires, tonight."

"Tonight?"

"Yes. So I will probably be home a little late tonight. Do you want to come?"

"No thank you. I've got some work I need to do. You go enjoy McGuires. And make sure they don't pay for their meal by pulling any of the dollars off the ceiling," she said, obviously referring to the fact that McGuires had over one million dollar bills stapled to the ceiling.

"I'll tell them that in America money just grows on the ceiling," Mark said with a laugh, before hanging up.

Mark was at the front door of McGuires promptly at seven. As usual, there was a line, but off to the side, two Asian gentlemen in business suits stood by themselves scanning the crowd. Mark walked up to them. "Are you Mr. Chin?" Mark asked.

"Mr. Williams?" was the reply from one of them in accented English.

"Yes," Mark said, holding out his hand to shake. Instead, both gentlemen bowed to Mark as they stated their names. Mark dropped his hand and bowed back. 'Odd,' he thought. 'Last time the Chinese had bowed, but they had also shaken hands. I will have to remember to ask them about that custom.'

"Our colleague has reserved us a table," one of the Chinese was saying. "Please follow me." He then led Mark to one of the back rooms where two more Asian looking gentlemen already occupied a corner booth.

They both half stood and bowed while introductions were made. They motioned Mark to join them and Mark slid into the booth next to one of the Chinese. The others joined them so that Mark was sitting between two Chinese on his side, while two others sat across from him. Fortunately, McGuires' booths were spacious or it would have been a tight fit.

The next hour and a half was spent eating and talking about China and the U.S. legal systems. Most of the conversation on the Chinese side was conducted by the two men sitting across from Mark, a Mr. Chin and Mr. Liang, both of whom spoke very passable English. Mark tried to include the two individuals sitting on either side of him into the conversation, but they merely smiled and nodded. He could not tell how much they were actually following. Mark recalled that last year only one of the three lawyers spoke any English, while the others had to rely exclusively on the interpreter. Although Mark tried to ask them about their legal system and customs, the Chinese kept most of the conversation on U.S. practice.

Despite the slight language difficulties, the only awkward moment was when they asked if Mark had ever visited China. Mark had not anticipated that question and it took him by surprise. He tried to cover his hesitation by taking a big bite of steak, taking the time to chew to formulate his answer, finally deciding to deny any visit.

After they finished their meal, Mark walked out into the parking lot with the Chinese. "We have not seen your beach," Mr. Chin was saying. "Could you show us where your beach is?"

"It is easy to get to," Mark said, as he started giving directions.

"Would you mind coming with us and showing us," Mr. Chin said. "You could ride with us and then we could bring you back here. We would really appreciate it."

Mark agreed and they had him climb into the back of the Chevy mini-van that they were driving. He ended up sitting between the same two Chinese men he had sat between at the table, while Mr. Chin sat in the front passenger's seat and the other gentleman drove. As they drove over the three-mile bridge towards Gulf Breeze, Mr. Chin turned so he could talk directly to Mark.

"You do not remember me," Mr. Chin said. "But we have met before."

Mark looked at him quizzically. "I'm sorry," Mark said. "I just can't place you."

"I was with Colonel Lui when you met him in the tunnels."

Mark immediately tensed up. He became painfully aware that he was sitting in the back of the car between two Chinese men, who now appeared more like soldiers than lawyers. They were eyeing him intently. Mark did not know how to respond. He watched as Pensacola Bay rippled beneath them as they continued to drive over the three-mile bridge. Soon they would be in Gulf Breeze. Mark doubted whether he could forcibly get out of the van. It was four against one, three, if you did not count the driver. 'Sergeant Jeffreys could do it,' Mark thought. 'Actually, did do it. Against five armed soldiers while they traveled in China. But here I am in my home town and I am defenseless.'

"Yes, I was there," Chin continued. "You were there with a Sergeant, looking for ..." Mark did not understand the Chinese word. "You called them blue-grays."

"What do you want?" Mark managed to say, hoping his voice did not betray his anxiety.

"I want to know what happened. Where are the blue-grays now?"

"Why don't you ask the government?"

"They tell us nothing," Chin said. "You were there. Yet somehow you are now here. You tell me what happened."

They were across the bridge and driving through Gulf Breeze. Mark glanced at the speedometer. Thirty-five. 'Damn!' He had hoped they were speeding. The speed limit dropped at the end of the bridge and Gulf Breeze was a known speed trap town.

"Tell me what happened," Chin repeated.

"You were there," Mark said. "Then you must know what happened." Even as he said it, Mark realized the stupidity of the statement.

"If I was there at the end, I would have been vaporized with Colonel Lui," Chin said ominously. "I was in the tunnels, back at headquarters. I was not at the blast site."

Mark thought furiously. Colonel Lui had ordered his soldiers to kill Mark and Sgt. Jeffreys. He wondered if Chin knew that. Or if there were any cameras at the scene that recorded the final moments, then Chin would know he was there. But then he would also know what happened. He would have seen it, wouldn't he? Or maybe the cameras were knocked out when the cats attacked. But then they would not have recorded Mark there. 'Stick as close to the truth as possible,' Mark thought.

"Sergeant Jeffreys and I were sent to look for the cube. Our vehicle was involved in an accident when it went into a ditch. We were all injured, the soldiers in the front were killed." 'Killed by the heavy machine gun from the vehicle behind,' Mark thought as he remembered the events. "When we recovered, the bomb went off."

"How are you here now?" Chin asked.

"We made it down to our embassy and they got us out of China. I really don't know the details."

"Then you were exposed to the radiation."

"Probably. I am being monitored by my doctor," Mark lied.

"What about the blue-grays?"

"What about them?"

"Where are they now?"

"I don't know where they are," Mark lied again.

"Did they win? Did they beat the cats?" Chin asked.

"I don't know. I was on the other side of the mountain. That's why I am alive. I don't know what happened anymore than you do." They were across Gulf Breeze and heading for the Bob Sykes bridge which would take them into Pensacola Beach. There was a toll booth at the bottom of the bridge, one with a person in it. Mark wondered if he could yell for help when they got there. The car could easily bust through the flimsy gate, but there was nowhere to go on Pensacola Beach and there was a heavy police presence for all the tourists. This might be his only chance.

Chin leaned between the seats towards Mark. They were approaching the tollbooth. There were only two cars between him and the booth. Chin said something in Chinese and the two men on either side of Mark pinned his arms to his sides. "I think you lie," Chin said in English. Mark started to protest when Chin slapped him on the thigh with the flat of his hand. There was a surprisingly sharp pain in his thigh. Mark looked desperately out the window, only one car was between them and the tollbooth. Chin was looking at Mark with a look of surprise on his face. Halo's formed around the brake lights of the car in front of them as Mark's head started to drop. The last thing Mark heard was Chin saying, "You have a cube."

## CHAPTER 14

Beth fell asleep before Mark came home. She woke up the next morning and Mark was not there. At first she assumed that he had gotten up early and gone out back to feed, but then she realized that he had not slept on his side of the bed. She went outside and the dogs and cats ran over, waiting to be fed. Glancing over to the driveway, she noticed that Mark's car was missing. A wave of fear passed through her.

'Don't panic,' she told herself. 'There is probably a perfectly reasonable and safe explanation for him not being here. And when I learn he is safe, I am going to kill him,' she added to herself. She went back in and checked for any notes on the kitchen counter. Finding none, she checked her phone for any messages. Again none. She called his phone and left a voice mail message. She called his office. The answering machine picked up. It was still too early for the staff to have come in.

Now she was really beginning to worry. Mark never stayed out late without telling her. Something must have happened. Surely the police would have notified her if there had been an accident. She checked the house again for messages and searched for any sign that he had been home. Still finding none, she quickly showered and dressed. 'What to do?'

She went out to the barn and walked between the hay bales to the back. Hands held out, she walked slowly forward until her hands hit the pod. It did not open. It never did for her. But it was still there. Mark had not flown to the moon or somewhere. She did not think that he had since his car was not home, but she had to check. 'What to do now?' she wondered.

She remembered that he had said he was meeting the Chinese lawyers at McGuire's. That's the last she had heard from him. If he had planned anything else, he would have called or at least texted her. She called his cell phone and office again, but both went into voicemail. She called the Florida Highway Patrol and asked if there had been an accident reported with his car. She repeated the call to the Sheriff's Department and the Pensacola Police Department. No such report. Calls to his cell phone and office again went to voice mail. 'I am going to kill him when I find him,' she told herself, while trying to tell herself that all would be fine.

'What to do now?' She decided to check his office. Maybe he decided to spend the night there and was still asleep. Unlikely, but she could not think of anything else. His car was not in the parking lot and the office was locked when she arrived and the staff had not come in yet. She knocked on the door anyway, but no one answered. Having run out of ideas, she drove over to McGuire's even though she knew it would be closed.

She pulled into the parking lot and spotted Mark's car sitting alone next to the hedge in the adjacent Sammy's parking lot. She looked inside the car. It was empty. She really had not expected him to be in it, although right now she no longer knew what to expect. She hadn't brought her extra set of car keys, so she could not open the car. She called his cell phone again, but it went to voice mail.

She called his office again. "Law offices," a female voice answered.

"Hello, Laura," Beth said, recognizing the receptionist's voice. "This is Beth. Is Mark there?"

"He hasn't come in yet Beth," Laura said.

"Did he leave any messages?" Beth asked, trying to keep her voice from sounding frantic.

"No."

"Is there anything on his calendar?" Beth asked.

"Not until 10 a.m. He has a client coming in then."

"Could you have him call me the second he comes in? I need to talk to him."

"Sure."

Beth hung up. She tried to assure herself that everything was fine, that there was a valid explanation for Mark's absence. But she could not come up with any reasonable, or even unreasonable explanation that made any sense. Not knowing what to do next, she left a note on the windshield asking Mark to call her and then drove to her office. She waited an hour, unsuccessfully trying to work. Every time she tried calling Mark's cell phone, it went into voicemail. She called his office again, but he had still not arrived.

She finally figured out how she could track down the Chinese lawyers. Mark had said it was another State Department visit. Beth knew the local representative for the State Department. She and Mark had hosted a high school girl from Iraq for a couple weeks as part of a State Department program. The leader of the Pensacola group had told her that he also coordinated the visits for adults. 'What was his name?' Beth wondered. She searched her phone. It was not under State Department. 'What was the name? She could picture the director's face, but could not remember his name. 'Diplomacy something is the name of the group,' she remembered. She typed in diplomacy and the contact popped up, Gulf Coast Citizen Diplomacy Council. She dialed the number.

"Jeremy Landers please," Beth said, her heart in her throat.

"This is Jeremy, how may I help you?"

"Jeremy, this is Beth Williams."

"Oh, Hi Beth, how are you doing?"

Beth wanted to scream 'not well, you idiot,' but her southern upbringing required her to go through the formalities. "I'm fine. But I wanted to talk to you about a recent program you have," Beth quickly said to cut off any more small talk.

"We aren't bringing in another group of high school students until February," Jeremy said.

"No, not that one. I'm talking about the Chinese lawyers you have here now. I wonder if I could meet them?"

"Chinese lawyers? We don't have anyone here now," Jeremy said.

Beth could feel her pulse pounding in her ears. "Yes, you do," she said. "Mark met with them last night at McGuire's. Someone called and asked him to cover the dinner since the local representative got sick. I thought maybe that was you."

"No. The last group of adults we had were schoolteachers from Brazil. That was last month. We are not due for another group of adults for a while."

"You don't have any Chinese adults here now," Beth repeated, trying to keep the pleading out of her voice.

"No."

"Could another group be hosting them? They said they were here on a State Department visit."

"Not likely. We have the contract for Pensacola. The next closest group is Jacksonville."

"What about Mobile?" Beth asked frantically.

"No. There isn't a group there. Why?"

"You are absolutely certain no Chinese would be here with the State Department?" Beth asked.

"Not on a cultural visit. No. I would know."

"Okay. Thanks." Beth hung up, unable to speak anymore. Dread filled her as she realized that something was seriously wrong. She had been trying to convince herself that Mark had gone to Sammy's and spent the night. Although completely out of character, it was still a better scenario than the one that faced her now: the Chinese had come and captured him. Resisting the almost overwhelming urge to break down and cry, she forced herself to consider her next step. After some careful thought, she picked up her phone and dialed another number.

"Sheriff Anderson, please, Beth Williams calling."

"Beth, how are you doing?" Sheriff Anderson answered a few moments later.

"Not well, John. I need your help. Mark is missing. I think he has been kidnapped."

John's tone immediately got serious. "Kidnapped? Are you sure? When?"

"Last night. It's a rather complicated story," Beth said. "I really need to tell you in person."

"Sure. You want to meet at my office?"

Beth paused. "I found his car downtown. How about we meet there?"

"Ok. Where is it?

"It's in the Sammy's parking lot on Gregory."

Beth could hear the silence on the phone. "Beth…"

"Oh for Pete's sake," Beth said. "You know Mark. He would drop dead before he stepped foot into Sammy's. He met some people at McGuire's last night and we always park on the other side of the hedge at Sammy's because that area is always empty. He didn't come home last night and he did not show up at the office today."

"Ok, Beth. I can be there in about ten minutes."

"I'll be waiting for you," Beth said as she hung up. Beth's office was only a couple blocks from McGuire's. She pulled into the parking lot and parked next to Mark's car. A minute later an unmarked Crown Victoria pulled into the parking lot. An officer got out and walked over to Beth, who had exited her car.

"Are you Beth Williams?" the officer asked.

"Yes."

"I'm Detective Johnson. Sheriff Anderson asked me to meet him here. He should be here in a minute." As he said it, a Sheriff's Blazer pulled into the parking lot and Sheriff Anderson got out.

"Thank you for coming John," Beth said.

"So what is this all about?" John asked.

Beth explained about Mark's call requesting that he meet the Chinese lawyers, his call to her that he was going to McGuire's and then her conversation this morning with Jeremy Landers when she found out there were no State Department visitors here. When she finished, John looked skeptical.

"Did you ever meet these Chinese lawyers?" John asked.

"No."

"Did you talk to the State Department people yesterday?"

"No."

"So all of your information about this visit was from Mark."

"Yes, but…"

"That is not a lot to go on," John said, glancing over at Sammy's.

"He did not spend the night with some girl from Sammy's," Beth said. "We've been married over twenty-five years. He has never not called or stayed out. Never."

"It would not be the first time someone suddenly had mid-life crisis," John said. "We see it all the time."

"You know Mark. That is not him."

"Agreed. But perhaps we should wait a little longer," John said. "Mark's absence doesn't mean he was kidnapped."

Beth counted to three to control herself. She would have to make John understand what was going on. There was no one else that she could call. "I'll tell you why I think something is seriously wrong," Beth said. "Remember last year, when I had that NSA agent lurking about the farm. Your boys arrested him, but then you had to let him go because Washington insisted?"

"Yes. I never did get a good explanation for that," John said.

"Well, I can give you that explanation. Mark works for the CIA." Beth let the statement hang.

"He what?" John said.

"Not full time," Beth admitted. "He has done a couple of missions for them. One was last year when he was away and we had that incident."

"But why would the NSA be spying on you if Mark is with the CIA?" John asked.

"I don't know," Beth said. "Maybe political infighting. Anyway, the important thing is that three months ago Mark was called to do another mission, in China. He was there when that nuclear explosion took place in China. He personally briefed the President as to what happened." Beth paused to let her statement sink in. "Yesterday, Mark called me and said he was meeting with four Chinese lawyers on a State Department visit. He has done that before, meeting with Chinese, Korean and other lawyers who were visiting. But those visits were all scheduled well in advance and were held at lunchtime at the courthouse or a local law firm. This one was last minute. He didn't think anything of it. Was excited about meeting them. But there were no State Department visitors here. I checked. I think the Chinese have come and kidnapped him."

Now it was John's turn to be silent. "If this is true," John finally said. "Then it takes it way out of my jurisdiction. Who did Mark report to at the CIA?"

"I don't know. The only one in the government that I know of is the President of the United States. I know Mark has reported directly to him more than once."

"Are you sure?"

"Absolutely."

"I also remember him mentioning a Navy Captain. I can't remember his name right now. He is the Captain of the *USS Ronald Reagan,* an aircraft carrier in the Pacific Ocean. That was the staging area for one of Mark's assignments."

"This is way out of my area," John said. "We need to contact the FBI."

"Then call them. I'm sure they will listen to you more than to me."

Sheriff Anderson made the call and fifteen very long minutes later a dark sedan pulled into the parking lot and two FBI agents got out. Any other time Beth would have laughed as the two looked like they had stepped out of central casting, both had gray slacks, blue blazers and matching sunglasses. She proceeded to tell the entire story to the two agents. Despite Sheriff Anderson confirming the portion about the NSA agents last year, it was obvious that the FBI agents were not buying Beth's story.

"You are saying that your husband is a covert CIA agent, but you don't know who his contact is, but you know he reports directly to the President?"

"Yes," Beth said, knowing that this would not convince the agents. Both agents glanced over at Sammy's.

"Is that all you guys can think about?" she said in disgust. "What is it with you? It seems natural that after twenty-five years of a happy marriage, a man will suddenly spend the night with some dancer from Sammy's? Let's even say that is true. My husband is not stupid. Don't you think if he was going to do that he would come up with some ruse? Wait until I am away for the weekend? He is missing appointments today. Even you must have some more control than that!"

There followed an uncomfortable silence. "What do you want us to do?" one of the agents asked.

Beth nearly screamed in frustration. "You're the cops. What do you do when someone is missing?" Beth paused. "Okay. I know you don't believe me. Why don't you try to confirm my story?"

"You don't expect us to call the President?" the second agent said.

"I really do," Beth said. When the silence deepened she added, "Why don't you go over to McGuire's and see if they have any surveillance video? Mark told me he was meeting four Chinese lawyers at seven p.m. at the front of McGuire's. See if I'm right."

That did the trick. Sheriff Anderson was keen to check on it, while the FBI agents grudgingly followed. It took thirty minutes for them to locate someone at McGuire's who had access to the surveillance video and another fifteen minutes to set up the computer to start reviewing just before seven p.m. They only had to watch for five minutes before Beth spotted Mark entering McGuire's with an Asian looking individual. They fast-forwarded the playback until they saw him leaving with four Asian looking men about an hour and a half later. They located the feed from a parking lot camera and could just make out Mark getting in the back of a van with the four men and driving off. When the playback ended Beth was sick. She had secretly hoped she was wrong and now she had seen Mark being escorted away. She looked over at the agents, tears forming in her eyes.

"I wish I was wrong," she said, trying to keep the sob from her voice.

"This does not confirm your story," the first FBI agent said. Beth did not remember their names.

"The only one who can confirm my story is the President," Beth said as fear for her husband's safety almost overwhelmed her. If these agents would not believe her, how would she get Washington to pay attention? She needed them to act now, not a week from now. She had one more card to play, but she would have to play it very carefully. "You have to get a message to the President right now," she said. "And I will give you the message. Tell the President that Mark Williams is missing. He was last seen with four Chinese looking men. Tell him that Mark is in possession of a fully functioning blue-gray cube and that both Mark and the cube are missing and that his wife thinks the Chinese have got them both."

"What is a blue-gray cube?" one agent asked.

"That is a code word. The President knows what it means. Very few other people know. If the President gets that message I guarantee he will be calling here within five minutes."

"You don't expect us to get a message to the President of the United States just on your say-so?" the agent said.

Beth looked him in the eye, surprisingly calm for the rage she felt building inside her. "Listen to me. My husband was in China at ground zero shortly before that nuke exploded. He is probably the only person alive who knows exactly what happened there. He personally briefed the President on it after being evacuated to the *U.S.S. Ronald Reagan*. The Chinese aren't the only people who have nukes. We have them all over the place. Let's just assume for a moment that my story is true. Don't you think the President would want to know? Think about it, the worst terrorist attack in history - a nuclear detonation. And now the only person with first hand knowledge of it has been abducted by unknown Chinese agents." Beth paused. "Or do you want to be the agents who sat on this information and gave them the time they need to carry out what ever their plans are here?"

The agents blinked first. "Ok. We'll send this upstairs."

"Make sure you send my message. The President has to be told that Mark has a fully functional blue-gray cube and that he is now missing, believed to be taken by the Chinese. I don't care what else you say, but that part of the message has to get to the President. That's the code. And most people don't know it. I don't even know if your FBI Director knows that code. But I know the President does."

When the agents left to deliver the message, Beth sat down, emotionally drained. "What do we do now?" she asked the Sheriff.

"We will get to work," John said. He turned to his detective. "I want this case worked up priority. Bring as many people as you need into this. Let's get copies of this tape and see if we can get an I.D. on the vehicle and where it went. Check the local street cams. Interview McGuire's servers and see if we can get any information on these four guys. Get someone to check the airport. And," John added as the detective started to make a call, "keep all the information about the CIA and the President secret. Don't tell anyone unless I personally okay it."

"Yes, Sir." The detective replied.

## CHAPTER 15

Beth was still with Sheriff Anderson when her cell phone rang.

"Ms. Williams?"

"Yes."

"This is Agent Philips, with the FBI. I met with you a little while ago."

"I remember."

"The President would like to speak to you."

Beth resisted the urge to say, 'no kidding.' Instead she simply said, "Ok."

"Can you come to our office so that we can make a secure call?" the agent asked. When Beth agreed, he gave her directions. It was only a few blocks away. When she hung up, Beth turned to Sheriff Anderson.

"I have to go. The President wants to talk to me." In any other situation, that would have been a fun line to say. But under the circumstances, Beth didn't even notice it. But Sheriff Anderson did.

"The President?" he asked.

"Yes. That was Agent Philips. They got my message to the President and he wants to talk to me. I have to go to their office so they can set up a secure phone call."

"Ok," Sheriff Anderson said. "I'll keep you posted on what we find here."

"Thank you John. I really appreciate your help. And your belief in me when no one else would listen."

Sheriff Anderson only nodded as Beth hurried to her car.

Fifteen minutes later Beth was sitting in front of a video screen as the agent finished setting up a secure video conference call. A minute later the President came into the camera view and sat down.

"Good morning, Ms. Williams," he said.

"Good morning, Mr. President."

"I understand that you believe Mr. Williams has a functioning blue-gray cube and has been kidnapped by the Chinese. Can you give me the details?"

"Yes," Beth said, wondering why no one had briefed him yet. She proceeded to tell him the same information she had told Sheriff Anderson and the FBI agents about Mark's last minute invitation yesterday and the fact that he was now missing. She also added that the Sheriff's department had found surveillance video showing her husband getting into a SUV with four oriental looking males and driving off and were trying to get further information on the vehicle. She noticed the FBI agents squirming off-camera as they had left McGuire's without doing any investigating, probably thinking she was some nut. But fortunately, at least they got her message through.

"What about the cube?" the President asked, interrupting Beth's thoughts. "We were not aware that he had a cube." Beth wondered if she caught irritation in the President's tone of voice.

"He didn't tell anyone about it," Beth said.

"No one?"

"No one. Other than me, of course."

"Where did he get it?" the President asked.

"It was the personal cube from the blue-gray who died in China. He brought it back with him from China."

"And it still worked? He could still access it, even after the nuclear explosion?" the President asked.

"Yes," Beth simply replied.

"How? The personal cube from the dead blue-gray on the *Ronald Reagan* ceased functioning when their ship was lost in the worm hole."

"I don't know," Beth answered. "All I know is that he had it and it still worked."

"Why didn't he turn it over to us?" the President asked. Beth clearly caught the irritated undercurrent to that question.

"He didn't trust you," Beth said without hesitation. "Not you, Mr. President, the government. He didn't trust the government with the cube. Not after the NSA agents drugged him last year and tried to spy on me. He said that the power of the cube was unimaginable and that he was afraid of what would happen if that technology got out."

"What does the cube do?"

"I don't know that it 'does' anything," Beth said. "I tried to access it, but it does not work for me. Mark said that it contains the blue-gray's knowledge. He described it like being inside the Library of Congress, with the world's knowledge at your fingertips. You just have to choose what to learn."

"What had he learned?" the President asked.

"He was exploring the blue-gray's culture, their civilization," Beth answered. "Mark was taking it slow. To use Mark's Library of Congress analogy, he said that you couldn't pick up an Advanced Physics book and understand it. You had to start at Physics 101 and then take it in order. Also, he was having trouble translating the blue-grays' information into terms that he could understand. After all, the cube was not in English."

"How did he understand it then?"

"I really don't know. He said that he understood it perfectly when he was connected to the cube. It was only after he disconnected that the translation problems arose."

"So why was he afraid to share this with the government?" the President asked.

"You know about the control cubes, right?" Beth asked.

"Yes."

"Mark said that the control cube technology was probably contained in the cube he had. He was terrified that if that technology got out, who ever had it could literally control the world."

"So what was he planning to do with the cube?"

"We talked about that at length," Beth said. "We discussed destroying the cube so no one could get it. What Mark finally decided was that he would cautiously explore the cube and see if he could find some advances, perhaps in medicine, that he could share with the world. He was afraid that too big a technological jump, particularly if it could be used militarily, would be very dangerous. And Mr. President," Beth said.

"Yes."

"I agree with him."

There was a pause. Finally the President said, "So how did the Chinese find out about him and the cube?"

"I have no idea," Beth answered. "We tried to be pretty careful. Mark was convinced that the NSA was still spying on us, so we did not talk about it in the house and took great pains to shield our conversations so they could not be overheard. I have no idea how the Chinese found out. Unless it is from when he was over there last time," Beth added.

"Anything else?" the President asked.

"No, Sir," Beth lied. "That's about it."

"We will find your husband and the cube," the President said. "We will keep you posted."

"Thank you, Mr. President," Beth said. She was concerned that she had told about the cube, but knew that without that information, the government would not act promptly. Now, she knew they would put all their resources on finding Mark. She hoped and prayed that it would be enough.

Later that day Beth received a phone call from Sheriff Anderson. "I don't know what you told the President," the Sheriff said. "But whatever it was, it did the trick. Federal agents have descended on Pensacola like locusts. They have taken over the investigation. So I am really calling to tell you that I probably will not have any more updates for you as our investigation is being shut down. However, don't worry, they have far more resources than we do. I am sure they will find Mark."

"Thank you, John," Beth said. "You have been very helpful."

"I wish I could do more," the Sheriff said. "Just so you are up to date, we haven't found that van yet. We got its plates off the cameras at the Pensacola Beach tollbooth. It was a rental van. But the credit card used to rent it has been a dead end so far. We did interview the waiters at McGuire's and one of them remembers waiting on Mark and the Chinese. He didn't notice anything out of the ordinary and said that it appeared that all were having a good time. They paid cash, so there is no credit card history there. So far we have not found where they were staying, although we were trying to trace it with the card. The feds will probably do that now."

"You did mention that to them?" Beth asked.

"Oh, yes. I had my men brief them on everything we had done. They seemed quite interested and professional about it. I suspect they may do it all again, but that's okay. It never hurts to be thorough. Right now you just have to wait. There are a lot of people looking for him and you can't just disappear, certainly not in today's world. We'll find him."

"Thank you again."

"Well, if there is anything else I can do, either personally or professionally, don't hesitate to call. You have my cell number."

"Thank you, John. I will."

# CHAPTER 16

Stuart Deering was a junior at the University of West Florida, majoring in Hospitality and Resort Management in the College of Professional Studies, locally known as COPS. He was working nights at the Pensacola Aviation Center, the private terminal across from the Pensacola International Airport terminal. This terminal catered to those who flew their own planes into the airport, and management insisted that they be treated with the utmost respect. Stuart prided himself on his people skills and always 'talked up' the clients. His theory was that you could never go wrong if you showed an interest in a person's business.

Tonight was busier than usual, as several small jets had landed at Pensacola, Gulfstreams by the look of them. Each were carrying ten to fifteen people, mostly men, who taxed Stuart's ability to engage in small talk as they all seemed to be very brusque. He had been told that they were FBI agents, which was good, as he would have panicked when he noticed that several of them were armed, their shoulder holsters bulging under their sport coats. By the end of the night four planes had come in and delivered their load of agents and mysterious metal covered containers before departing. The agents were picked up by a fleet of nondescript SUV's and departed, having barely said a word to Stuart.

The next night, Stuart's shift started at 7p.m. When he arrived he noticed eight FBI looking individuals in the lounge. "They're waiting for their flight," Amber, the attendant he was replacing, told him as he came on duty. "It got held up by the weather. Last account, it should be here within the hour. They are not a very friendly bunch," she added as she signed out on the computer.

Stuart took that as a challenge. After he clocked in and took care of the basic administrative details, he casually walked around the lounge, ostensibly tidying it up. As he did, he tried to talk with the agents, asking if they needed anything or whether they had a nice stay in Pensacola. His attempts were met by grunts or merely ignored. Miffed, he returned to the front desk. A short time later a youngish looking agent came up and asked him for some bottled water, which was complimentary.

"You are the hardest group of people to talk to," Stuart said with a smile as he handed the agent the bottle. "Are you trained not to talk to people?"

The young agent responded to Stuart's smile. "No, we are just busy."

"So what are you doing? Looking for America's most-wanted? Or can't you say," Stuart quickly added, afraid that he may have gone too far.

"We are looking for someone," the agent said rather tentatively.

"Really," Stuart said, brightening up. "Who? I haven't seen anything on the news."

"We are looking for these people," the agent said, pulling a folded piece of paper out of his inside jacket pocket and opening it up on the counter. A slightly grainy photo of five people was printed on the paper. The view was from above and in front of them.

"Looks like a store surveillance photo," Stuart said as he looked at the photo.

"You're pretty good," the agent said.

"Can you tell me why you are looking for them?"

"Possible kidnapping," the agent responded as he reached over to retrieve the photo as another agent called over to him to get his bags as their plane was landing.

Stuart held on to the photo. "Wait a minute." He paused and studied the photo.

"I've got to go," the agent said, now clearly in a hurry.

"Wait, I've seen them," Stuart said, refusing to release the paper.

"You serious?" the agent asked, obviously torn between following his boss and continuing the conversation. The other agents were walking out the door towards the waiting plane.

"Come on, plane's ready," one of them yelled back.

"Yes," Stuart said. "These four are all Asians, right? It's kind of hard to see in the photo. And this one's American."

"Yes," the agent said.

"They were here two nights ago. Caught a late flight out, sometime close to midnight."

"You are absolutely sure of this?" the agent said.

"Absolutely. It was a real slow night and they were the only ones. Businessmen. They were partying pretty good. I remember the American was real drunk. They had to help him to the plane, he could barely walk."

The agent stared at Stuart for a moment and then said. "Wait right there. Don't go away, I'll be right back." He ran out the door toward the plane. A minute later he was back, followed by the other agents.

# CHAPTER 17

"What do you have, Arthur?" the President asked the FBI director. Several members of the intelligence community were sitting across from the President on matching mustard colored sofas in the Oval Office.

"Well, Mr. President. We are fairly confident that Mr. Williams has been smuggled to mainland China. The information provided by the attendant at the flight terminal is pretty detailed and he seems very reliable." The Director did not mention that they stumbled across this lead by accident, probably because none of the agents admitted that to their boss. "It was a Gulfstream jet that arrived in Pensacola two days before Mr. Williams disappeared. It arrived from Cancun, Mexico, with four Chinese nationals and a Chinese pilot, with a stated mission of exploring economic opportunities on the Gulf Coast. Two of them had a meeting at the Pensacola Chamber of Commerce and then met with the Pensacola Mayor. Nothing formal was accomplished, just a fact-finding mission, a perfect cover story. Anyway, the plane left at 11:38 the night Mr. Williams met with the Chinese, with a flight plan back to Cancun.

"Here's where it get's interesting. The plane refuels and then immediately takes off for China. No customs, no inspection, since they were not stopping. It refuels in Canada and then flies to Shenzhen Bao'an International airport in south China where, according to CIA sources, five Chinese nationals disembark. But one of them is taken off in a stretcher and loaded into a waiting ambulance. It was reported that he was burned in a fire in Mexico and his face was covered in bandages and he was wearing an oxygen mask. Two of the men from the plane accompanied this mysterious passenger on the ambulance. The Chinese customs saw this mystery man's passport, but of course never saw his face. We are currently trying to identify the four other men in the plane as well as the pilot."

"So far," the CIA Director interjected, "we have not been able to identify where the ambulance went. We have not found any reports of a burn patient being admitted in any of the nearby hospitals."

"I imagine the hospitals don't just give you their records," the President said.

"We have different ways to track it down," the CIA Director said. "We have a female Chinese agent who posed as a distraught wife trying to find her burned husband and was confused as to where he was taken. We also have a lot of ELINT from NSA that we are combing through, trying to find an electronic record of an admission. So far, nothing."

"You are certain that he is already in China?" the President asked.

"We have a high degree of confidence in that opinion," the FBI Director said. "We have kept a number of agents in Pensacola to follow up leads, though. We found the vehicle in the surveillance video and are processing it, but we have nothing concrete from it at this time. The credit card used to rent the vehicle was a phony. I don't anticipate learning a lot from that in the short run. We know where they stayed, based upon the plane's manifest and customs forms, but the rooms were re-rented twice before we got there and they are clean.

Best bet is that they flew Mr. Williams to China, via Mexico, that very night."

"How did the Chinese know about the cube when we didn't?" the President asked. The question was met by silence. Finally the CIA director answered.

"We have no idea, Mr. President."

The President turned to the NSA Director. "Ms. Williams said they thought you were monitoring them after they got back. Were you?"

The NSA Director looked embarrassed. "As it turns out, we were, Mr. President."

"And you didn't know anything about the cube?"

"No, Sir. They did not discuss it on the phone, on their computers, in their house, yard, or offices. And we did not see it. But we had backed off on the surveillance. Recently, we were only monitoring their phone and computers."

"You were spying on them at home and work?" The tone of the question indicated that the President did not expect an answer. "Did you have a FISA Court order or did you just do it?"

"Do you want an answer to that question, Mr. President?"

The President shook his head no. "Maybe Mr. Williams was right about not turning over the cube." His comment was met by silence. "Anything else, Gentlemen?" the President finally asked.

"No, Mr. President," chorused the members.

"Find Mr. Williams," the President said. "Find him and find that cube. If Ms. Williams is right, this could be the most dangerous threat we have ever faced. Do what ever you have to do, but find that cube."

## CHAPTER 18

Dang Hu was a Chinese national. He was born in Shanghai to Chinese parents and lived there until age sixteen when his parents moved back to the mainland to be with their own parents. Dang hated the move. After having had virtual freedom in Shanghai, he felt oppressed by the rules imposed on the mainland. Worse, his access to the Internet and his friends on Facebook was severely limited, his first introduction to politics. He started to hang out with a group of Internet hackers, reveling in the freedom and excitement of such a rebellion. Then the state security forces moved in and arrested the leaders of the group. Dang was terrified that he would be next, but the expected knock on the door never came. Either he was too low in the group, or the government never knew his involvement. He never did see the group leaders again and was afraid to ask around to find out what happened to them.

At seventeen, he wanted to change his world. He continued to visit his friends in Shanghai yearly and the contrast between mainland and Shanghai could not be more apparent. On one visit a friend introduced him to an American businessman. He started having political conversations with him, complaining about the censorship of the Chinese government. One thing led to another and now Dang was a CIA operative. That visit was fifteen years ago.

Typically, Dang's assignments required him to perform some type of cyber espionage, hacking into one system or another. This time he received an urgent request to meet his contact, a Chinese-American female named Na Jinjing. Na's cover was her employment with a multinational corporation doing business in China. She was in her early thirties. Dang had originally met her at a social function. Thereafter, their meetings tended to be in restaurants, bars or clubs, as if he was trying to date her. It was a perfect cover; she was beautiful and Dang found her presence to be exciting, both personally and professionally.

Dang met Na for lunch at a local restaurant and secured a corner table where they could have some privacy and could watch the rest of the patrons without being obvious. "I haven't seen you in a while," Na stated after they ordered their meal.

"I had a new contract come in that took some time to complete." Dang was a freelance computer programmer who took on independent assignments from various companies that did not have their own tech department. This arrangement allowed him to stay in the computer field and also allowed him the freedom necessary to complete assignments for the agency.

"I hope you are free," Na said. "I have a new job that's a real rush job, one of those drop everything and do it now type."

"When will those corporate types learn to manage their affairs so they don't have to rush, rush, rush?" Dang asked.

"Hopefully, never," Na said with a delightful light laugh. "Handling their self imposed emergencies is how we make our living."

"I guess you're right," Dang said.

"I'll send the information over to you and you can contact them," Na said before changing the subject and talking about something else. During the course of the meal Na checked her phone for a text message and then laid it on the table. A little later Dang checked his for a text and casually laid his phone next to hers. 'What a great way to pass messages,' Dang thought as he glanced at his phone. The data passed between the two phones without going through a tower, virtually untraceable. When they finished their meal each picked up their phones and pocketed them. "See you soon," Na said as she left the restaurant. "I'll get that info to you."

Dang headed for his small office. He would open the file there.

When Dang arrived at his office, he entered the encryption code into his phone and opened the file Chou had transferred. There was a photo of five men, four Chinese and one American. The men looked like they were in a hallway, perhaps a restaurant, judging by what appeared to be a waiter next to them. The accompanying file told him that the Chinese men were suspected of kidnapping the American.

Intelligence believed the American was being held at an abandoned air force base southeast of him. Dang needed to confirm whether the American was there and identify any of the Chinese, if possible. It also noted that Washington was unsure whether the Chinese government sanctioned the kidnapping. The communiqué noted that information was needed on the situation immediately and that Dang should take any and all steps possible to obtain this information as soon as possible.

Dang looked at the picture again. 'I don't know who you are,' Dang thought. 'But you must be one very high-value target to get this type of attention.' Dang scrolled through the file until he came to an aerial photo of the base. Dang was used to obtaining information for the Americans, typically through his skill with computers, although sometimes he had to set up surveillance devices. Those were the riskier missions, the ones that made you feel alive. Dang did not consider himself a James Bond. He did not carry a gun, something that would be very foolish in China. Nor did he engage in any of that other Hollywood nonsense. But he did gather information and he was quite good at it.

'Now how to get confirmation that the American was there?' he wondered. He could set up a wiretap, monitor any communications coming or going from the base. But since it was supposedly closed, they probably were not using the landlines. And that type of surveillance usually took time, something that he apparently did not have. Dang finally decided that the best way would be to go on the base and look. He did not consider sneaking on the base and skulking around. Besides, if he were caught there would be no excuse for his presence. No, he would have to take another route. He would have to be on base legitimately. 'Who could get on a closed base?' he wondered.

Here his computer skills came in handy. In China, like the U.S., garbage collection was becoming big business. He found a local garbage collection company and hacked into their computer system. He accessed the personal system and hired himself as a garbage man with his first day being tomorrow. Then he sent the garbage company an email, requesting immediate garbage service on the base. Finally, he waited until the company assigned a truck to the base and then he assigned himself to the truck as the lowly garbage handler.

The next day Dang reported to work early, changed into his company uniform, and reported to his driver for the day. This was the part that Dang loved. He played the part of a rather slow worker, who did whatever the driver wanted. He didn't talk much and acted very respectful, something that went a long way with his colleagues. He was not too concerned about his role. As far as the company was concerned he was legitimate. And he figured that probably the worse that would happen on the base is that they would refuse the truck access because they had not placed the order. However, as the driver was authentic and the company paperwork was official looking, he did not think anything more would come of it. Nevertheless, he felt a surge of adrenalin as their collection route neared the base.

When they pulled up to the gate the driver handed the clipboard with their collection route to the gate guard while Dang sat beside him, holding his breath. The guard glanced at the paperwork and waved them through. 'Hiding in plain sight,' Dang thought. 'Works every time.'

They drove onto the base and followed the route Dang had sent the company when he forged the email. He had set up a rather circuitous route that allowed him to see most of the base while traveling between the dumpsters he spotted on the aerial photo. As they made their way towards the target dumpster, dutifully emptying already empty containers, Dang watched carefully, looking for guards. He spotted them in the entranceway, two with machine guns slung over their shoulders. They pulled around the back of the building and found some more garbage pails by the back door. Dang walked over to the pails, noting two more guards at the door. He bowed to the guards as he carried the pails to the truck and emptied them. These actually had garbage in them. Frustration welled up. He was so close, yet so far. There was no way he could get into the building.

As he replaced the last can and headed back to the truck, one of the guards yelled at him to stop. Dang forced himself not to panic. What had he done wrong? He shuffled over to the guard, making sure to smile like a simpleton as he did. 'Don't show that you are nervous,' he told himself. He bowed to the guard. "There's more inside," the guard told him gruffly. He followed the guard inside and collected another load of garbage from a kitchen and small barracks area. He passed eight other soldiers lounging around, but with their weapons nearby. This did not look like a garrison in a closed base. He carried out the last of the garbage, bowed to the guard when he replaced the empty can, and then climbed into the truck and they drove away.

When they arrived at the dump, Dang offered to empty the truck by himself, explaining that he always picked through the trash as his family was poor and he often found useful items. His driver was more than happy to avoid this unpleasant task, so he went to the shack while Dang worked. Dang had kept the base's garbage separate when he loaded the truck, so he checked it first, before emptying the truck. When they left the dump, Dang had a large black plastic bag filled with his treasures. He started to show them to the driver, but the driver quickly lost interest after the third pair of mismatched shoes and smelly socks.

Back at his house, Dang didn't wait to shower before he pulled the items from the bottom of the bag and started photographing them for his report. Langley would have to check the labels, but Dang felt that he had hit pay dirt.

# CHAPTER 19

"Mr. President," the CIA Director started the briefing. "We now have firm information that Mr. Williams is in China. We believe he is being held at a deserted Chinese Air Force base in Southeast China."

"Let me get one thing straight," the President interrupted. He was not in a good mood. "I want to know your source. I want to know why you think he is there. My predecessor invaded Iraq based on a belief. He was wrong and it cost thousands of lives, millions of dollars and years of war. I don't intend to make the same mistake, particularly not with China."

"Yes, Mr. President. Our information is all HUMINT, not ELINT. We haven't found any electronic information. But we do have someone on the ground. We have been trying to track down the ambulance that took the mysterious passenger from the plane. We received a report, really a rumor, that someone had seen an ambulance near this base. That would be odd since the base should be deserted. We started some surveillance on the base and noticed some activity. In order to get on base and investigate we created a fake work request to the local garbage collector to collect waste on the base. We placed one of our assets on the garbage truck and he got on base as a helper. The driver of the truck is a legitimate Chinese garbage man.

Anyway, our man noticed several soldiers with Second Artillery insignia on their uniforms. That is the same unit that Colonel Lui belonged to. That unit has no business this far south and on a deserted air force base. Anyway, our man removed the trash and when he searched it, he found Mr. Williams suit in the trash."

"Are you certain it is Mr. Williams' suit?"

"Yes, Sir. Mr. Williams has his suits made by Brooks Brothers in New Orleans," the Director said as he handed the President some pictures of a crumpled business suit." The suits have a code label on them, which you can see in this picture. We contacted Brooks Brothers and confirmed that these were made for Mr. Williams."

"How old is this information?"

"About sixteen hours, Mr. President. We just confirmed with Brooks Brothers in the past hour."

"Do we know if he is still there?"

"We have never laid eyes on him. We have his suit, and we have had people monitoring that location since we were first alerted it was a possibility. I can't guarantee that he is there or that he has not been moved, but the greatest possibility is that he is still there."

"Ok, gentlemen, keep me posted. I can't emphasize how important it is that we track this down as fast as possible. I shudder to think of the possibilities if the Chinese have access to a functioning cube."

Later that evening the President had another meeting with the Joint Chiefs of Staff, National Security Advisor, State Department, and the head of the CIA, FBI, NSA and a handful of support personal. It had been tricky bringing them all in without the media picking up on it.

"Let's table whether we should for now," the President said. "Let's focus on how. If we confirm Mr. Williams is there, how would we get him out?"

"Helicopter," General Abromson said. "That is the only reliable way. Ground transportation is too slow. Once the Chinese know we are there and start to mobilize, our window closes. We have to get in and out before they know we hit them."

"What do you suggest?" the President asked.

"Send in a couple Pave Low's," the General answered. "We used them to lead the attack in Iraq. They are the most technologically advanced helicopter in the world, terrain-following and avoidance radar, forward-looking infrared sensor, and projected map display. They can get us in by making a low-level approach. They are armor-plated, can pack a multitude of firepower options, and can transport 38 troops. We could send in four Pave Low's and that would put 152 special operations soldiers on the ground. Back that up with four or five Apache's with Hellfire missiles, like we did in Iraq, and that would present some incredible firepower. We go in, get the cube and your man, and get out. Do it fast and it is over before the Chinese know we were there."

"You are talking about an act of war," the Secretary of State objected. "This is China, not Iraq or Pakistan. We are talking about the second most advanced country in the world. And let's not forget that they are a nuclear power, a major nuclear power, with delivery capability."

"There is no way we could get those helicopters into China undetected," Admiral Lindquist interjected. "I am assuming you mean to launch from a carrier. China monitors our every move by radar and satellite. They will watch those choppers the minute they launch. Their radar sites in that region alone…"

You can't treat China like Iraq, Afghanistan or Pakistan," the Secretary of State interrupted. "You can't invade them."

"We are not invading," the General objected.

"What do you think we would do if China sent four Pave Low's and a handful of helicopter gunships and attacked one of our bases in California? I'll tell you what we would do," the Secretary continued. "We would call it another Pearl Harbor and all hell would break lose. You can't play those games with nuclear powers."

"John, what do you think?" the President asked his Vice President.

"I don't like the gunship option. If something went wrong... And things always go wrong on military missions. We have been lucky lately. But those missions were small and the target was not well defended. This is China, a very different animal. If it went bad, the political repercussions alone would be dreadful. And if we were successful in getting in and out, the Chinese would still find out about the mission. Maybe too late to do anything militarily to the mission, but the political fallout would still be incredible. It could be to cold-war levels, but this time with China. And on the world stage we would have a very hard time justifying what would be seen as an unprovoked attack on a sovereign nation."

"They kidnapped one of our citizens," the General said.

"And we have people being held all over the world, including North Korea, and we have done nothing militarily. Why the over reaction here?"

"Because he has the cube."

"Right. And you are going to tell the world that?"

"Gentlemen," the President interrupted. "We are just discussing possible plans. Let's focus. What do you think, Jim?" the President asked the Director of the CIA. "You got Mr. Williams into China last time."

"That was very different, Mr. President. We need a lot more intel before we can even formulate a plan and then it would be black ops. I doubt we could sneak him away without being observed. And the timeframe to just reconnoiter to create a plan is probably months, not weeks."

"You got someone on the base already," the President noted.

"Yes. We did. A one shot mission that provided us general information. We still don't have eyes on Mr. Williams or know much else. We need more time."

"We don't have time," the General objected. "By then the situation will be totally different. He probably won't even be there any longer."

"Exactly," the CIA head said. "My point exactly. I am afraid I do not have a viable option for you at this time, Mr. President."

"Helicopters are the only option," a Navy Captain said from the back of the room. Heads turned. "But it should be a Seahawk, not a Pave Low."

"A Seahawk doesn't have the optics and it only holds twelve soldiers. You would have to send in three Seahawks for every one Pave Low just to get the troops on the ground. That would be twelve Seahawks just for the troops. Add some Apaches and now you have sixteen helicopters trying to evade Chinese radar," the General objected.

"I'm talking one Seahawk," was the response. "We can't invade China. The numbers just don't work in our favor. So the key is to be stealthy. I agree with you, the more helicopters we send, the greater the chance of being intercepted before we arrive on target. Once the Chinese know the game is afoot, they scramble a couple of fighters and the game is over. So we send one Seahawk, flown high, and let the Chinese know it is coming."

"We can't tell them what we are doing…" someone objected.

The Captain held up his hand to silence the interruption as he continued. "We hide in plain sight. We send in the helicopter on a ruse. Say a medical evac from our embassy in in that area. The flight plan is close enough if we move our carrier. We get permission to medevac someone out. The chopper flies over or near the target area and the special ops folks parachute out. The chopper continues to the embassy while the ops folks infiltrate the base. Timing here will be critical. The chopper has to leave so that it will be in the target vicinity at the right time for extrication. It flies out low; we would need a medical reason for a low altitude flight. Then it drops down and extricates the special ops and heads back to the carrier.

"The key to this plan is that the special ops folks cannot create a disturbance. The Chinese claim 200 miles of territorial waters. That means about ninety minutes of flight time to clear Chinese airspace. If the Chinese are alerted by a large firefight, then all bets are off. The only way to protect the chopper would be to send jet fighters into Chinese airspace and that would create some serious escalation."

"What if the special ops just got him and the cube out of the target area. Could they go to ground in China and then the agency smuggle them out?"

"That is a possibility," the CIA Director said. "But you could expect a huge manhunt once the Chinese knew what we had done. It could be very difficult getting everyone out. The cube, however, that would be a lot easier to hide."

"But is the cube any good without Mr. Williams to access it?"

"I am a bit concerned about Mr. Williams' intentions," the FBI Director said. "He has evidently had this cube since his return from China several months ago. Yet he told no one. What has he been doing with it? What are his plans for it? What are its capabilities? Perhaps Mr. Williams should be treated as a hostile."

"Do you think he defected with the cube?" the President asked.

"No," the FBI Director said. "Our information is that he was smuggled out in a drugged state. I do not think he went voluntarily. But the question remains, what were his intentions with the cube?"

"Gentlemen," the President interrupted. "We digress. I want you to work on options to get Mr. Williams and the cube out of China. Flesh out the details and give me a workable plan, one that you can present with a degree of confidence and which does not start World War III. Once we have some realistic options, we can debate whether we should go in. Without a workable option, the question is moot. Any questions?"

A chorus of "No, Mr. President," followed and the meeting broke up.

# CHAPTER 20

Mark woke up slowly, completely disorientated. He was lying on his back, which was cramping, the light was too bright and his stomach was objecting to whatever he had eaten. He tried to roll over, hoping that lying on his side would relieve the pressure on his stomach and his cramping back, but his arms would not obey. No, they were stuck. Claustrophobia took over and he yanked frantically at the blankets, but could not get free. The action was too much for his fragile stomach and he started to retch. Desperate now, he tried to roll over as he started to vomit, only managing to turn his head, which was just enough to keep him from choking despite the fact that he did not have much in his stomach.

When the bout of nausea passed, he looked down and realized that he was on what looked like an ambulance gurney and his wrists were tied to the railings on each side. As his head started to clear, he looked around. He was in a small cinder-block room with naked fluorescent lights on the ceiling. He figured he was in a hospital. He could not believe the poor care. He could have choked to death being left unattended like that. The lawsuit they were asking for was unbelievable. But he did not want to sue, he just wanted off this gurney. His back was already cramping from being immobile for so long.

But why was he here? And where was he? He could not remember anything. He looked around. It sure did not look like any hospital he had ever seen. No medical equipment. No medical charts on the wall. No computers. Nothing. Just a bare room. He yelled out, his voice surprisingly hoarse. He yelled again.

A Chinese soldier carrying a machine gun walked into the room. A wave of panic coursed through Mark. They had caught them. Where was Sgt. Jeffreys? Where were the other CIA agents? What would the Chinese do? And then he remembered. He was not in China. They had escaped in the pod. He was back home. But then, why was there a Chinese soldier in the room with him? An armed Chinese soldier!

"What's going on? Where am I?" Mark asked.

The soldier simple stared at him and then turned and left the room.

"Hey! Come back," Mark yelled, his voice still coming out hoarse. The soldier closed the door on Mark's request. Mark yelled a couple times more to no avail and then just lay back on the gurney. He yanked at his arms again, but they were held fast. He looked down and inspected his bonds. He was tied to the railings with cloth, probably folded pillowcases. There was a good three or four inches of material on his wrist that guaranteed a secure hold, while at the same time ensuring that his wrists would not be cut by the bonds or the circulation cut off. They were secured with wraps of duct tape. He remembered a nurse describing this type of restraint to him during a deposition, very simple, yet very effective.

'What's going on?' he asked himself again. 'Where am I?' He tried to think back. The trip to China was long over. He was now certain of that. So what was going on with the Chinese soldier? He was home, in Pensacola. He was working on cases… He was meeting four

Chinese at McGuire's. The memory came flooding in. He tried to remember the details and what came next. The best he could do was a recollection of a car. Try as he might, he could not recall any further details.

Sometime later the door opened and another soldier came in, an officer judging from the epaulets on his shirt, but Mark could not remember what rank they indicated.

"You have finally awakened," the officer said.

Mark recognized the voice. The man from McGuire's, he was certain. The memory came back clearly now. It was the same man he had dinner with at McGuire's. His name was... he had to think. It was Chin. They had talked through dinner and then they wanted to go to the beach. He had been in a van. He had, he had... He could not pull up any more of the memory.

"What's going on?" Mark asked. "Why am I tied up? Where am I?"

"You know what is going on," Chin said. "Don't try to deny it."

Mark was confused. "I really don't," Mark said, wondering if Chin knew he had been in China when the bomb went off. 'Maybe he thinks I'm responsible for detonating the nuke?' Mark thought. 'But how could he know that? The cats had killed everyone there before I came out of the woods. Maybe there was a remote camera. But what to do now?' That question kept coming back to haunt him. 'Where am I and why are these soldiers in uniform?'

Mark guessed that the uniforms were to intimidate him. That realization had a calming effect on him. So they wanted something and were playing psychological games to trick him into giving the information. Somehow that thought helped, he felt calmer, more in control.

"You cannot lie to me," Chin was saying to him.

Mark did not respond. Chin reached into his pocket and pulled something out. Mark could not see what it was. Chin waited until Mark was staring at his hand before he held out his hand, palm up, and opened his fingers. Chin was holding the cube.

Panic welled up in Mark. Chin had the cube. If he knew what it was, if he could access it… Chin closed his fingers around the cube and then pressed his closed fist against Mark's arm. Mark screamed as Chin's consciousness flooded into Mark's mind, threatening to take over. Mark's screams filled the tiny room as he fought his restraints and fought the attack in his mind.

And then all was black.

Once again Mark woke up groggy and disorientated. But this time his headache was worse than his cramping back. It felt like a migraine from hell and Mark tried to squeeze his eyes shut to block out the glare from the overhead fluorescent lights. His head slowly cleared and the migraine lost some of its power. When Mark was able to think again, he tried to recall past events. Oddly enough, the more he forced himself to remember, the quicker his headache evaporated. He thought back to the attack, Chin's mind trying to take over his. Mark had fought back with psychic muscles he did not know he had and had never used. The memory ended when he blacked out and Mark hoped that meant the attack ended, rather than the attack succeeded, as he had no recollection of what happened next.

What to do? Mark was still tied to the gurney. He was sore, tired, and now that he thought about it, very hungry and thirsty. He should come up with a plan, some way to overpower the guard and escape. But what? How? He always enjoyed watching Tom Cruise and Bruce Willis movies. They always knew what to do, but he did not have a clue. Calling out, he yelled to the guards that he was thirsty. A short time later the door opened and two guards entered, along with Chin with the cube. 'Not again,' Mark thought. He did not have the energy to fight back, but fortunately it was not another attack.

"He will take care of you," Chin said, pointing to the first soldier. "You will not do anything to him. You will not touch him. You will not try to control him. If we even suspect that you are trying to control him, he will be shot. And you will be severely punished. If you want to eat, to drink, to move off that bunk, you will have to obey. Do you understand?"

Mark did not understand. 'Try to control him? What was he talking about?' Mark looked at the first soldier and realized he was unarmed. The second soldier was standing by the wall with his machine gun held ready, aimed at the first. Chin was standing next to the armed soldier. They would shoot their own soldier, but not Mark. That was a plus anyway. But none of this made any sense. How could he control him?

"Do you understand?" Chin repeated.

"Yes," Mark answered.

Chin spoke in rapid fire Chinese. The unarmed soldier approached Mark warily and cut Mark's bonds. Mark rubbed his wrists and then sat up, the movement giving him a moment of vertigo. A plastic canteen was placed on the gurney. Mark reached over and opened it. Water had never tasted so good. He resisted the urge to gulp it down, trying to ration himself to small sips. He did not know how long it had been since he last ate or drank and did not want to get nauseous. The soldier placed a plastic bowl on the gurney and Mark picked it up. It was some type of cold soup. Mark drank it slowly, wondering how his stomach would react. When he had finished, he tried to hand the bowl back. The soldier jumped back and pointed to the gurney. Mark placed the empty bowl on the gurney and the soldier retrieved it, before backing away.

"Why am I here?" Mark asked Chin. "What do you want from me?"

"You will obey me," Chin said. "The rules are simple. You will not touch a soldier. You will not try to control them. If you touch a soldier, he will be shot. If you try to control them, you will be shot. Do you understand?"

"I don't understand why I am here."

"Do you understand the rules?" Chin repeated.

"Yes," Mark said. "What do I do when I have to go to the bathroom?" Mark asked as Chin turned to leave.

"A pot will be brought in when you need it," Chin said and then all three soldiers left and the door was closed. Mark heard the lock click.

"See if I leave this hotel a good review," Mark muttered to himself, surprised that he could joke under the circumstances. But what else could he do? At least they had left him untied. Mark lowered the rail on the side of the gurney and slowly swung his legs over. He stood up carefully, holding the gurney for support as a wave of vertigo washed over him. His whole body ached and his back was stiff. How long had he lain there?

Mark slowly walked around the room, using the walls as support. He noted for the first time that he was wearing what looked like Chinese clothes, much like what he had worn when he and Sergeant Jeffreys had been flown to meet Colonel Lui. Black cloth pants, a rough linen shirt and cloth slippers. He did not have any of his own clothes, including his wedding ring. Everything was gone.

'Where did that leave him?' Mark wondered. Kidnapped by four Chinese and held in a cinderblock room. He could be anywhere. They were wearing Chinese military uniforms. Why? He could not figure that part out. And, he came to the most important fact last: Chin had the cube and could access it. He was trying to use it as a control cube against Mark. Mark thought he had fought it off, but could he be sure? Would he know if he was being controlled? Probably not. They were afraid of him. Chin clearly thought Mark had the ability to control his soldiers. Why else all the elaborate precautions? But what could Mark do? He could not fight the cube. He could not fight the soldiers. He couldn't even get out of this room.

Despair filled Mark as he considered his options and realized that there was nothing he could do. The Chinese had the cube and could use it. He should have destroyed the cube when he came home. He should have left it in the pod. Why had he taken it to the office? He should not have tried to use it. Oddly, he never felt guilty about not giving it to his government, as the result would be similar. No, he should have destroyed it. That was his failure. And that would have to be his goal now. More important than anything else, he had to destroy the cube.

Mark was sitting on the gurney the next time Chin walked in, flanked by two machine-gun toting guards. The guards took position on either side of Chin, who sat down in a wooden chair that was brought in for him. Mark had a million questions, but he just waited for Chin to start. The silence stretched for several minutes. Mark thought this was getting stupid and considered breaking the silence. Then he wondered if it was some type of test. Since he could not go anywhere, he finally just lay down on the gurney and closed his eyes. A few minutes later Chin spoke.

"Tell me what happened."

Mark opened his eyes and sat up on the gurney. "Tell you what?" Mark asked.

"What happened?"

"What happened when?" Mark asked. This guy was really not being very clear.

"When you were here in China. Tell me what happened," Chin said.

"You should know," Mark said. "You said you were there. You have the cube."

"If I was there, I would be dead now. I am not dead. Tell me what happened."

Mark was confused. Chin had the cube and could access it. So he had to know what happened since all but the last part would be recorded on the blue-gray's cube. Was this a test? What should he say? What did this Chin guy want? What was going on? Mark's mind whirled, until part of Chin's question caught his attention. Chin had said 'here in China.'

"Where am I?" Mark repeated.

"You can make this easy on yourself. Or you can make it very hard," Chin said. "Answer my question. What happened?"

"What happened when?"

Mark was not ready for the response. Without warning, Chin leaned forward and swung his hand, slapping Mark across the face. The blow knocked Mark down onto the gurney and left his face stinging. He could not believe how much a slap hurt. He sat up and rubbed his face, moving his jaw experimentally to see if it was broken.

"What happened?" Chin repeated ominously.

"When?" Mark asked. This time he saw the blow coming, but still did not have time to react. Although Chin hit him open handed, Mark saw stars. He sat up and rubbed his face again, surprised that he was not bleeding or had a broken jaw.

"We can do this the hard way," Chin said.

This is the easy way? Mark thought. He was confused. What did Chin want to know? And why shouldn't Mark tell him?

"What happened?"

"Tell me where to start," Mark said, flinching as he did not want to get hit again, but still not sure what Chin wanted to know.

"When you were here last," Chin repeated.

That was certainly not helpful, Mark thought. But what was the harm in telling Chin what happened. Mark had no interest in being tortured and no thoughts that he could withstand torture. More importantly, he could not figure out why he should not tell Chin. What harm could come of that? Why not tell Chin the same thing he had told his government? So he did.

"I was trying to find the cube," Mark said.

When he didn't continue, Chin hit him again. "Did you find it?"

"No, Colonel Lui found it first," Mark said, and cringed, waiting for the next blow.

"Tell me what happened," Chin repeated.

Mark took that as a starting point. "I was flown over to meet with Colonel Lui," Mark said. "He had the cube. I told him my government was intent on destroying it, but I disagreed. I wanted to help him. I had been in contact with a cube a year before on the *Ronald Reagan*. I told him I wanted to redeem myself after my failure a year before and asked how to help. He sent me on a decoy mission. He never told me his plans." Mark paused, but then continued, fearing he would be hit again. "And then the nuke went off. After that it was just a matter of getting away. Getting out of the country."

"How did you survive?" Chin asked.

Mark wondered if Chin was referring to surviving the nuke or surviving the attack by the other soldiers. Did Chin know about the Colonel's plans to kill Mark and

Jeffreys? Did he find the shot up Humvee and dead soldiers? They probably survived the explosion as they were outside the valley. But they were so close to the blast area, the radiation would probably make that area unsafe to search. What did Chin know? If Mark guessed wrong and lied to Chin, then he was in for a beating. But Mark had survived and he knew the other soldiers had not. Chin would know that they had never reported back in. Mark tried to buy himself some time.

"I was not near the blast. There were several mountains between me, so I survived it. Then it was just a matter of sneaking out of the country. You can imagine my government was very interested in getting me out and debriefing me."

"And what did you tell them?"

"Basically the same thing I just told you," Mark said.

"The Colonel never told you what he planned?" Chin asked.

"No. I offered to help. But he said I could help by being a decoy. He said he had other things to do, but never told me what they were."

"You lie!" Chin said as he struck Mark again.

Mark found himself lying on the gurney again, his face burning from the slap. Before he could sit back up Chin stood and pushed his closed fist against Mark's head. His fist held the cube. Mark screamed as Chin's consciousness pushed into his mind.

Mark awoke slowly. His back was stiff and he felt groggy. But he knew where he was, unfortunately. He opened his eyes and the bare walls of his prison confirmed it. He closed his eyes, but could not escape to a better place. Remorse filled him. He knew he would not get out of this alive, or if he lived, he would be broken, under the control of Chin, which would be infinitely worse. But what haunted him more was his sense of absolute failure.

He had kept the cube a secret to protect mankind from its power being abused. He had not destroyed it in hopes of using some of its knowledge to help mankind.

But by keeping the cube, he had allowed it to fall into the hands of Chin, a man who had been under the influence of a control cube and who hated the United States. Now the cube and all its power and potential would be used to destroy the United States. He had not trusted the U.S. with the cube, but he certainly did not want anyone else to get it. He should have just destroyed the cube when he had the chance. Or placed it in the pod and sent it off to space.

But he could not. He wanted to explore the cube. He wanted to use the pod. He could not give them up. It was his weakness. No, it was his greed that caused all this. He lay on his bunk in misery, his mind torturing him. He started to think about his family. He would never see Beth or his kids again. There was so much he wished he had told them. So many things he had never said. He tried to remember whether he had told them that he loved them the last time they had called. He did not think that he had. His son had called with a plumbing question. Wanting to know how to fix a broken toilet. He certainly had not ended that conversation with "I love you."

He could not recall when he spoke with Claire last. Oh, yes. She had called when he was with a client. He had taken the call, but told her to call Beth as he was busy. Busy. Too busy to talk to his daughter? He had been a good father, he had worked and supported them. But had he been a good Dad? Doubt filled him as his depression deepened. At least he had said, "I love you," to Beth. Beth always made a point of saying, "I love you." She said it was in case she never saw him again. Mark had always kidded her about the idea. But now…

The door to his room opened and a Chinese soldier walked in. Panic filled Mark as he realized he was not in a fit state to withstand an encounter with the cube. The soldier placed a tray of food on the floor and stepped out. Mark breathed a sigh of relief. That was close. He would have to control his thoughts. He had to be ready for another meeting with Chin. He could wallow in self pity some other time, he told himself. But now, he had to be ready for the next encounter with the cube.

The routine was getting predictable. The door opened and two armed guards entered, followed by Chin. The guards took their positions by the door, while Chin advanced. Mark had been lying on the gurney. He sat up, thinking that Chin would start asking him questions. Instead, Chin strode over and pressed his hand against Mark's head. Mark's screams filled the room.

*Chin's demands filled Mark's head. "What happened? Show me what happened."*

*Mark and Sgt. Jeffreys were meeting Colonel Lui for the first time.*

*"This is Colonel Lui Jiang," the officer on the right stated in acceptable English. Mark nodded to the Colonel sitting in the center, wondering if the introduction was typical for the Chinese or if the Colonel did not speak English. "You are to explain your mission to him," the officer continued.*

*"I lied to him here," Mark thought. "I can't let Chin know. Can Chin hear what I am thinking?" Mark fought to change the scene. To avoid showing Chin what came next.*

*The scene froze, wavered. Now Mark and Jeffreys were riding with their Chinese guards on Colonel Lui's decoy mission.*

*Mark was quiet for a moment and then said, "Anyone here speak English?" There was no reply from the soldiers. He repeated the question, again without any results. He then turned to Jeffreys. "Let me see that map," Mark asked Jeffreys. They spread the map out on the Chinese soldiers legs and Mark pointed to it while he spoke rapidly to Jeffreys, hoping that none of the Chinese could understand English, but figuring he had nothing to lose even if they could.*

*"We have a problem," Mark said quickly. "When we get to this point on the map the Humvee behind us is going to open fire with that machine-gun on their roof and kill everyone in this vehicle."*

*"I can't let Chin see the firefight," Mark thought. But Chin's control was too strong. The scene continued.*

*"What are you going to do?" Mark asked, watching the curve quickly approach.*

*"I'm going to take this weapon and go out my side," Jeffreys said evenly, smiling at the soldier between them. "Do you have that?"*

*"Yes," Mark said uncertainly.*

*"You can do it," Jeffreys said. As they approached the curve Jeffreys continued conversationally, "Ok, get ready, get set, go."*

*Mark yanked on the door handle while Jeffreys struck the soldier between them with a vicious elbow strike to the temple. The soldiers in the front yelled and the driver hit the brakes, slowing the vehicle, which was fortunate Mark thought absently as he jumped out and rolled, ending in a ditch, stunned.*

*The second vehicle slid to a stop next to Mark. The sound of machine gun fire filled the air as the soldier in the turret opened fire. Hot metal rained down on Mark, burning him. He winced, waiting for the searing pain of the gunshots, before his brain finally registered that it was hot empty shell casings ejected from the machine gun that were hitting him. He heard the sound of another machine gun firing, faster, but at a higher pitch. It came in short bursts, followed by a scream, and then another burst. Then all was quiet.*

*Mark lay in the ditch on his stomach, his ears ringing despite the silence. He told himself to get up and run, but his body would not obey. He heard footsteps, light and quick, and his mind screamed for him to run, but still he couldn't move. The footsteps came nearer and then stopped.*

*"Are you okay?" Jeffreys voice. Relief flooded through Mark as he tried to get up. A helping hand grabbed his arm and lifted. "Are you okay? Are you hit?" Jeffreys repeated.*

*Mark stood up slowly and looked around. Jeffreys was holding Mark with his left hand. His right hand held the assault rifle in a ready position as he quickly scanned their surroundings before looking back at Mark. Mark shook his head to clear it. "I'm okay," he said, his voice sounding quiet after the gunfire.*

*Unable to resist, Mark rested as the scene played out, playing the events from Mark's mind. When the scene ended, Mark attacked, trying to wrestle control of the vision away from Chin.*

*The vision swirled, he was a blue-gray walking in a jungle, he was sitting at the controls of a spaceship, he was running down a corridor, he was studying dinosaur DNA, he was…*

…Lying on the gurney gasping for breath. Sweat poured down his forehead like he had been doing a strenuous workout. Mark saw Chin stagger back and support himself on the far wall. Chin steadied himself and without another word led the guards out of the room.

So these sessions were as hard on him as on me, Mark thought with pleasure. Except that he was underfed and tortured. Mark would have to figure out how to maintain his strength so he could fight Chin in the cube. Chin had clearly won this round, Mark thought. He had seen what happened to the soldiers following Mark and Sgt. Jeffreys. Now Chin would want to see what happened next, what happened in the valley? Mark would have to keep Chin from finding out about the Pod. He couldn't let him have that prize also. But how could he prevent it. Chin was clearly getting better at controlling the cube. And now he was physically stronger than Mark. Between the two, Mark did not have a chance. He had to find some way to destroy the cube before he got too much weaker.

Some time later the door opened and two armed guards entered, followed by Chin. Mark tried to mentally brace himself as the guards took their positions by the door and Chin advanced.

*"Show me what happened," Chin's command filled Mark's thoughts. "Show me the blue-gray."*

*Mark tried to resist, but Chin's control was too strong. The memory swam into focus.*

*Suddenly, a fiery streak shot out of the sky and landed about 100 yards from the missile truck.*

*"Watch it, cats are here," Jeffreys warned. They lay prone, just their binoculars over the lip of the ledge as they watched the scene below. A number of people were running. Others just stood and stared.*

*"Where did it go?" Mark asked as he scanned the valley with his binoculars. One person detached himself from the crowd at the missile and walked toward an empty space in the valley. Suddenly a blue-gray emerged, walking towards him. "It's not the cats," Mark said. "The blue-grays are here!"*

*Mark tried to control the scene, but it barely wavered before Chin managed to reassert his control.*

*They were about to stand up and move on when another meteor streaked out of the sky. Jeffreys grabbed Mark and they rolled to the base of the rock outcropping. Seconds later the sky lit up with lightning bolts and the sound of automatic fire. Explosions rocked the valley as the fire teams opened up. Mark's skin tingled and his hair stood up as static electricity filled the air. The ground shook and Mark's ears echoed with the sound of gunfire, rockets and explosions. Just as quickly as it had started, the firefight ended and all was quiet, except for the ringing in Mark's ears.*

*Smoke drifted across the valley as the two trucks and some bushes burned. Nothing else moved. They scanned the valley with their binoculars. "Look at the missile," Jeffreys whispered in Mark's ear. Mark trained his binoculars on the missile, which was sitting on the cradle next to the burning truck. He waited for the smoke to clear. On the ground near the missile lay the blue-gray, his legs blown off. A cat stood over him and appeared to be torturing the blue-gray. Jeffreys was scanning the other mountain and the valley with his binoculars.*

*"The cats won," Jeffreys whispered.*

*The scene wavered as Mark made a half-hearted attempt to control the memory.*

*The cat came bounding out of the tunnel. Mark was trying to track the cat with his sights when Jeffreys' shot streaked at the cat. The cat leaped in the air and fired, while the missile slammed into a small boulder and exploded, spraying the cat with shrapnel. The cat hit and rolled, apparently injured, but not down.*

*Mark had to wait. He would have to save his strength and then he would have one chance. He tried to keep these thoughts deep in his mind so that Chin would not sense them. He waited as the scene played out.*

*The blast slowed the cat enough that Mark could take aim and fire, concentrating on short bursts. Aim, then another short burst. Mark fired until his magazine was empty and then fumbled for another magazine. He slammed the magazine home and took aim again. The cat was not moving.*

*After the cat was shot, Mark made his move. The scene shifted...*

*He was in space, at the controls of a ship staring at a view screen that hovered in the air above him. Bolts of light shot out from a ship in the distance directly at the view screen. A number of the views flicked out of existence and an alarm sounded in the distance. The blue-grays appeared agitated as they worked on their controls.*

*Mark knew this scene well. He had lived it, barely. And he knew how it ended. But Chin did not. They would both die. The only thing that had saved Mark last time was Dr. Stewart. Even then it had been close. Mark would force Chin to live this scene. And he would force Chin to die with this scene. He concentrated on the scene for all he was worth, with all his saved energy. This was his last chance. The scene continued...*

*More views flicked out of existence. Alien symbols danced over Mark's head. The tension among the blue-grays was palpable, actually worse than before as Mark accessed the blue-gray's emotions. Suddenly, an explosion behind Mark's host sent debris shooting past his head, only to hit the wall and float back. Mark's seat spun so he faced the blasted airlock. A cat creature wearing a form-fitting suit, complete with a clear helmet and faceplate, leaped into the room. The cat pointed an object at the blue-gray next to Mark. A blinding white beam shot out and the blue-gray's head disappeared in a cloud of black particles as a snapping sound filled the air. Mark's host was still sitting as he brought up the metal rod Mark had seen used on the cats before, but not fast enough. The cat twisted in the air and brought its weapon to bear on Mark's host. A dazzling white light filled Mark's vision as a beam of light flicked towards him, hitting him in the chest. Time stopped, then searing pain flooded Mark's senses…*

Mark opened his eyes. Chin was lying on the floor. One frightened guard pointed his gun at Mark while the other reached for Chin and dragged his body out of the room. 'Got you,' Mark thought, before the pain in his chest took over. Then all was black.

# CHAPTER 21

Mark opened his eyes and the walls of his prison came into focus. 'I'm not dead,' he thought. 'Was Chin?' He did not know how long he had been unconscious. He didn't know why he was still alive. Perhaps the fact that he knew what was coming had saved him. Or that he knew it was not real. Well, it was real, but just not for him. Did Chin survive?

Mark looked around his small cell. There was no food or water set out. No empty plates either. He had no idea how long he had been out. But his stomach was telling him that it was a long time. He thought of getting up or calling for a guard and asking for food. But that required too much energy. So he just closed his eyes. He was alive. And hopefully Chin was dead. He would worry about finding and destroying the cube later. Right now, he would sleep.

*Chin's consciousness forced itself into Mark's mind without warning. Mark tried to marshal his strength, to control the vision, but he was too tired. Chin quickly overrode Mark's defenses.*

*The scene shifted, the blue-gray was dying, but not before he had set a detonator on the nuclear warhead. Mark had to get away. He dragged Sgt. Jeffreys to the pod and climbed in.*

*Mark watched in helpless horror as the scene played out to him sending the pod away and then as the scene shifted to him opening the pod's hatch in his barn.*

*Triumph filled Mark's consciousness, Chin's triumph. "I have won! I am the master! And now I know where the pod is. With the cube and the pod, the U.S. is mine for the taking. No one will be able to stand against me. I will rule the world."*

The connection broke. Mark was lying exhausted on the gurney with Chin standing triumphantly over him. 'Rule the world. Wasn't that a bit cliché?' Mark thought. Did anyone really say that? But with the pod and the cube, Chin might actually be right. Chin was clearly learning to master the cube and the alien technology had been designed to control worlds. Now Chin had it, and soon he would have a completely stealthy means of transportation to go with it.

Mark tried to raise his hand, but he was too weak. He was even too weak to speak. Chin had won. And it was Mark's fault. All of this was Mark's fault. He should have destroyed the cube and sent the pod back to the Mothership where they would both be safely out of reach of mankind. Mark lay there miserable as Chin stepped out of the room.

Chin paused at the door and turned back to Mark. "After I retrieve the pod," Chin said to Mark. "I will put you out of your misery." And then he strode out with the guards, the door closing with an audible click behind him.

# Part III

# CHAPTER 22

Sgt. Jeffreys checked his gear again as the Seahawk helicopter cruised at 10,000 feet over the Chinese mainland. Below them the Chinese countryside glowed with lights as they crossed urban areas. "Too many lights," Sgt. Jeffreys thought. He much preferred the dark for night operations. Darkness would conceal him and his team and give them the edge they needed with their night vision goggles.

Sgt. Jeffreys had been assigned to accompany a squad from the SEAL Team that had been tasked with this mission. SEAL teams did not like to take outsiders. But the orders came straight from the President, upon recommendation from Captain Peters, who had pointed out that Sgt. Jeffreys was intimately familiar with the cube and its effects on Mark and that his knowledge could be extremely important. That Sgt. Jeffreys was a Marine, jump qualified, and had been involved with the cube in China previously clinched his assignment.

The SEALs had to accept the order, but did not have to be happy about it. Sgt. Jeffreys understood the SEAL team's reluctance. He had not trained with them and they did not know his capability, although they did recognize his experience. The SEALS treated Sgt. Jeffreys as baggage and assigned him to follow one SEAL and otherwise stay out of their way. They issued him a HK

MP7A1 submachine gun fitted with a suppressor. It was a lightweight compact weapon, weighing less than three pounds and only 16 inches long, about 26 when you added the silencer. Although it had an effective range of 200 meters, its small size was better suited for close quarter fighting. It was ideal for firefights inside buildings and tight spaces as it was easily maneuvered and had a rate of fire of 950 rounds/minute. However, as the magazine only held 40 rounds, one had to be judicious using ammunition.

Three of the SEALs were similarly armed with HK MP7A1's, while two of them carried Mk-11 sniper rifles, also equipped with silencers. One SEAL carried an M249 SPW, which was their compact version of the popular SAW or squad automatic weapon. It could fire over 750 rounds per minute from a collapsible canvas bag, rather than a traditional magazine. It was replacing the older M-60, which although heavier, was always a favorite weapon of Sgt. Jeffreys. However, he hoped it would not be needed as it was not equipped with a silencer and was for laying down cover fire. If they needed it, then their mission would be in jeopardy as their plan envisioned them getting in and out stealthily. They also all carried silenced Sig Sauer pistols in shoulder holsters or on their hips.

One of the SEALs held up his hand, fingers spread out. Five minutes to drop. Sgt. Jeffreys did a last check of his gear and then the SEALs checked each other's gear, paying particular attention to the parachutes and ensuring nothing was hanging free which would get caught up during the jump. At two minutes they positioned themselves by the open doors. Sgt. Jeffreys consciously controlled his breathing as adrenaline coursed through his body. Night jumps were always more dangerous as it was harder to judge your landing. He did not want to sprain an ankle or break a leg jumping into China.

Three, two, one. The jump began. Sgt. Jeffreys shuffled to the door, watched the SEAL in front of him disappear into the blackness and then leapt out. He felt that initial surge of vertigo in his chest and then orientated himself before pulling the cord on his chute. A hard yank on his harness told him his chute had deployed and he quickly looked around as he checked on his location. He spotted two other SEALs below and to his side and angled for a dark patch of ground, which he hoped was their target. The plan was to land on the far end of the runway, hoping that this area was far enough away from their target to be observed and flat enough for a clear landing.

The jump seemed to take forever although it actually lasted less than a minute. Even in the dark, Sgt. Jeffreys always felt horribly exposed during a jump, secretly fearing tracers racing up to pick him out of the sky. But no tracers appeared and no alarm sounded. Sgt. Jeffreys hit the ground and rolled, quickly standing back up and pulling in his chute. Once free of his chute, he freed his MP7 from its harness and sprinted over to his teammates. They had landed on target at the end of the runway. Once all were accounted for, they stowed their chutes in a rough pile. There was no time to bury them. Hopefully by the time the parachutes were discovered, the team would be long gone.

Sgt. Jeffreys' world glowed green though his night vision goggles. The view bobbed as they jogged to the edge of the old runway and made their way down in a running crouch toward the buildings at the other end. This was the riskiest part as the team was exposed with very little cover other than the darkness. Satellite reconnaissance had shown no activity on this side of the field, but they all knew that could easily change. They made it to the first building without incident, and although keyed up, Sgt. Jeffreys felt himself relax a bit as his back pressed against the side of the building. The fighting was about to begin, but at least they were no longer in the open where they could be picked off.

Guttural commands came though Sgt. Jeffreys' earpiece as the team fanned out and moved through the building complex. Throat mikes keeping the words inaudible to the enemy. The target building was on the other side of this complex. They moved silently from building to building, weapons ready. Sgt. Jeffreys stayed near the rear of the team, along with the SEAL carrying the SAW.

"Contact," Sgt. Jeffreys heard in his earpiece. Everyone froze. More commands were issued and the team moved into position. The snipers moved forward, positioning to cover both ends of the building. There were two Chinese guards lounging at the front of the building. Two other guards were on foot patrol near the rear. Satellite recon informed them that two other guards were on foot patrol on the far side of the complex. Sgt. Jeffreys would have liked to take them out first. But the positioning of the troops would not allow for that.

The snipers moved into position and the command was given. No sound betrayed them. The only evidence that the attack had commenced came from Sgt. Jeffreys' earpiece.

"One down. Two down."

The second sniper's report quickly followed. Four sentries down and not a sound, that left the barracks to the right and the target building to the left. Four SEALs positioned on the barracks while Sgt. Jeffreys and the other four SEALs headed for the target building. They got to the front door when the alarms went off. Sgt. Jeffreys did not know what went wrong. But there was no wondering now, only reacting. Sgt. Jeffreys pulled off his night vision goggles as floodlights lit up the area and a siren pierced the night air.

"Go, go, go," the command came through his earpiece. Sgt. Jeffreys followed the four SEALs into the building. Behind him he heard the unmistakable whoosh of a LAW rocket as the other squad sent two rounds into the barracks, twin explosions sounding in quick succession. As Sgt. Jeffreys moved down the hall, he could hear the rapid fire of the SAW shattered the night.

'So much for surprise,' Sgt. Jeffreys thought.

Sgt. Jeffreys ran down the hall. The lead SEAL turned a corner and Sgt. Jeffreys heard the unmistakable 'click, click, click' as the MP7 fired and heard the metallic sound of empty shell casings hitting the tile floor. Rounding the corner, weapon held ready, Sgt. Jeffreys had to step over three dead Chinese soldiers as he followed the SEALs. Another corridor, another 'click, click, click' and more dead soldiers.

Here two corridors branched, Sgt. Jeffreys and one of the SEALs went left, while the other two SEALs headed right. As they rounded another turn, automatic weapons fire filled the hall. The SEAL in front of Jeffreys spun around and fell. Jeffreys dodged right and brought up his MP7. 'Click, click, click, click.' The Chinese soldier fell. Jeffreys went over to check on the SEAL. Miraculously, he was unharmed. Although two of the Chinese rounds had hit him, they had hit his ammunition magazines. That and his Kevlar vest had saved the SEAL. Sgt. Jeffreys helped the SEAL up and then moved cautiously down the hall. They heard running boots and both crouched. A Chinese soldier ran around the corner and died as both MP7's opened up.

Together Sgt. Jeffreys and the SEAL cleared several rooms, all the time listening to cryptic reports of the ongoing battle in their earpieces. They were painfully aware that time was against them and they would have to find Mark and the cube and get out soon, before the entire Chinese army showed up. They came to a locked door. They positioned themselves on either side of the door, weapons ready. Sgt. Jeffreys pulled a flash-bang grenade from his vest and stood to the side. The SEAL kicked in the door and jumped aside while Jeffreys tossed the grenade inside.

The explosion reverberated out into the hall and the SEAL and Jeffreys rushed into the room, crouched low, weapons held ready. There was a man lying on the floor. There was a bed, and otherwise the room was empty. Sgt. Jeffreys went over to the body and rolled it over, while the SEAL stood guard at the door. It was Mark. Sgt. Jeffreys pulled off a glove and checked Mark's pulse. He was alive. "Located Mr. Williams," Sgt. Jeffreys said in his throat mike. He did a quick body scan for injuries and then gently shook him. "Mark, it's me, Jeffreys. Wake up."

Mark moaned and opened his eyes. He stared at Jeffreys for a minute and then appeared to focus.

"Mark, we have to get out of here. We don't have much time," Jeffreys urged.

Mark shook his head. "Did you just try to blow me up?" Mark asked.

Jeffreys smiled.

"If I wanted to blow you up, you would be blown up," Jeffreys said. "Now we have to go."

"Chin has the cube," Mark said. "We have to get the cube."

"Do you know where it is?" Jeffreys asked.

Mark closed his eyes. Opening them, he said, "Yes."

Sgt. Jeffreys helped Mark to his feet and they left the room, Jeffreys supporting Mark as the SEAL led, weapon held ready.

"The cube is dangerous," Mark said as Sgt. Jeffreys helped him down the hall. "Chin is using it as a control cube. It is much more powerful than the cube we saw on the island, much more dangerous. We have to destroy it."

"The SEALs have come for the cube," Jeffreys said. "I came for you."

Mark smiled. Then he frowned. "Chin's coming. He's getting close. That way," Mark pointed down the hall, and then grabbed his head and slumped to the floor. Jeffreys bent down to assist Mark. "He's using the cube," Mark gasped. "You have to kill him. He is too powerful..." Mark's voice trailed off.

Jeffreys heard a noise and looked up. At the end of the hall a Chinese soldier stood. Jeffreys was still crouched over Mark, who now appeared to be unconscious. The SEAL was standing between them and the Chinese soldier, weapon held ready.

"Shoot," Jeffreys said, when the SEAL did not react. "Shoot him!"

The SEAL just stood there. Jeffreys tried to bring his MP7 up, but his mind suddenly became sluggish. He watched as the Chinese soldier raised his arm, almost as if in slow motion. He saw the dull grey of a gun barrel and then the bright flash as the Chinese shot the SEAL with his handgun. The SEAL collapsed in slow motion while Jeffreys still tried to bring up his MP7, but his arm would not obey. The Chinese soldier walked down the hall towards him, stopping several feet away.

"I told you I am your master," the Chinese said to Mark's unconscious form. "Why do you try to fight? I have won."

The Chinese turned to Sgt. Jeffreys. "And now you will die." He raised his arm, pointing his sidearm at Jeffreys face.

It was like a nightmare, Jeffreys thought. One of those where you could not run or hide or even fight, you could only watch. Jeffreys held his MP7 in his right hand, but he could not lift it. He just had to raise it a little and he could fire, but his arm would not obey. Time seemed to slow and Jeffreys' senses became acute. He became aware of every little sound. Every color seemed brighter, every detail more intense. The gun barrel loomed large in front of him and he could see or sense the muscles of the soldier's finger tightening on the trigger. Jeffreys' mind screamed to lift his gun, but his arm refused to move.

"Shoot him!" Mark's command filled Jeffreys' mind.

Jeffreys' arm shot up, followed up 'click, click, click, click, click' and the sound of empty shell casings bouncing off the wall. A resounding boom filled the room and Jeffreys was partially blinded by the flash of the soldier's handgun in his face.

When Jeffreys' vision cleared, he was still crouched over Mark. The SEAL was lying on the floor and the Chinese soldier was lying on his back in a growing puddle of blood. Jeffreys' MP7 was empty, the receiver locked open, awaiting a fresh magazine. Jeffreys shook his head, as his mind seemed to clear. "Man down," Jeffreys said into his throat mike. Turning to Mark, he asked, "Are you okay?"

"Yes. I am now," Mark replied. "The cube. He has the cube," Mark said, pointing to the dead Chinese. "In his left hand. But don't touch it! It's very powerful. We need to destroy it."

The sound of running feet filled the hallway. Jeffreys turned but did not fire as two SEALs rounded the turn. One SEAL tended to the downed SEAL. The other turned to Jeffreys. "Where is the cube?"

Jeffreys pointed. "Left hand. Make sure not to touch it."

The SEAL reached into his gear and pulled out a black container, slightly larger than the cube. He opened it and pushed the cube out of the dead Chinese's hand with his boot and scooped it up with the container. He closed the padded container around the cube and stowed it in his web gear. "We have the cube, Mr. Williams and one casualty," the SEAL reported on his throat mike. "We are headed out the North side."

When they emerged from the building, Sgt. Jeffreys saw that the barracks were completely engulfed in fire and partially collapsed. Bodies were strewn around the ground. "Area is secure," Sgt. Jeffreys heard in his earpiece. "But it won't be for long."

In the distance Sgt. Jeffreys could hear sirens. 'Fire department, probably,' he thought. That did not worry him. They would also be sending police, which the SEALs would easily outgun. The issue was whether any army units were also approaching. They had to get out of here. Jeffreys heard one of the SEALs contact the helicopter and they made their way out of the building complex to get to the airfield where the helicopter could land. Jeffreys assisted Mark, who was quickly getting stronger, while two SEALs assisted the wounded SEAL, who amazingly, was still alive.

When they cleared the buildings, they could hear the helicopter in the distance. The SEALs set up a quick perimeter and one of them activated an infrared beacon. When the Seahawk touched down, they loaded Mark and the injured SEAL and then the rest of them piled in, the SEAL carrying the SAW on the outside so he could train his weapon on any developing threats.

Sgt. Jeffreys never felt so glad to feel a helicopter take off as he did this time. As they rose, he saw the lights of approaching vehicles and the flames from the barracks reaching up to the night sky. The helicopter quickly climbed as the pilot pulled on the collective. And then the tracers came. Off to the right a line of red climbed lazily into the night sky towards them. Jeffreys heard someone shout a warning over the roar of the engines and then he felt the helicopter shudder as it was hit. The helicopter banked and swerved, trying to stay away from the deadly tracers. One more time Jeffreys thought he heard the ping of an impact and then the tracers were behind them. He breathed a sigh of relief and then he heard an engine sputter. He glanced forward to the cockpit. He did not understand the displays, but there certainly appeared to be a lot of red lights on.

And then it was quiet as both engines quit.

Mark was squashed into the back of the helicopter, surrounded by soldiers. He was lying on the floor, pressed against the back wall. He could not see anything but camo and gear. He felt the helicopter lift off and saw a nearby soldier trying to talk to him.

"Are you okay?" the soldier yelled.

It was Jeffreys. Mark barely recognized him in the dark. But the voice was recognizable. Mark managed a weak smile. The engines were too loud to try to talk and Mark was too tired to yell. Jeffreys smiled back and squeezed Mark's shoulder, then he looked back out the side door. The weight of the world seemed to lift off him as the helicopter took off. Chin was dead and they had the cube. Mark could now destroy the cube before any more trouble came from it. But right now he could relax. His ordeal was over. Mark did not have headphones on, but he could hear yelling over the sound of the engines. Suddenly the helicopter shook and then it started to bank and swerve. Mark hoped the maneuver was intentional. There was some more yelling and then silence.

Had they landed? The feeling in Mark's stomach as they suddenly dropped told Mark that they were not on the ground. Not yet anyway. But they would be soon.

"Brace yourself," Jeffreys yelled at Mark.

There was nothing Mark could do as he was pressed against the back wall by all the soldiers, he could not move if he wanted to. He wondered how high they were and how long it would take to hit. He wondered if it would hurt. It was amazingly quiet, only the sound of wind going by the open doors. None of the soldiers said a word, they just held on. Mark wanted to scream, but he could not be the only one. Somehow he held it in.

Suddenly the nose of the helicopter pitched up. Mark tightened his grip on something. Then the nose dropped and they hit and bounced and hit again, before sliding to a stop. Mark sat there dazed. They had stopped. They were not dead. There was a moment of silence, before someone from up front yelled, "Everyone out!"

The soldiers bailed out of the stricken craft, Sgt. Jeffreys dragging Mark. Mark could not see in the dark. He thought they were in a field. There was high grass under his feet. He looked around. Jeffreys had pulled his night vision goggles over his eyes, giving him a mechanized robot sort of look.

"This way," Jeffreys said, grabbing Mark by the arm and half pulling him, half leading him across the field, while Mark tripped and stumbled over the rough terrain.

Mark was winded when they got to the tree line. "Where are we going?" he asked.

"We have to get away from the chopper," Jeffreys responded.

"Where is everyone else?"

"They're here," Jeffreys said.

Mark looked around, but could not see anyone in the blackness. Suddenly, there was a loud "whoomf" and orange light shown through the woods. Mark saw three soldiers crouched nearby in the light.

"Ok, we have to go," Jeffreys said. "This way."

"What was that?" Mark asked.

"Helicopter blew."

Mark did not ask anything else. He had to save his breath. Jeffreys set a fast past. Mark still could not see very well in the dark, so Jeffreys had him by the arm and was guiding him through the woods. Mark held his free arm in front of his face to ward off stray branches. Before long Mark's breathing was coming in ragged gasps and he did not know how much farther he could go. If only Jeffreys would set a slower pace. He could jog a couple miles, but not at this pace.

"Come on, Mark," Jeffreys encouraged. He did not even seem out of breath.

"I can't jog out of China," Mark managed to gasp.

"Just consider it a motivational run," Jeffreys said.

"Only a marine," Mark had to pause to gasp for breath, "would use motivational," another gasp, "and run," another gasp, "in the same sentence."

They ran on in silence. Mark was relieved when they got to a path or small road. At least now he was not tripping all the time, but the SEALs picked up their pace. Mark's heart was racing and his breathing came hard. Sweat was pouring down his face. He was slowing them down. Jeffreys was pulling on him more and more.

"We are going to have to either slow down, or stop and rest for a minute," Mark managed to say.

Sgt. Jeffreys said something, but Mark did not hear it. A moment later a SEAL came up and grabbed Mark's other arm and between the two of them they practically carried Mark on the run.

'This is humiliating,' Mark thought. But there was nothing he could do about it. He could not keep up on his own. He did, however, try to run as much as he could so he was not completely dead weight. Time seemed to blur. Mark concentrated only on putting one foot in front of the other and trying not to stumble. And breathing, he had to concentrate on breathing. After an eternity, they finally halted. Mark collapsed on his back, arms spread out, gasping for breath.

"Are you okay?" Jeffreys asked.

"Just shoot me," Mark managed to gasp.

"I'm going to check on the others. Stay here," Jeffreys said.

'I'm not going anywhere,' Mark thought, but did not have the air to say.

Jeffreys disappeared into the dark and Mark lay there panting. Mark had not recovered when Jeffreys was back. "Up and at 'em," Jeffreys said. "We need to get moving."

"Are we really going to run all the way across China?" Mark asked as he struggled to his feet.

"We have to get some distance between us and the helicopter," Jeffreys said.

"I hope there is more to the plan than just running," Mark said.

"There is, we have a spot not far from here that we can hole up in. We need to get there before sunrise."

"Don't tell me how far it is," Mark said. "I don't think I could take the news." Mark took a tentative step and stumbled. "Aagh," he said. "My legs are cramping."

"That's okay, we'll make it," Jeffreys said as he took Mark's arm.

A SEAL materialized out of the dark and took Mark's other arm and they set off at a brisk jog. The rest of the night was a blur. Mark concentrated on running and breathing. Trying, unsuccessfully, to carry his own weight. There were brief moments of rest followed by the endless running. Jeffreys and the SEAL were breathing hard when Mark realized that he could see much clearer. It was only minutes later that he realized that sunrise was approaching. 'Weren't they supposed to be stopped by sunrise?' Mark thought. It was getting noticeably lighter when they stopped next. Mark would have commented on it, but he felt too bad and needed all his air just to breath.

"We're there," Jeffreys was saying. "The SEALs are checking it out." A couple minutes passed and Jeffreys said, "Okay, it's clear. Come on. Last little bit." Mark tried to get up, but his calves cramped and he fell. Jeffreys picked him up and the other SEAL took his arm. Mark tried to walk, but felt that the soldiers were really doing all the work. They carried him across another field and then slid down into a ditch. When they put Mark down, he just laid there, eyes closed, concentrated on breathing and trying not to vomit.

## CHAPTER 23

When Mark woke up, it was dark. His legs felt like rubber, painful rubber, and his back was stiff from lying on the hard ground. He tried to roll over and heard a soft moan, then realized that he was moaning.

"Shhh," Jeffreys was at Mark's side.

"Sorry," Mark whispered. "Where are we?"

"In a drainage culvert," Jeffreys said.

Mark felt the ground with his hand. It felt like cement. "What time is it?"

"Ten-fifteen."

"Morning or night?" Mark asked.

"Morning. You haven't slept that long."

"Can we talk?" Mark asked.

"Yes. Just not too loud. We don't want any echoes."

"Tell me what is going on."

"You remember the helicopter crashing?"

"Yes. And then we went on that endless marathon run," Mark said.

"We had to get some distance from the crash site," Jeffreys said.

"Was anyone hurt?"

"Not really," Jeffreys said. "Bumps and bruises. Nothing serious. The pilots are with us now."

"The more the merrier," Mark grunted. He tried to put out of his mind that all these people were risking their lives because of him. "So what is the plan?"

"We hide here while command tries to figure out what to do."

"That's a plan?" Mark said. "That sounds a lot like my 'run like hell' plan."

"Yea. I didn't like that plan much either."

"So why can't someone just come and get us?" Mark asked. "And how did you get here anyway?"

Jeffreys proceeded to tell Mark about the SEAL team and the details of the mission. He ended with, "So with the element of surprise gone, along with our ride, command has to figure out how to get us out. It's not like they can just send another helicopter. We've been hearing jets and helicopters flying overhead all morning. We've stirred up a bit of a hornet's nest."

"Are we safe here?" Mark asked.

"We are safe as long as we are not found," Jeffreys answered truthfully. "We can't fight our way out of China."

Mark was silent for a minute. "The cube," Mark started to say.

"We have the cube," Jeffreys finished.

"I know."

Jeffreys looked at Mark. "You can feel it? Like the control cube?"

"Yes," Mark said.

"What kind of cube is it?" Jeffreys asked.

"It's the blue-gray's personal cube. I took it from him after he died. You didn't know because you were unconscious."

"And you didn't tell anyone?" Jeffreys asked.

"No," Mark admitted. "Unlike the blue-grays cube on the *Ronald Reagan*, this cube continued to work. I don't know why. It's very powerful. I was afraid to give it to the government for fear someone like those NSA gentlemen would get their hands on it and abuse the power. In hindsight, it was a mistake, a huge mistake. I should have destroyed it."

"What happened?" Jeffreys asked.

"What do you know? What did Washington tell you?"

"We were told that you were kidnapped by the Chinese and that you had a working cube. We also knew that the Chinese was Colonel Lui's number two man."

"Ok. Here's the rest of that story. Chin was under control of Colonel Lui and continued to be under its control even after Colonel Lui was killed and the control cube destroyed by the nuke. Remember I explained that typically the control cube plants a goal in your head and then you figure out how to obtain the goal. Chin was still under the control and desperately needed answers. He did not know what happened, as he was deep in the tunnels when the attack occurred, which is why he survived the blast. He knew we had been there and when I turned up back in Pensacola, he and some of his officers came for a visit. When he kidnapped me, he discovered I had a cube."

"How?"

"He felt it. Just like I could feel the control cubes."

"You had the cube with you when you met Chin?" Jeffreys asked.

"No. I wasn't quite that stupid," Mark said. "But I did have it at my office, which was stupid enough. It was like a drug, I couldn't resist keeping it around me," Mark explained. "Anyway, Chin sensed it and must have retrieved it after he knocked me out. He can access it. But he was under control of the control cube. So his access was different. The personal cube has all the blue-gray's knowledge. It also has elements of the control cube in it. Somehow Chin accessed the control portion of the cube and started using it as a super control cube. All of his soldiers were under the control of Chin through the cube."

"Like those Chinese on the island in Qiando Lake," Jeffreys said.

"That, and he had direct mental contact with his soldiers."

"Like telepathy?"

"Something like that," Mark said. "It's hard to explain. But it is constant contact."

"That may explain why the alarm went off so quickly when we attacked the base," Jeffreys said.

"Yes, he knew the minute you took out the four sentries. He felt them die."

Jeffreys looked sharply at Mark. "How do you know about the four sentries?"

"I had contact with the cube also," Mark said. "I could sense it though him. Something like a party line. I could listen in."

"Were you under his control?" Jeffreys asked.

"No. Although we fought for control," Mark said, trying not to remember the painful details of the fight. "It was a fight in our minds. It was horrible. In the end, he won. He couldn't control me," Mark added when he saw the look of alarm on Jeffreys' face. "But I could no longer control the cube."

"What was that like, the fight?" Jeffreys asked.

"I can't describe it," Mark said. "But you felt a part of it. Remember when Chin showed up in the corridor and you tried to shoot him, but you couldn't move?"

"It was like one of those nightmares when you are running in quicksand or in slow motion," Jeffreys said.

"That was the cube. He was using the cube on you."

"But he didn't touch me," Jeffreys said.

"You don't have to. Not with this cube. You just have to be close enough."

"But then I heard you say, 'shoot him,' and I was suddenly able to move. What happened then?"

"Chin made a mistake. He walked over to you rather than shooting you like he did the SEAL. By the way, how is that SEAL?" Mark asked.

"Hurts like hell I suspect, but he is okay. Kevlar vests stop handgun bullets pretty well. It's the assault rifles that do the real damage."

"Good. Anyway," Mark continued. "When he got close, I could access the cube directly. He was distracted by you and in that second I was able to get enough control to send you that command and break his hold over you."

"You said that to me telepathically, not verbally?"

"Yes."

Jeffreys was silent for a moment. "Did I shoot him of my own free will or did you control me into shooting him?"

Now it was Mark's turn to pause. "You were trying to shoot him anyway," Mark explained. "But he was holding you back. I released the hold. But," Mark added, "My command may have forced you to shoot him even if you did not want to. Sorry."

"Don't apologize," Jeffreys said. "He needed shooting. But that cube stuff is scary."

"That is why we have to destroy it. There are others who can access it. And as you discovered, if they control the cube, they can control anyone. Chin's goal was to destroy the United States. He developed that from the control cube. The original goal of the control cube was to attack the blue-gray's enemies. When the blue-gray was killed, we became the blue-gray's enemy. And with the cube, he would have won."

"Won against the United States? All by himself?" Jeffreys asked, disbelief clear in his voice.

"Yes. And he would not have been alone. With the cube he could control anyone. He could control the Chinese government."

"Make them launch an attack against the U.S.?" Jeffreys asked.

"He could. Or he could go to the U.S. and take over the government. You don't understand the power of the cube," Mark said. "I always suspected that the blue-grays were telepathic, that they communicated by touch. I never realized until delving into this cube, how that really worked. The blue-grays developed as a telepathic species. They communicated telepathically by touch. But it wasn't just conversation like we have. Rather than asking someone to do something, or trying to convince them that they should by reason, every time a blue-gray communicated it was a battle for control. The control cubes just mirrored their day-to-day communication, a constant mental battle with the stronger mentalities becoming dominant in their culture.

"The cube focuses this energy so who ever controls the cube, can control Earth. It seems that mankind does have telepathic abilities. Many have suspected this for centuries and there are hundreds of books written on the subject. But we don't know how to control it and we, as a species, have not yet developed it. And we have no mental defenses against it. Actually, we do have defenses. But they are weak and untrained. Much like my legs feel like right now. But that is why we have to destroy that cube. To keep this from happening again."

"That could be a problem," Jeffreys said.

"Why? We destroyed the control cubes. We just do the same thing with this one. Problem solved."

Jeffreys lowered his voice. "The purpose of the mission was to get the cube," Jeffreys whispered. "Not you. You were secondary. Captain Peters talked the President into allowing me to come because I had past experience with you and the cube. They thought that might be critical. But the orders were to get the cube at all costs. I don't think they will allow us to destroy the cube."

"But I can explain the danger to them," Mark said.

"The only reason that I agree with you is because I was with you for our past… adventures," Jeffreys said. "They weren't. They will follow their orders and their orders are to get the cube at all costs."

Mark was silent.

"If we get out, it will be okay," Jeffreys said.

"No it won't," Mark objected. "You don't think our government has people like Chin. It will be the same thing, only we will be the bad guys, not the Chinese. We've had these conversations before. This technology is too advanced for us. It will destroy us. We are not ready for it."

"So what are you suggesting?" Jeffreys asked.

"One way or the other, we have to get that cube and destroy it."

"We? Can you touch the cube? Isn't it like the control cubes?"

"I can touch it. I have been touching it for months. It can be used as a control cube. Or, I should say that Chin used it as a control cube. I don't know if I could."

"But you told me to shoot him."

"That's true. But you wanted to. I don't really know if I could have forced that. I never delved into that aspect of the cube. Part of it I didn't even know was there until Chin accessed it. The whole thing is very confusing."

"Can you access the cube right now, like you did at the camp, without touching it?"

"No. I could access it then because Chin had it and he was contacting me. I can't access it now, although I can sense it. I know it is here. Like I said, it's very confusing."

"But the bottom line," Mark continued after a long silence. "Is that the cube is too dangerous to allow anyone to use. We must destroy it."

Mark was trying to run, but his legs would not move. The enemy was getting closer. He could not hide. He had to run. But all he could do was stand there while they came.

Mark woke up with a start, the dream fresh in his mind. He was lying on his side in the culvert. He was stiff and sore all over. Painfully, Mark sat up. His legs still hurt from last night and he wondered if he could walk. With some effort he tried to stand up, but hit his back on the culvert roof. The culvert was only about three feet high. Fighting a bout of claustrophobia, Mark crawled down the culvert until he spotted a light in the distance. He got half way before Jeffreys stopped him.

"Where you going?"

"Thought I would get up, see if I could still walk," Mark said. "Besides, the beds here are a bit too hard for my taste."

"You might as well sit back down. We won't be walking for a while," Jeffreys said.

"Do we have a new plan?" Mark asked.

"Yes. The SEALs got a SAT link to command. They want us to get down to a local fishing village and get out to sea on a boat. Once there, a submarine will pick us up. We move out at nightfall. It's too dangerous to go out there now."

"A submarine?"

"Yes. I know how much you like them. Maybe it's the same one you were in last year. I know how well you hit it off with its Captain," Jeffreys chuckled.

"Just my luck," Mark said. "And we will probably have to dive down to it because it will be too dangerous for it to surface."

"I hadn't thought of that," Jeffreys said. "You're probably right."

"Sure I am," Mark said morosely. "You don't think SEALs do anything the easy way, do you? They're probably just like you Marines."

"I knew I liked them," Jeffreys said.

"You would. By the way, is there a menu around here? I'm starving."

"You missed room service," Jeffreys said. "But they left this power bar for you. And you can have a few swallows from this canteen. But don't finish it off. It's all we have until we find a place to replenish."

Mark took the power bar. He was starving. As he started unwrapping it, he asked, "Have you eaten?"

"No," Jeffreys said.

"Then we split it," Mark said.

"You need it," Jeffreys argued.

"You're the one who carried me all night. We split it. I should be on a diet anyway."

They ate the power bar slowly. All the while Mark's dream kept haunting him, the enemy was getting near, he had to run. He tried to push it away. Jeffreys cocked his head, like he was listening to something.

"What?" Mark asked.

Jeffreys tapped his ear. "Sniper reporting. We may have a problem."

"Great," Mark said, the dream looming larger in his consciousness.

There was a bustling in the culvert as the SEALs started quickly gathering their gear.

"What is going on?" Mark asked.

Jeffreys got up and started putting on his rucksack. "The Chinese are coming. They are searching the culverts. They are at one about a mile away. This one will be next. We need to move out."

"I thought you said it was too dangerous to go out in the daytime."

"Not as dangerous as it will be getting caught in here," Jeffreys said as he checked his weapon.

Sgt. Jeffreys and Mark moved down to the end of the culvert. Mark looked around. Dark clouds were building in the distance. Maybe they would get lucky and it would storm. At least that would give them some cover. As they stepped out of the culvert a second SEAL joined them. 'Great,' Mark thought. 'They are already assuming I can't keep up. But, of course they are right,' Mark thought glumly.

"You stand out too much," Jeffreys said. "We need to give you some camouflage." With that, Jeffreys and the other SEAL reached into the mud and started smearing it all over Mark's clothes.

"Why don't I just roll in it," Mark said sarcastically.

"Good idea," Jeffreys said.

Mark stood there for a second before he realized that Jeffreys was serious. Sighing, Mark got down on his hands and knees and then started rolling in the dirty mud at the base of the culvert. When he was completely soaked and miserable, Jeffreys said, "And now your head, cover your hair and face." Mark reached down and smeared smelly, muddy goop on his head and face. When he had finished, Jeffreys added some more until he was satisfied.

"Well, that's better than nothing," Jeffreys said to the SEAL, then turned to Mark. "Okay, lets get going. Stay with me. Do what I do. Just like on the mountain."

Mark wanted to joke, but he was too scared and miserable to think of anything to say. Instead, he merely nodded. The team formed a line as they moved out of the culvert. They stayed in the drainage ditch, moving in a low crouch. When the ditch became shallower, they crawled so they would not be seen from the road. When the ditch became deeper, they jogged through the muddy water crouched over. 'This is much worse than last night,' Mark thought as he wondered how long he could keep up.

"How do we know where we are going?" Mark whispered to Jeffreys when they were crawling through the mud in a shallow area. "We have a sniper in front and a sniper in back of us," Jeffreys said. "They are the team's eyes right now."

Mark glanced behind him. The only person he saw was carrying a big machine gun. It looked to Mark something like an M-60, although perhaps a bit smaller. Either way, Mark was glad he was not carrying it right now.

Jeffreys started moving again and Mark tried to mimic his movement. He was crawling through the ditch on his elbows and knees. It was maddening having to crawl. They were not making good time. Mark felt like a sitting duck.

"Down!" Jeffreys whispered. Mark flattened in the dirt, willing himself to be invisible. Mark lay still, heart pounding, his face in the dirt. He wanted desperately to look around, to see what was going on. But Jeffreys had been very specific about what to do. He would tell him when to move. Mark lay there as instructed, only his ears giving him any clues as to what was happening. An eternity seemed to pass before he heard the sound of an engine, some type of truck by the sound of it. It was approaching. Mark tried to sink deeper into the ground. They were in a shallow area of the ditch, so there was not much to hide in. The truck approached and then passed. And stopped. He heard Chinese voices, a yell. Then all hell broke loose. Gunshots came from the direction of the Chinese. The SAW opening up behind him deafened

Mark. The fight was over as quickly as it had started. Mark had not even moved.

"Come on!" Jeffreys yelled, grabbing Mark's arm. "To the truck."

Mark stumbled to his feet, while Jeffreys pulled him. He climbed out of the ditch and headed for the Chinese truck. A dozen Chinese soldiers lay dead around the truck. They were halfway to the truck when two more Chinese trucks came around the corner in front of them at high speed. They were the Chinese Humvees that Mark had travelled in before. And one had a machine gun on the roof. The Chinese gunner opened up, sending puffs of dirt flying around the truck. The SEALs dove for cover and the gunner stopped firing when he was hit by one of the snipers. The SEALs opened up and the first Humvee swerved and crashed into the ditch. The second Humvee stopped and the several Chinese soldiers bailed out, shooting wildly at the SEALs. Several dropped when the SEALs returned fire, but not all of them.

Jeffreys grabbed Mark again. "Back to the ditch."

"What about the truck?" Mark asked as he ran for the ditch.

"It got shot up," Jeffreys yelled back. "And we have more company coming from down the road. Get down in the ditch."

Mark dove into the ditch and tried to find as deep a spot to disappear into. There was not much cover, just two or three feet. But it was better than being out on the road. The rest of the team moved back into the ditch, taking up firing positions. Another truck came up the road, but stopped before getting too close. It was like an American deuce and a half, a troop carrier. Mark looked on in despair when Chinese soldiers poured out of the truck. He saw another truck coming up behind the first.

Mark ducked down as the air filled with the sound of automatic weapons fire and bullets whizzed overhead. Most of the noise came from the Chinese. Mark saw the SEALs return fire, but their weapons, except for the SAW, were silenced. Mark noticed that Jeffreys was firing single shots and realized he must be trying to conserve ammunition. 'How many rounds did they have?' Mark wondered.

'This is it,' Mark thought. There was no getting out of this. Bullets whizzed by Mark, thudding in the dirt nearby. 'Click, click, click.' A scream. "I'm hit," an American voice. "Ammo." "Take the truck, take the truck." Mark saw a SEAL slump. Wanting nothing more than to just lie still, Mark crawled over to the SEAL and turned him over to check on him. He appeared to be dead. Mark glanced up and saw the Chinese advancing. Looking down the ditch, he counted only five SEALs. He did not know if the others were dead or somewhere else. But this battle would only end one way.

Mark realized the dead SEAL had the cube. He could still sense it. He searched the body and found the container. He had to destroy the cube before the Chinese won. If nothing else, he would at least destroy the cube. He opened the container and the cube dropped into his hand.

# CHAPTER 24

Mark's hand closed around the cube.

*The power of the cube coursed through him like a drug to an addict. Memories flooded his mind, vast open vistas under a purple sky, traveling through space, dinosaurs roaming in fern covered valleys, an asteroid plummeting towards the Earth, Chinese soldiers guarding a building... The memories threatened to overwhelm Mark. He typically braced himself before accessing the cube to avoid being overwhelmed in the initial contact. But this time he had just grabbed it, forgetting to concentrate, and the memories washed over him.*

*Pain washed over him, but it was not a memory, how he could tell he did not know. The pain was from the SEAL lying beside him. He was not dead, but was badly wounded. The SEAL's mind was open for Mark to read: pain, fear.*

*"I'll get you out of here," Mark said, wondering as he said it whether he could deliver on his promise. The pain focused Mark. He concentrated on the cube and the familiar pathways opened before him, the recent history of the blue-grays, their time on Earth, their gene-splicing experiments with the dinosaurs 65 million years ago and then their recent experience the last year. Mark spotted the path that Chin had taken, the control cube side. He had not been aware of that area when he had the cube, but had only first glimpsed it when he fought with Chin. He dove into that area now, feeling the power of the cube. He reached out like he had felt Chin do, like*

he had done when Chin attacked Sgt. Jeffreys. He saw Jeffreys fifteen feet away, crouched in the ditch, searching for targets. He entered Jeffreys mind. Emotions swept through him; pain, fear, rage, determination. Determination was dominant, controlling the other emotions. Mark was awed. Jeffreys knew the tactical situation. He knew they were outgunned, yet he fought on, determined.

"Ammo," Jeffreys yelled as he fired his last round from his MP7.

"Out, out, out," were the replies Jeffreys heard over his earpiece, replies Mark heard in Jeffreys' mind.

Jeffreys tossed aside the useless MP7 and pulled out his 9 mm handgun. 'Twelve rounds in the clip and two spare clips,' Jeffreys thought, and Mark heard in his mind. 'Close range only. No penetration power. Need to make them head shots,' Jeffreys told himself.

The SAW stopped firing. 'SAW's out,' a voice said.

Mark reached out farther. He felt the SEAL's minds. Desperate determination. Grim. He reached out and found the Chinese.

Mark was looking down a gun barrel, shooting at the Americans. He was running across for cover, spraying the ditch with rapid fire from his Chinese SKS machine gun. He was sighting his rifle carefully, waiting for the American to pop his head up again. There, the cross hairs were on the soldiers' face, Sgt. Jeffreys' face. He squeezed the trigger...

"Jeffreys, duck!" Mark screamed.

Jeffreys ducked, the shot grazing the top of his head, enough to sting, to break the skin, but only that. Jeffreys glanced quickly at Mark, nodded, and resumed his firing position.

The sound of firing changed. The Chinese guns still rang loud, but the SEAL's counter fire slowed as they ran out of ammunition. The battle was all but over. The Chinese heard the difference too. They knew the SEALs were running out of ammunition.

Bloodlust replaced fear. Hatred. They would teach these people a lesson, the people who had killed their comrades. They would kill *them all. The Chinese let out a war cry and charged the ditch, weapons blasting.*

*The Americans waited. "Hold your fire, make every shot count," someone instructed.*

*Mark felt Sgt. Jeffreys brace himself. The first Chinese soldier came within range and Jeffreys fired, hitting him in the face. He pivoted and shot the second and then turned for the third. Bullets ricocheted past him.*

*Mark saw the battle from every perspective, from every soldier, Chinese and American. He rushed the American line, firing wildly while yelling, only to die when he was shot in the face. He was crouched in the ditch firing desperately. He was running, his comrade falling next to him. He swung his SKS towards the lone American who was crouched with a handgun, pointed away from him. He was Jeffreys firing at the second soldier, then pivoting back to a third who was swinging his SKS towards him. The American was pivoting too slowly, he would die…*

"NOOOOOO!"

Jeffreys was firing methodically. He no longer tried to keep down. It no longer mattered. The Chinese were charging the ditch. He knelt and fired his 9mm as soon as the Chinese crossed the edge. Point and shoot, pivot, point and shoot. This would not last long. Part of his mind wondered if he would have a chance to reload before he was gunned down. Another soldier to his right. He pivoted. The Chinese was bringing up his SKS. This was going to be close.

The Chinese war cry turned into a primal scream that sent chills down Jeffreys' spine, causing him to flinch just enough to miss the shot. The Chinese went down anyway. Jeffreys spun, getting ready for the next shot. No one showed. He swung his 9mm back and forth searching for targets. No one showed. It was quiet. Deadly quiet. His ears rang from the shooting, but he heard nothing else. No shots, no screaming.

He quickly holstered his 9mm and grabbed the fallen soldiers' SKS, checked the action, and prepared to fire. Still no targets. Still no noise. Nothing. Slowly he looked over the edge of the ditch. The road was covered with fallen Chinese soldiers. No one moved. He looked around carefully. Nothing.

"Report," someone said over the comm link.

"No one's moving," someone else said.

"They're all dead," another report.

Jeffreys saw a couple SEALs dart out onto the road to retrieve Chinese weapons and ammunition. He covered them, but no shots rang out. A couple more sprinted across to the trucks, weapons held ready.

"All dead," came back the reports.

The reports were scarier than the firefight. What had happened? What killed them? Apprehension, almost a dread threatened to overcome him, but he forced it down. He had work to do.

The SEALs started to recover. "Mike, check out that second truck to the left. See if it runs. Sam, you and John collect some weapons and ammo. The rest check on our team," the commands came over the net.

Jeffreys went over to Mark. That was his first priority now. His heart sank when he saw Mark laying face first in the ditch. Had he been hit? He could not tell for all the mud and dirt on him. But he was not moving. Jeffreys lay his SKS on the ground and bent over Mark, gently turning him over, afraid what he would find. Mark moaned. There was no sign of blood on his shirt.

"Mark, Mark, are you okay? Are you hit?" Jeffreys ran his hands quickly over Mark's body, doing a quick combat medic blood check. There was blood on Jeffreys' hands. He checked again, then realized it was his blood, not Mark's. Blood was running down Jeffrey's arm. He would tend to that later.

Mark moaned again and opened his eyes. Jeffreys thought he recognized that look from the times Mark had accessed the cube. Jeffreys saw the cube clenched tight in Mark's right hand. He tried to take it away, but Mark resisted, his grip surprisingly strong for his condition.

"Truck runs," Jeffreys heard on his earpiece and the sound of an engine confirmed the report.

"Drive it up here and we will load up. We need to get out of here before more company arrives," another voice said.

"Mark, wake up," Jeffreys said. "We need to get out of here." Jeffreys did not know where they would go, but going sounded good to him. He slung Mark over his shoulder and crawled out of the ditch. He staggered over to the truck where a SEAL helped load Mark into the back. It was a troop carrier, so there was plenty of room. The other SEALs climbed in or helped load the injured into the truck. Everyone appeared to be wounded, but three were critical. They were tended to as the truck started to drive away. Jeffreys glanced out of the open back of the truck at the scene they were leaving. Several vehicles were left in the road, one smoking. The ground was littered with dead Chinese soldiers. Jeffreys estimated there was at least a company of dead on the road. What had happened? How had they survived?

Jeffreys glanced around the truck. Two SEALs rode in the front. Three more lay on the floor, being tended to by their comrades, while the others were stationed on either side of the truck, weapons ready, looking for enemies. Although Jeffreys was glad for the ride, he realized they could not do this for long. They were too exposed. The SEALs knew that too. They headed down the road as fast as they could. They needed distance from this firefight and cover. A passing convoy or a helicopter and they would be done. They were 32 clicks from the coast. Might as well be a million, Jeffreys thought. He checked his captured SKS and picked up some extra magazines from the pile on the floor. He would need the ammo, probably sooner than later. Then Jeffreys turned to check on Mark, who was curled up in a fetal position on the floor of the truck. When Jeffreys reached over to touch him, he realized Mark was shaking. No, he was quietly sobbing.

Jeffreys had seen it before, all sorts of reactions after a battle. Crying, swearing, bragging, false bravado, fear, or no emotion, the 1000 yard stare as they called it. He wondered if he should just leave him be, to get over it, or try to comfort him. He was tempted to leave Mark alone. But their position was precarious and it was very likely they would have to abandon the truck very soon. If so, Mark would have to be able to walk or run on his own. Jeffreys leaned down.

"Mark, it's okay. We made it. You have to shake it off." No reaction.

"Mark," Jeffreys said harsher, hating himself for doing so. "We don't have time for this. I need your help. I can't carry you. You have to pull your own weight. Now shake it off."

The sobbing stopped, although Mark remained curled up in a ball. He said something, but Jeffreys did not make it out.

"What did you say?" Jeffreys asked.

"… are all dead."

"No," Jeffreys said. "We made it. We're banged up a bit, but we made it."

"No," Mark said, clearer this time. "The Chinese are all dead. Every one of them."

"Yes," Jeffreys said. "It was them or us."

"It's my fault," Mark said, slightly inaudible.

"It's not your fault," Jeffreys replied. "You didn't know they would kidnap you. You were trying to do the right thing."

"No," Mark said. "I killed them."

Jeffreys shook Mark. He had to get him over this pity party. "We've talked about this," Jeffreys said. "You made the best decision you could make. It's not your fault."

"No," Mark said. "It is. I killed them. With this." And Mark held up the cube, still clenched in his hand.

"You didn't know. Maybe in hindsight you should have destroyed it, but you have to stop blaming yourself."

"*I killed them*," Mark said, and Jeffreys realized that Mark's lips had not moved. He had spoken directly in Jeffreys' head.

Jeffreys stared at the cube in Mark's hand, sudden realization dawning on him. "With the cube," Jeffreys whispered.

"*Yes*," Mark answered in Jeffreys' mind.

# CHAPTER 25

Jeffreys was worried. He was worried about the mission. He was worried about Mark. He was worried about having enough ammunition. He was worried that he would fail the team. He was worried about getting out of China alive, although that worried him the least. Mark had at least stopped sobbing, but now he just sat on the floor of the truck staring at the cube. He had been that way the last ten minutes while the truck headed south on a back road that command had instructed them to take.

They were trying to get to a small fishing village where they could hopefully commandeer a boat to get out to the submarine. However, the village was twenty-eight clicks away and they still had an hour of sunlight left. A group of American combat soldiers in a Chinese troop carrier was not an easy thing to hide. So far they had been lucky, their route had been deserted. But Jeffreys knew you could not count on luck for long, particularly in combat. Any minute now he was expecting to see an enemy convoy or helicopter converge on them.

The SEALs were tense, keeping a sharp look out. Their instincts told them to hide somewhere, but they knew they had to get some distance from the massacre. Once that was discovered, the place would be crawling with troops and helicopters with infrared sights. No, they had to stay in the open and make a run for it and hope for the best. They were armed again, but only with small arms, Chinese SKS assault rifles. That was better than nothing, but would be useless against bigger weapons, or a helicopter. That was their biggest fear, a helicopter. It would be able to stay out of range and coordinate an attack. Or, it could call in an attack helicopter or a jet fighter. That would be the end of the story. The SEALs only hope was to remain undiscovered for as long as possible. But driving down this back road they were exposed. Jeffreys wondered how long their luck would hold.

Mark stirred. "Tell them to slow down," Mark said.

"What?" Jeffreys asked.

"They are driving too fast. Tell them to slow down."

"We have to get off this road as fast as possible," Jeffreys explained.

"Tell them to slow down to normal traffic speed," Mark said in a tone that required obedience.

Jeffreys obeyed. "Slow it down," Jeffreys said into his mic. "We are too obvious racing like this. Take it down to normal speed."

Jeffreys was surprised when the SEALs obeyed him. Although the command made some sense, every instinct told him to run as fast as they could.

When they had slowed Mark said, "There is a Chinese convoy approaching us from the South, three Chinese Humvees and two troop carriers. They are around the next corner."

Jeffreys looked up alarmed. How did Mark know? Was he hallucinating? He sounded calm, almost matter of fact about it. Could it be the cube? Jeffreys could see the corner about a half-mile ahead. There was nowhere for them to pull off and hide. He was about to key his mic when he saw the lead vehicle make the turn and head towards him. It was a Chinese Humvee with a heavy machine gun mounted on the top. The SEAL driver must have seen it too as he took his foot off the gas and their troop carrier slowed.

"Tell him to keep going. Drive normally right past them," Mark said in a normal tone.

Jeffreys relayed the instructions, again surprised that the driver obeyed. The SEALs all tensed and Jeffreys saw them readying their weapons. It was an impossible fight. They had six effectives at this time with assault rifles. The convoy had to have at least a company or more of troops and at least two of the Humvees had heavy machine guns. Even if they took out the troops in the turrets, they would not be able to get past before the other troops opened fire. And even if they somehow managed that, the Chinese would have radios. One call and it would be over. But Jeffreys was not one to quit, ever. He readied his weapon and checked his spare magazines as the distance between them quickly closed.

"Wave," Mark said. "Everyone wave."

That was the stupidest command Jeffreys had ever heard. Yet he found himself waving at the lead Chinese Humvee. The Chinese soldier in the turret smiled and waved back. The soldier in the turret of the second Humvee did the same. Soon Jeffreys was waving to forty-some Chinese soldiers in the back of the troop carrier and they were all waving back. It was like a parade or something. As the last vehicle passed behind them, Jeffreys lowered his arm and started laughing at the idiocy of the whole thing.

"How did we manage to get through that?" one of the SEALs asked on the com link.

"Beats the hell out of me," another replied.

"Didn't they see us? Our camouflage is not that good. They had to see that we weren't Chinese."

Jeffreys looked down at Mark. He was slumped over, apparently unconscious, but still tightly holding the cube. Jeffreys reached down, concerned, and checked on him.

Mark's pulse was pounding and his breathing was fast and hard, like he had just exercised or had been running, rather than riding in the truck. 'What is going on with him?' Jeffreys wondered. This business with the cube was getting stranger and stranger.

They continued the drive for another hour without meeting anyone. Jeffreys moved towards the front of the truck so he could listen to the SEALs talking in the cab. They were trying to decide the best course of action. The truck was heading south, towards the target fishing village. Barring any further unforeseen events, like being discovered, they would arrive at the village in fifteen or twenty minutes. Just after sunset. The sun was already touching the horizon and Jeffreys could not remember being so happy about the coming of darkness.

"We have to find someplace to ditch this truck," one of the SEALs was saying.

'Once the truck is discovered, it won't be long before they track us down. We park the truck, then go in and reconnoiter. We have two choices as I see it. One, we go in and find the boat we need and take it. The other choice is to hide in the boat and take it and the crew when they arrive in the morning to take it out. My guess is that will be around zero four hundred."

"What's the downside of just taking the boat?" Jeffreys asked through the back window.

"There are several," the SEAL replied. "First, once it is reported stolen, then the Chinese will figure out that we have it and start searching for it. There is no cover for us once we get out on the water. So if they start looking for it before we link up with the submarine, we have problems. The second problem is that we don't know the vessel, and more importantly, don't have any charts for this area. We can probably figure out how run to the boat, but the chart issue really concerns me. It would not do to get grounded on a sandbar. That could ruin our whole day."

"I think," said the SEAL leader, "that the best option is to find a suitable boat, hide in it and then take it over once the crew boards. They can help us get out to the submarine and then we just turn them loose with their boat when we board the sub."

"We just have to make sure no one finds the truck before we are well out of the way."

"We don't have time to do that," Jeffreys heard Mark say. He was surprised, because he did not think Mark was awake. "We need to drive slowly into the fishing village and find the Captain and the crew and have them take us out with the rest of the fishing fleet in the morning. We can blend in with the rest of the fleet that way."

"There is no way we can walk into the village and do that," one of the SEALs objected. "One phone call to the authorities from anyone in that village and we are blown."

"*We need to drive slowly into the fishing village and find the Captain and the crew and have them take us out with the rest of the fishing fleet in the morning,*" Mark said again.

"We need to drive slowly into the fishing village and find the Captain and the crew and have them take us out with the rest of the fishing fleet in the morning," the SEAL commander said.

Jeffreys looked up in surprise. He looked back over at Mark, who was still lying slumped in the back of the truck. He shuffled over to Mark and gently shook him. "What are you doing? You're using the cube on him," Jeffreys said. "You can't do that. I know you helped us back there," Jeffreys continued. "But this is a combat operation and you are not combat trained. You can't assert your will like that. You have to let them lead."

Mark gave a weary smile to Jeffreys. "If we run this as a combat operation, we are all dead. Do you really think we can fight our way out of China now that the Chinese are looking for us? The only reason we made it out of that last firefight is because of the cube. The only way we have made it this far is because of the cube. The cube made that convoy we passed think that they were waiving at a fellow platoon. The cube has kept dozens of people from noticing us as we have driven down this road. And the only way we will get out of China is with the cube.

"I am exhausted. I am tired and hungry. I don't know how much longer I can keep it up. And when I can't, then everyone is going to notice our little band of soldiers sitting here in the middle of China. And we won't last ten seconds after that. So, we are going to drive right into that village. I'm going to find the Captain of the vessel we want and he is going to agree to take us out with him in the morning when he sails. And we are going to do it as fast as possible so I can rest."

Jeffreys was silent for a while. "You could at least tell the SEALs, rather than using the cube on them."

"You're right," Mark agreed. "But I don't have the energy. The only reason I am telling you is because you deserve to know what is going on. You have saved my butt too many times. But now I have to concentrate, more people are coming," Mark finished as he closed his eyes.

Jeffreys looked up. The truck was taking a turn. On the other side of the turn the road passed between two rice paddies. Jeffreys counted fifteen Chinese working in the fields. As they rumbled past, not a single one looked up. Jeffreys wondered if that was typical in China, or if that was the cube keeping them from being interested.

## CHAPTER 26

They drove slowly into the fishing village and down the only street. *"Stop,"* Mark said. They stopped and waited. The SEALs were tense, weapons held ready.

An old man came walking out to the truck.

"It's about time you got here," he said in fluent English. "Supper is ready. Get your things and come on in. Tan-lo will take care of your truck."

The SEALs looked at each other in disbelief.

*"Do what he says,"* Mark said.

The SEALs carefully climbed out of the truck, weapons held at the ready. The old man was all smiles, seemingly oblivious to their weapons, that they were carrying three wounded soldiers or that they were American soldiers. They walked into the old man's house and entered a large common room where an old woman spoke to them in Chinese while gesturing that they should sit. She moved to the wounded and pointed to a door. The SEALS complied, carefully carrying the wounded into the next room.

Mark was taken to a low table. He sat on the floor next to the table and the old woman brought food, steaming rice and some type of fish. Jeffreys chuckled as he remembered Mark's dislike for Chinese food, particularly their fish dishes. But Mark dug into the food ravenously, nodding his head to his hostess. She beamed in delight and bowed back.

Jeffreys squatted down next to Mark. "Want to tell me what's happening?"

Mark swallowed a mouthful of rice and fish. "We are distant cousins who have come visiting."

"What about the wounded?"

"They are being cared for," Mark said.

"But won't they notice they are bullet wounds?"

"No," Mark said. "They will treat them and not think anything of it. Tomorrow we are going to help him on his boat. We will launch about four a.m. Here, have something to eat."

Jeffreys shook his head, then rethought it and sat down. "This is all the cube."

"It's really very easy, this part," Mark explained. "I just planted the cousin part and their minds filled in the rest of the details. I didn't have to, which is good, because it would be too exhausting to do that. When I go to sleep you need to make sure the control holds. I think it will, but I have never done this before. So you need to make sure it holds. If it doesn't, you will have to wake me up."

"How is it that they speak such good English?" Jeffreys asked.

"They don't," Mark said. "That is the cube translating for you."

Jeffreys sat and thought for a moment. "I better brief the SEAL team leader on our position," Jeffreys said.

"Probably should," Mark muttered between mouthfuls. "Tell him to eat and rest now while he can. Tomorrow will be a long day."

Jeffreys went over and spoke with the SEAL team leader. When he came back, Mark was still eating. "Can you tell me what is going on with the cube?" Jeffreys asked. "It seems very different from the memory cube."

"That's an understatement," Mark said.

"So how does it work?" Jeffreys asked.

Mark paused between mouthfuls. "That's a hard question to answer. Since we haven't developed this capability, we really don't have words that adequately describe it."

"What are you doing right now?"

"Now? Pretty much relaxing," Mark said. "In the back of my mind I am monitoring our hosts, making sure they are staying with the cousin theme. But other than that, I am relaxing. Driving down here, that was a different story. I was scanning, which is the only word I can think of, searching out with my mind to see if I could contact other minds."

"You don't have to touch them?"

"No. I learned that from Chin. But they have to be within a certain range, a certain distance for me to access them."

"How close?"

"I don't know."

"You don't know?"

"No. I really don't. Sensing them with my mind is very different than seeing them physically or hearing them. There is no frame of reference to say how far they are physically. It is very different from what we are used to."

"But you knew that convoy was approaching," Jeffreys said.

"True. But I could see what they saw and what we saw and could tell that the two paths were coming together. It was a combination of the mind and the senses, so I could figure it out."

"What did you do with the convoy?"

"I just reinforced what they were expecting, another one of their trucks with their troops in it. They were not expecting to see us, so it was an easy vision to plant."

"Easy? I thought you were passed out."

"Easy in the sense that I did not have to change their initial impression," Mark said. "This whole mind cube thing is mentally exhausting."

"How long can you keep it up?"

"I don't know," Mark said. "I am using new muscles, so to speak. Right now, it is easy. The situation is relatively static and everyone is nearby. When we are on the road, the elements are dynamic and distances vary. I get spread too thin and lose control. When the helicopter came by, that was impossible."

"Helicopter? What helicopter?" Jeffreys asked.

"Right after we passed the convoy, a helicopter had us in its sights, long distance optics. We were targeted."

"You never said anything. You got to the helicopter?"

"No. It was too far. But they radioed the convoy and I had contact with the radio operator in the last vehicle. I had him radio back that they had made contact with us and we were one of their units, but our radio was out. That satisfied the helicopter pilot and he turned away."

Jeffreys was silent for a moment. "And all this is through the cube."

"It's not me, that's for sure," Mark said. "The cube has all sorts of parts to it. If you opened it up, it would be larger than the Smithsonian museum. The part I am in now is the control cube side, or hall. That's the part Chin accessed. I didn't even know it was there before he 'opened the door' so to speak."

"What happened back at the culvert?" Jeffreys asked.

Now it was Mark's turn to be silent. "That was bad," Mark finally said. "That was real bad."

Jeffreys waited for Mark to continue.

"The cube is complicated," Mark finally said. "It has hidden pathways in it. Pathways you don't even know are there. Like searching directories on a Mac, you go to 'Go' in finder and you see a list of the directories. But if you push the 'option' key, then the hidden 'library' directory suddenly materializes, which you had no idea was even there."

"What are you talking about?"

"You aren't an Apple person," Mark said.

"No."

"Too bad. It was a perfect analogy," Mark said. "Ok. You know that on computers there are hidden files that you have to know how to look for before you can even see them, right?"

"Yes."

"The cube is the same way. There are hidden files, or doors. I did not even know there was this control cube aspect to the cube until I accessed it through Chin. He found it, perhaps because he was already under the control cube's power. So that showed me that area of the cube. But there was another area, a deeper aspect to it as well. When we were under attack, I grabbed the cube so I could destroy it. I was panicking, not thinking. So when I opened the container the cube dropped into my hand. Of course I accessed it then. I had not intended to. I was not prepared. I went down the last path used in the cube, the control cube side. Suddenly, I could sense those around me. It started with the SEAL team and then I expanded outwards until I could start sensing the Chinese soldiers. It was very jumbled, hectic. Fleeting images, emotions, pain, anger, fear. No order to it. I was a Chinese soldier, a SEAL, another Chinese. I was shooting, being shot, dying. I felt it all."

"You felt people dying?" Jeffreys asked. "And you didn't?"

"Yes," Mark said. "A vast improvement from the last time."

"Last time it killed you."

"I think the difference is that last time I was fully involved with my host. This time the images were fleeting, more of an overview. I could still feel their pain, but it passed quickly. The whole thing was horrible. Not only was I watching the firefight, I was living it, from everyone's perspective."

"I can't imagine what that was like," Jeffreys said.

"I saw, felt…, I don't know how to describe it. I was the Chinese soldier sighting in on your head."

"Is that when you told me to duck?"

"Yes," Mark said. "That was the breaking point. I couldn't be the one who killed you, or watched as they killed you. There was another door in the cube, one farther down. It wasn't there when Chin accessed the cube. But it was when I did. I opened it and traveled down the cube. It was the blue-gray's fail-safe. It was how they controlled their subjects, how they made sure that the subjects did not rebel or turn on them. They could kill their subjects if they needed to. I went down that path. I entered all of the Chinese soldiers' minds and killed them. And they knew it. They knew what I was doing. But they had no defense against me. They just died."

"That was the primal scream we heard at the end of the firefight," Jeffreys said.

"Yes."

The two men were silent for a long time. "I can't do that again," Mark finally broke the silence.

"It was combat," Jeffreys said. "You do what you have to do. You saved us all."

"But I can't do that again. I could shoot someone if I had to. But to use the cube to kill I have to accept the blue-gray psyche. I'm afraid the blue-gray psyche will take over and I won't care about mankind, I won't have any of our moral or ethical checks and balances. There is no telling what I might do next. So I have locked that door and I can't, won't go back."

"But you don't have to," Jeffreys said. "You have learned to use the control cube. To control people, like this Chinese family," even as Jeffreys said this, the thought of such control, such power, even by Mark, gave him a cold chill. "You won't have to kill again."

"I am learning to use the cube, the control aspects," Mark agreed. "But I have a long way to go before I can master it, if a human can indeed master the cube at all. But it is scary. And the power, you can see how freaked out the SEALs are by my power, can't you?"

"They do seem a bit subdued," Jeffreys said.

"You should hear what they are thinking," Mark said. "They are terrified. They realize that the cube is the only thing keeping them alive right now. But they are terrified."

"You are reading their minds?"

"Yes."

"You said you couldn't read minds," Jeffrey said.

"That was before," Mark said. "But now I can. With this cube, with the depth that I have gone, I can read minds. Even as we speak, I am monitoring all around us."

Jeffreys looked startled. "You are reading my mind?"

"No," Mark said. "Everyone but you."

"You can't read my mind?"

"Oh, I can," Mark said. "I did during the firefight. I didn't have any control. I felt everyone. But now that I am getting more control, I have backed out of your mind."

"Why?"

"Because you are my friend and I consider it an invasion of privacy."

"Wow. That is scary," Jeffreys said.

"And that is why we have to destroy the cube," Mark said. "The power of the cube is incomprehensible, and we have no defense against it. We need to grow as a species before we can have this type of technology."

"If we ever can," Jeffreys said.

"True."

"Are you going to destroy it now?" Jeffreys asked.

"No. I probably should. But I promised one of the wounded SEALs that I would get him out of here. And I already know that I can't let you get killed. I need to get you all out of here. When we are safe, then I will destroy the cube."

"If you wait too long, they won't let you," Jeffreys said, referring to the SEALs.

"You miss the point," Mark said. "No one around me will be able to stop me. I control everyone around me, except you, of course. So I will be able to destroy it. Then if I lose control, which I suspect I will, it will be too late. The cube will be destroyed." They sat in silence. "Do you think I am wrong for wanting to destroy it?" Mark finally asked.

"No," Jeffreys answered carefully. "With what you have told me, I think you have to. It is too dangerous."

"Way too dangerous."

"Do you think I should destroy it right now?" Mark asked.

"I am kind of biased on that point," Jeffreys said. "After all, it is the key to getting us out of China. But if the choice were between getting us out or letting the Chinese get the cube, you would have to destroy the cube."

"Agreed."

"So what is your plan?" Jeffreys asked.

"Run like hell?"

Jeffreys laughed. "I never did like that plan."

"Neither did I."

"Seriously, what is your plan?" Jeffreys asked again.

"I need to get some sleep," Mark said. "You need to stay awake. Make sure that the control holds when I am asleep. I think it will because it did with Chin, but I need to make sure. If it holds, you need to rotate with the SEALs. Make sure someone stays on watch. And make sure that they know if anything happens, anything seems out of place, they need to wake me up immediately. And make sure no one tries to steal the cube from me while I'm sleeping. That would be very, very bad.

"In the morning, and I mean much too early in the morning, the Chinese will wake us up and we will board his boat and go out fishing. We will have to play it by ear then. I can get us out. The SEALs need to tell me where they need to go and I'll have the Chinese take us there. When we rendezvous with the sub, I'll destroy the cube, throw the pieces into the ocean where no one can put them back together, assuming we even could, and we will be out of here."

"What about after that?" Jeffreys asked.

"After that is not my problem," Mark said. "I go home to Pensacola and everyone goes about their business."

"Happily ever after?" Jeffreys asked sarcastically.

"Why not?" Mark said. "Oh, Washington will grill me, no doubt. But without the cube I have no value, no power. I can't explain any of the blue-gray technology without the cube. So they will question me for a while, but then I go back to meek, mild-mannered Pensacola lawyer."

"No super powers?" Jeffrey said.

"No super powers. And quite frankly, I'm good with that. I never intended to sign up for this gig. It's a bit too exciting for my tastes. My excitement level is about whether I am going to flip the Hobie Cat or whether my horse is going to make the jump. Not this. I like to watch firefights and international espionage at the theater. Let Tom Cruise or Bruce Willis play the part, not me."

"It certainly has not been dull hanging around you," Jeffreys conceded.

"Yes. And that is about to end. I am looking forward to dull, very dull. And right now I have to go to sleep so I can handle the cube tomorrow. Are you good on what you have to do?"

"Yes. I will take care of you."

"Make sure you get some sleep, too," Mark said. "I have a feeling that I will need your help tomorrow and you will need to be rested. Or as much as we can be."

"I promise," Jeffreys said. "Once I know we are safe, I will get some sleep. Besides, I don't need nearly as much sleep as you seem to need."

Mark laughed. The old woman came over a moment later and motioned Mark to the other room. Jeffreys followed and saw that it was a bedroom. Mark curled up on a Chinese bed and quickly fell asleep.

## CHAPTER 27

"Mr. President, we have another update." The speaker was Admiral Lindquist. They were seated in the war room in the White House. Large flat screen displays were on the walls, depicting satellite photos of China. "We have a new report from the SEAL team." The President nodded for the Admiral to continue. "They are holed up in a house in a fishing village located here, on the coast," the Admiral said as he pointed to a spot on the satellite photo. "They will go out with the fishing fleet in the morning and rendezvous with our submarine."

"Are they holding hostages?" the President asked.

"No, Sir," the Admiral answered. "The SEALs report that they drove into the village and that the Chinese greeted them like long lost cousins and are feeding and caring for them and that they will take them out on the boat to go fishing in the morning."

"They are treating armed Americans as long lost cousins?" the President asked.

"Not exactly, Mr. President," the Admiral answered, obviously uncomfortable with what he was about to report. "This is according to the SEAL report," the Admiral qualified. "There is a Marine, a Sergeant Jeffreys, with the SEAL team. He is taking care of Mr. Williams. Evidently, he has some history with Mr. Williams."

"Yes," the President interrupted. "I remember a Sergeant Jeffreys."

"Yes. Well, he is interacting with Mr. Williams. Sergeant Jeffreys informed the SEAL team that they are under the protection of the cube and have been since the last firefight. He says that Mr. Williams has hypnotized the Chinese villagers and the villagers believe the SEALs are long lost relatives. That is what they see. They do not see Americans, they see Chinese cousins," the Admiral finished, clearly uncomfortable.

"He has hypnotized the entire village?" the President asked.

"Evidently, Mr. President."

"First he kills a company of soldiers with his mind and now he has hypnotized an entire village?" Another speaker asked. "Are we sure these reports are accurate?"

"This team is our best," Admiral Lindquist responded. "If they are reporting this, then that is what is happening. Although I agree, it is hard to believe."

"They report that it is the power of the cube," the Admiral continued.

"This cube appears to be more powerful than we thought," The President said. "I thought Mr. Williams explained that it was like a computer, holding all the knowledge of the blue-gray world on it."

"He did, Mr. President," the Chief of Staff said. "That's how he described the cube after the *Ronald Reagan* incident. But this is a different cube. This one he got in China. And not only does it still work, but apparently it works differently."

"What did Beth Williams say about this cube?" The President asked.

"She described it like a supercomputer, a giant library" the Director of the FBI said. " She never described any control type activities, or anything like this."

"Perhaps we need to talk to her again," another speaker suggested.

"Do that," the President said. "Find out if she knows anything about these abilities the SEALs are reporting." Turning to the Admiral, he added, "What do you think about these reported abilities?"

The Admiral paused before answering. "It is hard to comprehend, Mr. President. But I would have to agree that something is going on. That SEAL team is good. But even they reported that there is no way that they could have gotten as far as they did without some outside help. They are just too conspicuous. An American combat team in China, it's not like they could blend in. As far-fetched as it seems, I would have to conclude that their report about the cube is accurate."

"That makes the cube even more powerful and more dangerous than we ever imagined," the Secretary of Defense said.

"And even more reason why we have to get it back. We can't let something that powerful fall into the hands of the Chinese," General Abromson said.

"Mr. Williams reported that the Chinese had access to the cube before the SEAL team arrived and intended on attacking the United States. He believed they would have been successful with the power of the cube."

"The Chinese cannot successfully attack the United States," the chairman of the Joint Chiefs of Staff interjected.

"The Chinese might not before," Admiral Lindquist said. "But this is alien technology. An alien ship took out the *Ronald Reagan* with one shot. Completely crippled it. We have no idea what this technology is capable of. How can we defend ourselves against something when we don't even know what it is?"

"Then we have to get it back. At all costs, we have to get the cube back," the Secretary of State said.

"What about Mr. Williams?" The FBI Director asked.

"He is way too powerful. He is dangerous," the NSA Director said.

"He is only dangerous with the cube," General Abromson said. "I say as soon as they get out of China, the SEALs take the cube away from him."

"And if they can't?" someone asked.

"If they can't, they shoot him, and then take the cube away," the NSA Director interjected.

"Isn't that a bit drastic?"

"He is too dangerous. If he does not give the cube up voluntarily, then we take it. We can always find somebody else to access it. He said so himself."

"I agree," the President said. "What is the military situation now?"

"It is deteriorating," the Chairman of the Joint Chiefs responded. "The SEALs have stirred up a hornet's nest. The Chinese are mobilizing their land forces, conducting a systematic search of the area. They have also increased their Navy patrols. It will be very difficult to get our submarine in undetected."

"Can we move our fleet in closer?" the President asked.

"The Chinese claim a 200 mile buffer off their mainland. It is already a hotly contested area. Moving our fleet in will be considered a provocation. Particularly in light of recent developments."

"They have a history of ramming vessels that get too close. Look what they have done with the Vietnamese."

"They wouldn't dare run into our boats," the President said.

"Actually, they would. We have had some close calls in the past," the Admiral said. "And our submarines play cat and mouse with them all the time."

"We need to get the cube and Mr. Williams out of there," the President said. "Can we do it any other way?"

"The submarine is our best option. We can't get a helicopter in there. Not anymore. The Chinese would shoot it down."

"Can we just tell the Chinese there is an American hostage and were going to get him out?" the President asked.

"With the Chinese?" The Secretary of State answered. "It would take weeks of negotiation and even then I couldn't guarantee that they would say yes."

"We don't have that time. We have to get them out now."

"So the military option remains the only one available," the President said, rather than asked.

"I'm afraid so, Mr. President," the Chairman of the Joint Chiefs said.

"Then move the fleet in as close as you can," the President said. "State, you put as much pressure on the Chinese as you can politically. I want that cube and I want Mr. Williams out of there in the next twelve hours. Understood?"

A chorus of "Yes, Mr. President," was said as the meeting broke up.

## CHAPTER 28

Mark felt drugged when Jeffreys woke him up the next morning. He had a moment of disorientation before he was able to ground himself. He was still holding the cube, so he immediately knew what was going on. What took him a minute was distinguishing who he was from the number of personalities he was experiencing. That was a bit odd. He wondered if it would be possible for him to submerge himself in someone else's personality and not realize who he really was? 'Great,' he thought. 'Yet another thing to worry about.'

The old Chinese man was bustling around the house, preparing to leave. The SEALs were already up and ready, the injured ready to be transported.

There was a surprising amount of activity in this village for four in the morning. But it was a fishing community and the fishermen were all getting ready for an early start. Mark stretched his mind to encompass the other villagers. Many had already been told by the old man that his cousins would be accompanying him today. They were easy as Mark only had to make sure that they saw the cousins, rather than heavily armed American soldiers. The other villagers were more difficult as they did not have the preconceived notion. Mark had to give them the entire memory, something more difficult, particularly at a distance and with as many as there were in this village.

The SEAL team was walking behind the old man, heading for the boat, which was tied to the pier. Mark staggered as he tried to maintain control of so many people. Jeffreys supported him and soon another SEAL came over and helped Jeffreys carry Mark between them, much like they had done during the run. But this time Mark was not embarrassed. He was doing his part. He was not just a liability.

"Are you okay?" Jeffreys whispered to Mark as he faltered.

"So many people," Mark whispered back. "So many."

Jeffreys looked alarmed and shifted his grip on his captured Chinese assault rifle. "Stay alert everyone," he said into his throat mic. To Mark he said, "Can you control them?"

"So far," Mark managed to say.

Jeffreys did not ask anything else, as he did not want to distract Mark from his task. They made it to the boat without incident and climbed on board. It was a thirty-meter steel fishing trawler. Old and rusty, it sat low in the water. The foredeck was bare, with a low gunwale so the nets could be pulled over the side. The back portion of the vessel had a wheelhouse, with cramped crew's quarters beneath. The SEALs took the wounded below deck and then hid after Jeffreys told them it would ease the strain on Mark. Now Mark did not have to change their appearances to the Chinese on the neighboring boats.

The old man and his crew cast off and soon they were sailing out into the pitch black harbor, the sound of water lapping on the hull and Chinese voices from the other boats coming across the water. One of the SEALs stayed crouched in the wheelhouse, while the others all stayed below deck. That way Mark only had to keep one SEAL disguised and that was only from their crew as the SEAL was not visible to the other boats.

"Are you better now?" Jeffreys asked as they sailed out into the harbor.

"Much," Mark said. "That was overwhelming. I don't have the mental muscles for this type of activity. That run we did yesterday seems easy in comparison."

"That's not good," Jeffreys said. "No offense, but you did not do really well during that run."

"No kidding. I thought I was going to die."

"And this is harder?"

"Yes," Mark said, obviously out of breath.

"Well, not much longer," Jeffreys encouraged. "We have to clear the harbor and meet up with the sub and then we are home free."

They were silent as they listened to the waves on the hull and the putt, putt, putt, of the old vessel's engine.

"Don't tell anyone that I told you I was going to destroy the cube," Mark said, breaking the silence.

Jeffreys glanced at the SEAL sitting next to him.

"He can't hear us," Mark said. "He thinks we are talking about the weather and sea conditions."

Jeffreys looked back at the SEAL. The SEAL simply nodded and smiled. "What do you think?" Jeffreys said to the SEAL, still having trouble believing Mark had such incredible control over people with the cube.

"It will get rougher when we clear the harbor," the SEAL said. "How much will depend on the weather out there."

Jeffreys turned to Mark. "That is weird. He's not getting any of this."

"The power of the cube," Mark said. "But I'm serious. When they ask, you had no idea. You were as surprised as anyone else. And couldn't do anything to prevent it. I'll make sure you are not even near me when I do it."

"Ok," Jeffreys said. "But why?"

"Because the SEALs contacted Washington last night and told them what is going on with me and the cube. Washington, or whomever they are reporting to, I'm assuming it is Washington, really wants the cube now. They are starting to realize that the cube has more power than just a computer with the blue-gray's knowledge. They are getting an inkling of its raw power. And they want it. They have ordered the SEALs to secure the cube as soon as they are clear, even if they have to shoot me to get it."

"Shoot you!" Jeffreys said in alarm.

"Don't worry," Mark said. "Those were their orders. But they don't remember them. Now they think their orders are to protect the cube and me. But you see, it has begun, the desire to obtain the power of the cube. It is irresistible. Governments won't be able to stop themselves from trying to get it. So it has to be destroyed."

"I still can't get over the fact they authorized them to shoot you."

"As long as I have the cube, I am a threat," Mark said. "I am not under their control. Worse, I could control them. The order makes perfect sense. But they don't understand the true power of the cube. If they did, they would have ordered them to shoot me last night when I was asleep and if that didn't work, they would level the building we were in with about six cruise missiles. That's what I would have done if I were in their shoes and knew the power of the cube."

"Don't you think that is rather dramatic, overkill perhaps?"

"No. It makes perfect sense. You can't take the cube away from me in person, since I will sense it and could control you. So the only way is to do it from a distance. And the cruise missile does that and ensures the cube is destroyed so no one else gets it. Washington doesn't get it. But neither do the Chinese. Fortunately for us, neither side comprehends the power of the cube, so they still think they can get it for themselves. So we are still alive."

"You always paint such a rosy picture of things," Jeffreys said.

"I think it is realistic."

"Why can't realistic be happy? Why always so gloomy?"

"Because gloomy is more realistic," Mark said.

"There you go again. No faith in your fellow man."

"If you knew what your fellow man was thinking, you would have little faith as well."

"But we do manage," Jeffreys objected.

"We do. True," Mark said. "But only just. History is full of missteps, tragedies. And they all involve new technologies or new weapons, power. Which is why everyone is now focusing on the cube."

"So what are you going to do now?"

"Same plan," Mark said. "I will get us out to the rendezvous and then destroy the cube before we board the submarine."

"How is that going to work?"

"According to our host, we will be clear of the harbor in an hour and then should be out to his traditional fishing area by sunrise. The SEAL team leader is trying to contact command right now on the SAT phone. We can then determine where the rendezvous is compared to our intended course."

"That could be a problem," Jeffreys said.

"How so?"

"These fishing boats have nets. I don't think submarines like nets. Tends to give away their position. Might also foul their propeller."

"We will have to make sure we are at the edge of the fishing fleet," Mark said.

"How many fishing boats are there?"

"There are thirty-three coming out of this harbor," Mark said. "I don't know how many in this area. Perhaps hundreds."

"And they probably all have radios," Jeffreys said. "It's going to be dicey for that sub."

They rode in silence, Mark monitoring everyone as they sailed. The gentle rocking of the boat increased as they cleared the protection of the harbor. Now the boat rocked harder, its bow crashing down on the waves. "I hope you don't get seasick," Jeffreys said as they hit a particularly large wave.

"Not typically," Mark said. "The wave action will make the transfer to the submarine much more exciting," Mark added.

"Yea," Jeffreys agreed. "I have some concerns about the wounded. Transferring them will be difficult."

"Speaking of difficult," Mark said. "We have a problem."

"What?" Jeffreys asked, reflexively looking around and checking his weapon.

"The SEALs were just informed that the Chinese have increased their off-shore patrols. They are even harassing the Seventh Fleet."

"Do the Chinese know we are our here?" Jeffreys asked.

"Washington did not say. Maybe the Chinese are just widening their search. The last known contact with us was not far from the coast and it doesn't take a rocket scientist to figure out that we are probably headed for the coast."

"Do the Chinese know about the cube yet?"

"I don't know," Mark said. "Washington has not said and the Chinese I have contacted don't know about the cube. But then again, I am only in contact with local soldiers or fishermen. The soldiers only know that there was a firefight."

"Maybe the Chinese are assuming it is a terrorist attack," Jeffreys said.

"No. They know it is Americans," Mark said. "When you attacked, Chin called for help. He said the Americans were attacking. The Chinese have probably already figured out that the helicopter going to the American embassy was involved. And it came from the fleet. They know the Americans attacked. They probably just don't know why."

"Then the politicians can explain it," Jeffreys said. "Tell them that we were rescuing a kidnapped American."

"And killed hundreds of Chinese soldiers in the process. I'm sure that will go over real well with the Chinese government."

"So we need to get to that submarine," Jeffreys said.

"The sooner, the better," Mark said. "I can't wait for this adventure to be over."

An hour and a half later the SEALs received another call from command. "More bad news," Mark said to Jeffreys down in the hold.

"Really?"

"SEALs are getting another update. The Chinese have helicopters out pinging for the sub."

"They know it is there?" Jeffreys asked.

"They did not say. It may be that they are just getting pro-active. They certainly must know a submarine is attached to the fleet. But evidently there is a lot of saber-rattling going on."

"Leave it to the politicians to screw things up."

"I'm afraid I probably screwed this up by keeping the cube. We can't blame it all on the politicians. And we probably did not help any by fighting our way down here. I need to know what is going on. We are so isolated out here on this boat."

As Mark said that, a jet roared close overhead.

"What was that?" Jeffreys asked.

"Chinese," Mark said.

"You could tell that from down here?" Jeffreys asked.

"Yes. He was low enough that I could sense him. But just."

"That is just too weird," Jeffreys said.

"Weird for you? You should be in here." Mark said as he tapped his forehead.

"Could you read his mind?" Jeffreys asked.

"No. He was too far away. I could just tell that he was Chinese."

"So how are you going to get the big picture?"

"I thought I would have the SEALs ask Washington for me," Mark said.

"You can try. But they may not get the answer. No need to know. Military is very funny that way." Jeffreys said.

They were silent as the boat continued to rock, the bow slamming on the waves. Mark tried to flex his new mental muscles. He could sense all aboard the fishing vessel, the SEALs and the Chinese crew. He reached out further and sensed the vessel closest to them. He could pick up on all the crew's thoughts, but not quite as clearly as those on his vessel. He reached out further, sensing a second and third vessel. When they had been in the harbor, he could sense them all. But now the vessels were spreading out as they cleared the harbor mouth and headed to their fishing grounds. He tried to get an overview and found that he could locate a number of the other vessels, although not with the details that he could sense them in the harbor. He also was not sure whether he could control them from this distance, or merely sense them. Another jet flew by. This one was American.

# CHAPTER 29

Captain Peters was standing at the bridge trying to make sense of events. The original plan was for the helicopter to pick up the SEAL team and deliver them to his ship. The revised plan was to have the SEAL team leave China on a Chinese fishing vessel and rendezvous with the fleet's submarine. Several problems were arising with that plan. First, intel put the SEAL Team on a Chinese fishing vessel leaving the Bohe Harbor. However, satellite reconnaissance showed over forty fishing vessels leaving from that harbor and literally hundreds more heading out to sea. Getting the sub close enough without encountering fishing nets was going to be a problem. An additional problem was that the Chinese navy was mobilizing and were now actively searching for submarines with sonar and sub-hunting helicopters, making it almost impossible for the submarine to move in close enough for a rendezvous.

The new plan, which Captain Peters thought was fatally flawed, was for him to move his fleet closer to Chinese waters and send in a helicopter to intercept the fishing vessel. Captain Peters was concerned that the helicopter would be intercepted, but his orders from Washington were clear, he was to recover the cube, and Mr. Williams if possible, at all costs.

With serious misgivings, Captain Peters ordered his fleet to proceed closer to the Chinese territorial waters. He directed the guided-missile destroyer USS Preble on a course west of the fishing fleet as a decoy and sent a Seahawk to intercept the fishing fleet. He sent another two Seahawks to follow as backup. Hopefully, the Chinese would not take action against the frigate or the helicopters. As an additional ploy, he broadcasted that they were on a rescue mission.

His answer came five minutes later when Chinese jets fired missiles at the helicopters. Two were destroyed and the third managed to escape. Captain Peters sent four F/A-18's to protect the remaining helicopter, but he knew that action was futile. The helicopter was too easy a target from a determined attack and the Chinese seemed determined. Minutes later a dogfight erupted with the F/A-18's. One was shot down, but the other three took out the Chinese attackers. But in the process, the third helicopter was downed. That left the frigate. Captain Peters wondered if he should send other helicopters, or if that action would be futile. Communications with the Chinese were stalemated with both sides making demands, but neither side giving anything in return.

Then three silkworm missiles hit the USS Preble, sinking it almost immediately. Captain Peters was stunned at how fast this situation was escalating. Washington was enraged. The next flash transmission authorized Captain Peters to ready, but not deploy, nuclear weapons. "Were they insane?" Captain Peters thought. "Nuclear?" Captain Peters was listening to all the traffic in the CIC. Part of his attention noted an air traffic controller trying to contact an F/A−18 that had made a low fly-by the Chinese fishing fleet to contact the SEAL Team and confirm which vessel they were onboard. After radioing back confirmation, the F/A-18 went to Mach speed and was now heading directly back to the *Ronald Reagan*. Minutes later it buzzed the tower, a maneuver that was frowned on in normal times and was incredibly foolhardy under the current situation. He would have that pilot's wings for that, Captain Peters thought. But a moment later his attention was diverted by a report that a helicopter had just landed on the *Ronald Reagan* with some survivors from the SEAL Team. Evidently, one of the helicopters had made it through. He wondered why he had not been told before now?

A few minutes later Mr. Williams and one of the SEAL team members entered the CIC. Mr. Williams looked exhausted. His clothes were dirty and blood stained. Behind him, in full combat gear, complete with brown and black face paint and a Chinese machine gun, was a SEAL. They had Mr. Williams! The mission was accomplished. Why hadn't anyone told him? Now he had to disengage the fleet before any more casualties.

"Captain Peters," Mark said. "I need to talk to you."

"I'm a little busy right now," Captain Peters said as reports continued to come in about dogfights and ship positions. The situation was deteriorating to a full-fledged naval engagement.

"Not too busy for this," Mark said in a tone that surprised the Captain. "The situation is escalating."

"I know that," the Captain said irritable.

"It has to be stopped before it is too late."

"What do you think I am trying to do?" the Captain snapped as another report of a downed F/A−18 came in.

Mark walked over to the Captain, grabbed his arm.

"Captain, we can stop this."

"How?" the Captain asked.

"With this," Mark said as he held up his right hand. He opened his fingers and the Captain saw the cube sitting in Mark's palm. The Captain had seen the Memory cube and the personal cube of the blue-gray who had died on his ship last year. This cube was the same shape as the personal cube, but the coloration was very different. Last year the colors were flat, almost drab. This cube was iridescent. Colors and patterns swirled inside it, barely perceptible to the eye, but somehow clearly seen. The effect was hypnotizing. The Captain stared at the cube, before pulling his eyes off it to look at Mark.

"How?" the Captain repeated.

"I can explain what has happened to the Chinese Captain."

"He won't believe you," Captain Peters objected.

"With this he will," Mark said and somehow Captain Peters knew he was right. "But I have to be there. In person."

"On his ship?" Captain Peters asked.

"Yes, we have to be there."

"What do you mean 'we'?"

"I can explain what has happened. He will believe me. But then you have to be there to stop this madness from escalating. It has to be you. I am only a civilian. You have the authority to stop this."

"I don't have that authority. My orders are coming straight from Washington. From the President."

"Captain," Mark said. "You are the highest ranking person here. Look around. You are witnessing the beginning of a nuclear war between China and the U.S., a war that will destroy both of our countries and poison the Earth with radioactive fallout. You have to stop this."

"You and the cube are here," the Captain said. "I can turn our ships around and leave. I have met my orders. We can disengage."

"And you think the Chinese will let you go, now that the fighting has started?"

"We will notify them that we are disengaging," the Captain insisted.

"And you will turn and leave at what, twenty, thirty knots?" Mark asked. "How many silkworm missiles do you think the Chinese have? How long will the *Ronald Reagan* be in range? Do you think the Chinese can let you go? They have to save face. They can't back down."

"They would not dare hit the *Ronald Reagan*," the Captain said, but with some doubt in his voice.

"Wouldn't they? They have already sunk one of your ships and how many planes? You think they will just give up? We killed over a hundred Chinese soldiers escaping from the mainland," Mark said. "We have started a war. I have started a war," Mark added wearily. "And you have the ability to stop it."

"It's not as bad as you say," the Captain protested.

"No? What do you think the President will do if they sink the *Ronald Reagan*? Do you think he will just sit back and talk about it? Do you think the Joint Chiefs will stand for that? And with the *Ronald Reagan* gone, what are his options? Missiles. Nuclear missiles. And China will retaliate. The problem with our society today is that we have the ability to destroy ourselves in a matter of minutes now. That is not enough time to let people cool down and reflect. And that is what you are watching now, the start of the end of the world."

Mark's comments were interrupted by a report of multiple launches of silkworm missiles. The target was USS Chancellorsville, which was the next closest vessel to the mainland. The Captain watched the displays as the missiles approached. Three were intercepted, but two struck. They were not nuclear tipped, but the damage was tremendous. The Chancellorsville was dead in the water.

"You have to stop this now," Mark said.

"How?"

"Call the Chinese Captain. Tell him that you want to end this. That you will meet with him on his ship. We will fly over in a helicopter. No threat. And discuss how to stop this."

"That's impossible," the Captain said. "I can't do that without authorization and I can't leave my post. We are at war here."

"We are at war, and you are the only one who can stop it. We don't have time to engage Washington with this. You have to do it. If you don't, this ship is dead. You are dead. And then the rest of the world is dead when Washington avenges your loss."

"The Chinese will never agree to it," the Captain said.

"Yes, they will," Mark said and he held up the cube again. The Captain caught his gaze being drawn into the swirling patterns of the cube and once again had to consciously pull his eyes away from it.

"Ok, I will call them."

Surprisingly, the Chinese agreed and within five minutes the Captain, Mark and the soldier, who the Captain finally realized was Sgt. Jeffreys, were flying towards the Chinese carrier in a Seahawk helicopter.

The Captain did not recall much of the helicopter ride to the Chinese command ship. It should have taken at least twenty minutes, but it seemed to take no time at all. The next thing he knew, the helicopter was touching down on the deck of the Chinese command ship, while soldiers aimed machine guns at them.

The crew chief was looking nervously out the window at the armed soldiers watching their landing.

"It's okay, Chief," Mark said. "Just open the door and let us out."

The crew Chief complied, sliding the side door open and assisting Mark out of the helicopter. The Captain and Sgt. Jeffreys, who was still in full combat gear, followed him.

"Better leave your assault rifle on the chopper," the Captain said to Sgt. Jeffreys as they stepped out. "Our hosts seem a bit nervous and you do appear rather lethal."

Sgt. Jeffreys' weapon was hanging on his chest. Making a point of keeping his hands away from the trigger, he lifted the weapon over his head and handed it to the crew chief. "Take good care of that," Sgt. Jeffreys said. "We may need it." He then followed Mark and the Captain across the deck towards the tower. The Captain did not think that Jeffreys looked any less lethal without the assault rifle, but it would have to do, particularly as Mark had insisted that he accompany them.

They were escorted inside to a conference room where they were told to wait.

"We don't have time for these games," the Captain said.

Mark appeared very tired, but surprisingly calm considering their surroundings. He seemed confident, in control. Maybe that was the cube's impact on him, the Captain thought. The entrance of the Chinese Captain interrupted these thoughts.

Mark bowed deeply to the Chinese officer. "Captain Zheng Mark said, and then proceeded to speak to the officer in Chinese. It was obviously an introduction as the officer then turned to Captain Peters and bowed slightly. Captain Peters returned the bow. He did not know that Mark could speak Chinese. Mark then continued in English. "Captain Zheng, if you will allow me, I will continue in English as Captain Peters does not speak Chinese and I know that you have a good command of the language."

'How does he know so much about this officer?' Captain Peters asked himself.

"I believe that I owe you and Captain Peters an explanation and an apology," Mark continued. "When I have finished, it is my hope that the two of you can stop this tragedy from continuing and prevent our countries from destroying each other in a nuclear war. First, my apology, it is my fault that we are here, that our countries are at the verge of war. And because of my actions, you two are the only ones who can save us."

Mark paused for a moment, obviously overcome with emotion. "Let me explain to both of you how we got to this point. Captain Peters knows some of this, but not all. You probably do not know, but this is what you are fighting over." Mark raised his hand, palm up, and presented the cube. It was as beautiful as before, with colors mysteriously swirling in its depths. Mark let everyone stare at it for a minute before he continued.

"This is not from Earth. This is an alien artifact, which I call a cube. It belonged to an alien that was killed three months ago when the nuclear bomb detonated in your country. Yes," Mark continued. "That was not a terrorist attack, the Earth actually got caught up in a battle between two alien species. One species - I call them the blue-grays - detonated that bomb in an attempt to kill the others. They both died, but in the process, I obtained this cube. I can tell you the details later, when we have more time. Only a few people in my country and yours know the true story. Both our governments hushed up the rest.

"By the way, Captain Peters is one of the few people, other than myself and Sergeant Jeffreys here, who has actually seen these aliens first hand. That occurred last year on the *Ronald Reagan* when they first arrived. I am sure that you were informed about the mysterious explosion on the *Ronald Reagan* last year. The aliens caused that.

"Here is the part neither of you know. In an attempt to obtain a nuclear weapon to use against their enemies, the blue-grays controlled a number of your officers. I will call it hypnotism, although that word does not adequately describe the control they obtained. But that is the best word I can use in English." Mark summarized the recent events for both Captains.

"As you can only imagine, this cube is very powerful. The knowledge it contains is so far advanced, it is like giving a cave man a nuclear weapon. Mankind is not ready for this big a technological leap.

"Somehow, and I don't know how, our President discovered where I was and that the Chinese had the cube. I kept the cube after the explosion, but I never told anyone that I had it. I kept it for myself. I wanted to explore it, but I knew how powerful it was and was afraid that if any government, including my own, obtained it, disaster would follow. That was my mistake. I should have destroyed it. But I couldn't. And that is my failure. That has led us to the brink of war.

"But I am straying. The President sent a team, including Sergeant Jeffreys here to rescue me, actually, to get the cube and perhaps me in the process. They succeeded in freeing me from my captors, but in the process of trying to flee China, the fighting began and is now escalating beyond anyone's control because the U.S. President is starting to understand some of the potential of the cube and I am sure he will do everything in his power to get it back. I don't think the Chinese understand exactly what is going on, what is at stake. Probably all they know right now, like you Captain Zheng, is that for some reason the United States is attacking their sovereign country and killing their soldiers and they have to defend their land." Mark paused.

Captain Peters tried to make sense of what he had heard. Why had he allowed Mark to talk him into coming here? And with the cube? Now the cube was back in Chinese control. How could he have been so stupid?

"So now you both know what is going on. Why we are here," Mark continued. "It is all over this." Mark held up the cube again.

The Captain could not believe what Mark was doing. He was telling the Chinese about the power of the cube and was basically giving it to them. The Captain looked at Sergeant Jeffreys, who appeared to be as stunned by the story as the Captain. The Captain noticed that Jeffreys had a nine-millimeter in a shoulder holster. But three Chinese guards had accompanied them and they were standing at the door with Chinese assault rifles. Then the Captain noticed a grenade in Sergeant Jeffreys' web gear. Maybe, if he could…

Mark recommenced his narration. "You probably are trying to figure out what to do with the cube," Mark said. "You don't have to worry about the cube. That part will be solved shortly." The Captain looked back to Mark. "As we speak," Mark continued, "a blue-gray ship is heading this way. They had not intended to leave the cube here. So that problem will be solved. Neither the U.S., nor China will be able to keep the cube. Captain Peters will tell you that there is no use fighting against these aliens. They are too advanced. A single alien scout ship took out the *Ronald Reagan* with one shot. So the reason for all this fighting is now, or soon will be, over. And I have to go with it. I have been in contact with the cube too long. It has infected me, for lack of a better description.

"And that is why I asked for the two of you to meet. You have to fix what I have started. You have to end the war before it is beyond stopping." Mark tilted his head as if he were listening to something no one else could hear. "You have about five minutes to end this war, or the Earth is lost."

"How?" Captain Peters asked, when it became apparent that Mark was finished.

"Talk," Mark said. "Mediate your differences."

"I don't have the authority to bind the United States," Captain Peters objected. "I have to call the President."

"I don't have the authority," Captain Zheng objected at the same time.

"You both have authority over the forces here," Mark said wearily. "And you do not have time to call anyone else. Even as we speak, irreversible actions are being taken. Lives are being lost. You have to stop this now before your leaders start launching nuclear missiles in retaliation. At that point it will be too late." Mark tilted his head again, listening. "You have four minutes. Talk."

Captain Peters did not know what to say. In the background he could hear frantic commands, and although they were in Chinese, he could tell that the battle was raging. He wondered what was going on in his ship, how many lives had been lost while he was here. "You have to call off your planes," Captain Peters said. "You sunk the Preble."

"You have invaded our land and killed our soldiers. Even now you are in our waters and threatening us with your ships and planes," Captain Zheng responded.

"We were on a rescue mission," Captain Peters said. "We have the right to protect our…"

"Stop it," Mark interrupted. "Stop it right now! You are wasting time. What is done is done. You are talking about history. You have to talk about the future." No one spoke. "Captain Peters, do you want to start a nuclear war?"

Captain Peters was shocked by the tone of Mark's voice.

"Well, do you?"

"No."

"Captain Zheng, do you want to start a nuclear war?"

"No, but we are defending…"

"Stop," Mark said with surprising force. "Yes or no. Do you want to start a nuclear war?"

"No."

"Do either of you think that your country would survive a nuclear war?"

Captain Peters hesitated, and then replied, "No."

"No," Captain Zheng said.

Mark tilted his head again. 'What was he listening to?' Captain Peters wondered.

"You have two minutes to make your decisions," Mark said. "No decision means war. I mean this quite seriously when I say the fate of the world rests on what the two of you decide right now. Decide wrong, or don't decide, and the U.S. and China destroy each other in a nuclear war and the rest of the world will slowly die from the fallout. The choice is yours gentlemen," Mark ended and sort of slumped as if all the energy was seeping out of him.

The Captains stared at each other for a moment. Then both spoke at once.

"I will pull back my ships and planes, order them to disengage," Captain Peters said.

"I will call off my fighters," Captain Zheng said.

"I have wounded sailors from the sinking ships," Captain Peters said. "I would like to send Search and Rescue helicopters to save them."

"I will assist you," Captain Zheng said. "But first we must order our fleets to disengage."

"Agreed."

"I will probably be shot when this is over," Captain Zheng said.

"You will be a hero," Captain Peters said. "But we will never command again."

"And now I have to go," Mark interrupted. "They are coming for me." Mark bowed deep to the Chinese Captain. "You are a brave man. And I will do what ever

I can to convince your leaders that you are indeed a hero."

Mark turned and shook Captain Peter's hand. "It was a pleasure working with you Captain," Mark said.

"And you," the Captain replied.

Mark stepped over to Sergeant Jeffreys. They stood and stared at each other for a moment and then Mark gave Jeffreys a big bear hug, which Jeffreys returned. When they pulled apart, Mark said, "I owe you my life Jeffreys. I will never forget that."

Jeffreys merely nodded.

Mark continued. "I need you to deliver a message to my family."

"Certainly," Jeffreys said.

Mark cocked his head again. "So much to say and so little time." Turning back to Jeffreys, Mark said, "Tell my daughter that I love her."

"I suspect she knows that, Mark."

"She probably does, but it bears repeating. You take family for granted, that they will always be there and that they know you love them. You forget to say it. Instead, you start dwelling on the things that drive you crazy, the quirks. Like leaving two wet towels on the rack after they shower or putting the toilet paper roll on backwards. You nag on the little things that drive you nuts. So what? It doesn't matter. You forget to tell them that you are so proud of them you could just pop. You tell them to tuck in their shirt, rather than telling them they are beautiful. Tell her that," Mark said.

"And tell my son," Mark cocked his head to the side again. "I have to go. Tell my son the same thing. But tell him he is handsome, not beautiful. Beautiful won't cut it at his age."

Sgt. Jeffreys chuckled. "Probably not."

"And Beth," Mark said. 'What could he tell Beth?' Mark wondered. He was running out of time. "Tell her I am going to the mothership," Mark said urgently. "Make sure to give her that message."

"I will," Sgt. Jeffreys said.

"But now I have to tell you one more thing." Mark leaned close and whispered to Sgt. Jeffreys.

"I need you to do one more thing. I need you to make sure this truce does not unravel when I leave."

"They have agreed to it," Sgt. Jeffreys said. "I don't know what you need me to do?"

"There is not much time left to explain," Mark said. "You have the best understanding of the cube. You have seen its power. You will all have a great shock when I leave. You have to keep them focused. Promise me," Mark said almost frantically.

"What do you want me to do?" Jeffreys asked.

"When I leave, the Captain has to do three things immediately. He has to turn the fleet away, he has to call the Chinese Captain and he has to rescue you and the other soldiers."

"But I am here," Jeffreys objected. "I don't need rescuing."

"Promise me," Mark said. "Those three things, immediately."

"I promise," Jeffreys said.

Mark gave Jeffreys another hug, before stepping back and snapping Jeffreys a perfect salute.

Reflexively, Jeffreys snapped to attention and returned the salute.

Before Sgt. Jeffreys could drop his arm from his salute, everything changed. He looked around. He was standing on the bridge of the *Ronald Reagan*. The Captain was standing five feet from him, looking completely bewildered as he glanced around. Spotting Sgt. Jeffreys, the Captain asked, "Sergeant, did that just happen?"

Jeffreys lowered his hand to his side. "Yes, Sir, I think it did." Jeffreys looked around. No one was paying any attention to him except the Captain. How had he gotten here? He should be on the Chinese ship. Or he should be on the Chinese fishing boat. How had he gotten off that? He wondered.

"What did Mr. Williams say to you?" the Captain interrupted Jeffreys' contemplation.

Jeffreys stared at the Captain. "Sir?"

"When he was leaving, Mr. Williams whispered something to you. What did he say?"

Jeffreys stared at the Captain. Wasn't he curious about what just happened? Surely he was aware of the impossibility of this moment. Indeed, the Captain looked very confused. Then Mark's words came flooding back to Jeffreys. Mark was relying on him. He had warned him they would be confused. Jeffreys did not know what was happening, but he would carry out Mark's last request.

"Sir," Jeffreys said. "Mr. Williams said we were about to have a huge shock."

"That's an understatement," the Captain said. "How did we get here?"

"Sir," Jeffreys interrupted. "Mr. Williams said it was imperative that you do three things as soon as he left."

"What three things?"

"You had to turn your ships away from China. You had to call the Chinese Captain. And you had to come and rescue me and the SEAL Team."

"But you are here," the Captain said. "Why do I have to rescue you?"

"I don't know," Jeffreys said. "I asked Mr. Williams the same thing, but he left before he answered. But he was absolutely adamant that I made sure that you did that. He said that of everyone, I knew the cube the best. I had to do it."

"What did he mean by that?"

"I don't know, Sir." Sergeant Jeffreys paused. "Unless it was a vision, Sir."

"A vision?" the Captain repeated. "Ensign."

"Sir?"

"Have I been off this bridge?"

The Ensign looked confused. "Not since we went to General Quarters, Sir," the Ensign responded.

The Captain looked at the computer. "Sergeant Jeffreys, look at the time. No time has elapsed since my last orders. We were gone a good hour, yet no time has elapsed."

"Then it was a vision," Jeffreys said.

"So it didn't happen? We are still about to start a war?"

"Sir, Mr. Williams was adamant about those three things. You have to turn your ships around and call the Chinese Captain."

The Captain stared at Jeffreys. "They will have my head if I am wrong," he said, really to himself. "Helm," he said louder. "New course, bearing one-seven-five."

"New course, Sir, bearing one-seven-five," helm replied.

"Comm," the Captain continued. "Get me a direct channel to Captain Zheng."

"Aye, aye, Sir," Comm replied.

"Let's hope Mr. Williams is right," the Captain said to Sgt. Jeffreys. The Captain glanced around. Sgt. Jeffreys had disappeared.

"Captain Zheng on the radio," Comm said.

"Captain Zheng, this is Captain Peters on the *USS Ronald Reagan*."

"Where did you go?" Captain Zheng asked. "One minute you were here, then you disappeared."

"You saw that too," Captain Peters asked, relieved that he was not the only one.

"Yes. You were here along with a civilian and a Sergeant. Now you are all gone and your helicopter is gone. And my crew says you were never here."

"But I was there. We talked. We had an understanding, an agreement," Captain Peters said.

"Yes," Captain Zheng agreed. "But what happened?"

"It must be the power of the cube," Captain Peters said. "My crew says I never left." There was a pause, then Captain Peters continued. "I won't pretend to understand what happened. But I will honor the agreement that we made. I have already ordered my ships to turn away. I will call in my aircraft. Do we still have an agreement?"

There was a long pause and Captain Peters held his breath.

"We have an agreement," Captain Zheng replied.

"Thank you."

"Our countries do not need to engage in a war," Captain Zheng said.

"I agree. May I have your permission to send search and rescue helicopters to pick up my men in your waters?" Captain Peters added.

"Yes. And I will send helicopters to assist. I will pull back my other ships."

"Thank you Captain Zheng."

"I think we have stepped back from an accidental nuclear war," Captain Zheng said.

"So do I," Captain Peters agreed.

## CHAPTER 30

Jeffreys blinked. He was laying on his back, staring at the blue sky, the sound of waves filling his ears. He sat up and looked around. He was back on the Chinese fishing boat. He got up and walked around the boat. Everyone was unconscious. As he moved around the boat, everyone started to wake up, but no one had a memory of being unconscious. That's when he realized that Mark was missing. No one had seen anything. He turned to the SEAL team leader and together they searched the vessel from stem to stern, but found nothing. Mark was nowhere to be found.

Before long two U.S. Navy Search and Rescue Seahawks showed up on the horizon. They hovered over the boat and slowly brought up the soldiers one at a time, the most injured ones first. As Jeffreys help move the third injured SEAL to the foredeck of the Chinese fishing boat, the soldier moaned and opened his eyes. He looked around and then focused on Jeffreys.

"Hang in there, buddy," Jeffreys said. "We're almost out of here." He had to yell to be heard over the chopper.

The SEAL forced a smile that looked more like a grimace. "Did everyone make it?"

Jeffreys paused before he answered. "Yes, everyone made it."

The SEAL smiled, this time it looked genuine. "The civilian? He made it too?"

Jeffreys looked puzzled. "Why do you ask?"

"It must be the morphine," the SEAL answered. "I had the strangest hallucination."

Jeffreys could barely hear the soldier over the noise of the helicopter.

"What hallucination?"

"He's next," another SEAL yelled as he moved over with a basket for the helicopter.

"Wait a minute," Jeffreys yelled back. Turning back to the wounded SEAL he asked, "What hallucination?"

"I was lying on the floor below decks, looking up the hatchway. I saw him step out over the rail."

"You saw him go overboard?" Jeffreys asked, panic rising in his chest.

"We have to load him now," the third SEAL said.

"Wait a minute," Jeffreys said, pushing the SEAL away.

"What did you see?" Jeffreys asked.

"He stepped off the rail," the injured SEAL said. "I thought he had died. I thought we were all dead. He stepped into an open door."

"A door? What door?" Jeffreys shouted.

"A door hovering over the back rail. It was just there. He stepped in and it disappeared."

"Did you see anything else?"

"Just the angel helping him."

"What Angel?"

"It was an hallucination," the SEAL said. "Angels don't have blue hands."

The third SEAL pushed Jeffreys aside. "We don't have time for this. We have to load now." With that he and another SEAL loaded the injured soldier into the lift basket in the helicopter pulled him up, leaving Jeffreys standing on the deck puzzled.

There were still three SEALs left when the second helicopter was full. As it left, a third helicopter arrived. It was a Chinese Search and Rescue. Sgt. Jeffreys and the last two SEALs were hoisted into the helicopter and flown to the *Ronald Reagan*. When the Chinese helicopter landed on the carrier, Sgt. Jeffreys noticed that one of the soldiers was lying on a stretcher, covered by a blanket, his face covered in bandages.

Odd, Jeffreys thought, he could have sworn they loaded all the wounded on the first helicopter. Maybe this one was a casualty off one of the stricken ships, he thought. Jeffreys helped one of the SEALs and the Chinese flight crewman pull the stretcher out of the helicopter and lay it on the flight deck. Sailors from the *Ronald Reagan* ran up and carried the stretcher off. Sgt. Jeffreys turned and saluted the Chinese flight officer, who saluted him back. Jeffreys stepped back and watched the helicopter lift off.

Jeffreys looked around at the flight deck of the carrier. It was organized pandemonium, helicopters coming and going, depositing a seemingly endless stream of wounded and wandering sailors. No one paid any attention to Jeffreys. Unsure of what to do, Jeffreys finally decided to seek out Captain Peters. He crossed the flight deck to the tower and climbed the stairs to CIC. Anywhere else he would've been a strange sight, decked out in full combat gear, black and brown stripes on his face, carrying a Chinese assault rifle. But under the circumstances, no one paid him any attention. Not until he walked into CIC. Captain Peters spotted him almost immediately.

"Sgt. Jeffreys," Captain Peters called across the room. "Is that you? Is that really you?"

"Yes, Sir," Jeffreys responded.

The Captain walked over to Jeffreys so they could talk privately. "Were you here before? On this bridge?" Captain Peters asked hesitantly.

"Yes, Sir," Jeffreys answered. "Or, I thought I was here. But, I don't think I really was. I think it was a vision."

"And the meeting with the Chinese captain, were you there also? Do you remember that?"

"Yes. I was there for that also."

"Do you think this is a vision also?" the Captain asked. "Or is this real?"

"I think this is real," Jeffreys said. "I think Mark, Mr. Williams, is gone."

"What happened?"

"After I was here with you on the bridge," Jeffreys said. "I woke up back on the Chinese fishing boat. Everyone was unconscious. Mr. Williams was missing. We searched the boat. We searched everywhere. We couldn't find him. As we were loading into the helicopters, one of the wounded SEALs told me that he saw Mr. Williams step over the rail of the boat into an open door and disappear. The SEAL thought he was hallucinating because of the morphine. I think he saw Mr. Williams step into a blue-gray ship. The same ship we saw in China. The same ship that brought me here last time. I think the blue-grays took him, just like he said they were going to. But that they took him from the fishing vessel, which is where he was."

"How did we have that vision if Mr. Williams was on the fishing vessel?" the Captain asked.

"The cube," Jeffreys said. "It is incredibly powerful, much more than the memory cube. It is more than simply a computer. It gave him powers. Mind powers. He could read your mind. He could control you. Give you visions."

"How did he get it?"

"He smuggled it out of China last time," Jeffreys said.

"Why didn't he tell us? What was he going to do with it?"

"He was afraid the power of the cube would be abused. So he was trying to explore it to see if it was safe to share some of its knowledge. But then the Chinese came and kidnapped him and stole the cube.

"You know the rest of the story. A Chinese officer who had been under the control cube accessed the cube and intended to attack the U.S. with it. When the SEAL team attacked, we killed him, but not before I found out firsthand what it was like to have the control cube used against you. Mr. Williams got us out of China, but in the process he had to go deep into the cube. Those were his words.

"I don't think he ever fully recovered from that. He tried to describe it to me, but said that we did not have the words to describe what was going on in his mind. He was convinced more than ever that the cube had to be destroyed or it would destroy mankind. It was too powerful and mankind was not ready for the psychic power that it contained. And from what you and I experienced here, I would have to agree," Jeffreys said.

# CHAPTER 31

Mark lay on the metal floor, listening to the sound of the helicopters engines as they flew towards the aircraft carrier. Sgt. Jeffreys sat morosely nearby, staring out the open door at the endless sea. In the distance Mark could make out smoke rising over the horizon, but did not know its source. Mark did not have much time. He was exhausted and did not know how much longer he could control those around him. Even controlling the eight people in the helicopter was taxing his reserves. The Chinese were easy, as they just considered him another American. The hard part was keeping Jeffreys from recognizing him. He hated to delude Jeffreys, but he had no choice. In Jeffrey's mind Mark was just another wounded sailor.

But all that would change when they landed on the *Ronald Reagan*. There were 5,000 people on that ship and Mark would not be able to control all of them. More importantly, there were cameras and they would show Mark to whomever watched them. Mark looked at the cube clutched in his hand. He had sworn he would destroy it and now would be the perfect time. And perhaps the last time that he could before he was overwhelmed. But did he dare? He had used the energy of all the people on the fishing vessel in order to do that last vision. But even then, he had barely managed to complete it and did not know if he had been successful. He assumed it must have been successful or this Chinese helicopter would not be flying them to the *Ronald Reagan*. But what if the truce fell apart? Without the cube he would not be able to fix it.

Mark stared at the ocean beneath the helicopter. He was sorely tempted to just toss the cube out the open door. But he could not. It was his fault that the war had started. He had to ensure it was over. He had to fix it. But he had to disappear. That is why he created the vision of him going with the blue-grays. He could not control everyone around him. Sooner or later someone else would steal the cube and he knew what would happen then. So he had to blend into the crowd, to disappear. Until he knew that he had fixed what he had started. And then he had to disappear for good.

But what to do about the cameras? What about all the people on the *Ronald Reagan*? He would be overwhelmed. He felt around in the minds of the people in the helicopter. The Chinese were carrying weary and wounded soldiers to the Americans. Wounded. That was the key, Mark thought. He planted that in their mind. The Chinese medic pulled out a stretcher and spread it across the floor. Mark stripped off his clothes and threw them out the open door. He could not be found wearing Chinese clothing. He lay naked on the stretcher. The medic covered him with a blanket and then wrapped his head and face with gauze, a burn victim.

When they landed on the *Ronald Reagan*, sailors ran up and carried Mark away on the stretcher, heading for sickbay. Mark reached out with his mind and found Captain Peters to ensure that the truce was holding. He let his mind quickly search the surroundings, careful not to be overwhelmed by the number of people on board. There was a triage area set up on the first landing that handled the sailors rescued from the other ships. He was placed among them and registered as a John Doe. A quick nudge in a medic's mind and he was quickly forgotten. He would ride a medevac flight back to the United States to avoid customs and then work his way back home to the blue-gray pod. He would have to avoid Beth, as she would be watched. That would be the hardest part. The disappearing act had begun.

## CHAPTER 32

Nyoko Konishi was replacing the access panel, making sure that none of the screws floated away in zero gravity. 38 years old, Nyoko was Japan's sixth astronaut to visit the International Space Station and this was her first spacewalk. She had been tasked to go out and replace a module in the cooling system that had been giving bad readings lately.

"Almost done," Nyoko said as she inserted the last screw. Fortunately, they were oversized, or they would be impossible to handle with her gloves on. And space was certainly not the place where she could take her gloves off. She tightened the last screw and then double-checked all the others. "Done," she announced.

"Stand-by while we check the circuit," Dan, the mission commander, said.

Now that the work was done, Nyoko could take a minute to enjoy the view. Although she was tethered to the space station, Nyoko still did not let go of the handhold. The thought of drifting off the station was not a pleasant one. She pivoted her body so she could gaze at the Earth. The blue and white disk hung in a black sky. As many times as she saw it, she would never get over its beauty. If she never came back to space, she would cherish this sight forever.

"Nyoko, you can stop sight-seeing now," Dan's voice crackled in Nyoko's helmet. "Circuit check is green, you can come in now. Good job."

Nyoko stared at the Earth a moment longer, taking every detail into his memory. "Look at that view," Nyoko said.

"It's just the Earth. No big deal," Dan said.

Nyoko chuckled at Dan's standard line. This was Dan's third trip to the ISS and he always made light of the view. But Nyoko knew that Dan was still awestruck, spending as much time looking out the windows in the cupola as everyone else. Nyoko pivoted back and slowly made her way back to the Quest airlock, being careful to keep her tether free of obstructions while maintaining good handholds. The suit was bulky and you had to concentrate. Space was not a forgiving environment.

"I'm at the airlock," Nyoko announced. "Securing the tether." Nyoko anchored herself to the hold next to the airlock and started reeling in the tether. It caught and she looked up to see what it was tangled on. From her position the Earth was behind her and she was looking across the space station's Quest airlock module, with the blackness of space and the multitude of stars in the background. "Hold on, tether has caught on something. I'm going to… AAHHH!"

"Nyoko, what is going on?" Dan said into the microphone, trying to keep his voice from betraying that Nyoko's scream had scared him to death. No response. "Nyoko, report!"

Dan looked at the monitor. The camera showed Nyoko standing still, staring into space. Nyoko's suit camera was aimed at the airlock. Nothing seemed wrong there.

"Nyoko, report. Do you copy?"

Dan looked at the external camera monitor. Nothing had changed. He glanced at Nyoko's suit monitors, pulse was elevated and respirations were short and fast. Careful to keep his voice calm, Dan repeated, "Nyoko, I need you to report. Tell me what is going on. Nyoko, do you copy?"

"Do you see it?" Nyoko's voice came back almost in a whisper.

"See what?" Dan asked.

"That," Nyoko whispered back and Dan saw her raise her arm and point.

"Nyoko, I can't see it. Point your suit camera at it." Turning to a nearby crewman, Dan said, "See if you can see what she is pointing at."

The crewman floated over to a bulkhead window above Dan and craned his neck so he could see in the direction Nyoko was pointing. "Oh my God…"

Samuel Johnson was monitoring the space walk from mission control in Houston. He was chomping at the bit to know what was going on, but had wisely stayed out of it, not wanting to distract the mission commander from whatever emergency had just arisen. He was monitoring Nyoko's vitals, which although elevated, were within safe limits. He wondered what had scared Nyoko. The scream had shocked them all. Now everyone at mission control was either staring at their consoles or at the screens at the front of the room, which showed split screen views of Nyoko standing, pointing, Nyoko's suit view of the hatch, and the inside of the ISS where Dan was talking on the microphone and another crewman was floating by a window. Samuel watched Dan ask the crewman, it was the Russian Serge, for a report several times. When none came, Dan floated up to the window and, pushing Serge out of the way, looked out and stared.

Finally, when Dan did not move, Samuel could wait no longer.

"ISS, this is Houston, report," Samuel said. "ISS, this is Houston, report."

Dan did not move, he just stared out the window. Serge floated out of camera view and Nyoko remained where she stood.

"Dan, this is Houston, report," Samuel repeated. "Dan, talk to me. What is going on?" Samuel said.

Slowly Dan disengaged from the window and floated back down to his station. With strain clear in his voice he said, "Nyoko, you need to come into the station. Now, Nyoko. Come inside, now." Getting control of his voice, he yelled to the astronauts inside the station, "Ok, people. Let's focus. Let's get Nyoko inside now!"

"Dan, what is going on?" Samuel repeated.

"We have company," Dan said.

Outside the ISS, Nyoko stared up into space. But instead of stars, a huge spaceship hovered not a hundred meters above her. It was sleek and smooth and gleamed a white and blue. The main body of the ship was circular, an alabaster white with purple designs pulsing across it. Two huge wing-like structures jutted out from the sides and pulsed an iridescent purple that was difficult to look at.

"Nyoko, you need to come inside, now," Nyoko heard Dan's voice in her headphones.

Tearing her eyes off the alien ship, Nyoko slowly pulled in her tether.

If NASA had any intent to hide the alien ship from the rest of the world, they never had the opportunity. An amateur astronomer, Ted Vickery, was in his back yard playing with his new camera adapter. He had an Orion SkyView Pro 180mm Maksutov-Cassegrain telescope and had just purchased a new camera adapter for it. As there was no moon tonight, he thought he would check it out by photographing the ISS as it passed by. It would be a tricky shot due to the speed that the ISS would cross the heavens, but he thought that with this new equipment, he would be able to do it. On schedule, the ISS started to cross his horizon. On his visual range finder, he thought he saw a double image. But he ignored it and managed to get several images taken during the three minutes that the space station was visible.

After the pass he stared in disbelief at his camera's display. He then went inside and downloaded the images into his laptop and again stared at the screen in disbelief.

Fifteen minutes later the images were all over the Internet. Forty-five minutes later, after several other amateur enthusiasts confirmed the findings, they went viral. By morning the whole world woke up to discover that mankind was not alone, news that quickly trumped the skirmish between the Chinese and the U.S. six days before.

# EPILOGUE

It was evening in Paris. The sky was dark and the city lights had taken over, casting their magical light over the Parisian landscape. Parisians filled the sidewalk cafes during these warm summer nights. Beth walked slowly up the Boulevard Saint-Germain to a sidewalk café. She chose an empty seat at a table set for two and stared out at the passing traffic. She and Mark had eaten here several times during one of their trips to Paris. Now the empty chair across from her mocked her. The waiter spotted her and brought her a menu, before turning to attend to another customer. Beth let the menu sit on the table as she continued to stare absently at the traffic.

Beth had stayed in Pensacola for six months after Mark had disappeared. But staying there was unbearable without him, so she finally gave notice at her job and sold their small farm and moved. She moved to Paris. She had always loved Paris and now, more than anything, she needed it. She had found a quaint little apartment on the fourth floor of an adorable building in the Latin district. The view of the street below was so typical French, she wondered why no one had painted it. Now, having lived here now for almost three months, her French was passable and improving every day. She had planned on taking a year off to adjust, after which she would decide upon getting a job or deciding how to occupy her time.

She sighed and glanced around, wondering where the watcher would be. She knew that someone was watching her. Sometimes she spotted them on the street, or in a car. Other times she just assumed they were there. They had questioned her rather intensely after Mark disappeared last year and had watched her before she left Pensacola. They had been easy to spot then as she knew the area and they stood out. She had made no secret about leaving for Paris and knew they would follow, until they finally got bored. Mark had been right, there was no way he could stay after they learned he could access the cube. It was too dangerous for all of them. The government, any government, would stop at nothing to gain that technology.

So here she sat, alone, at a sidewalk cafe in Paris.

"Bonjour, Madame. Est-ce que vous voulez de l'eau?" the waiter asked when he returned.

Beth had been too preoccupied to consider the menu. "Pourez-vous me server un verde de vin blanc, s'il vous plait," she said as she picked up the menu.

The waiter hurried off as Beth smiled. She loved France. Only here would it be perfectly reasonable to dabble over your menu while drinking a glass of wine. As she glanced around, she noticed a man staring at her from a far table. As she caught his eye, he looked away, but the move was clumsy. She glanced his way casually again and noted that he seemed out of place, sitting alone at his table, his cell phone held so it was pointed towards her. Photographing her? She was getting good at this game, trying to spot the watchers. This one was a bit too young and inexperienced. She got irritated and considered approaching him and telling him to leave her alone. But making a scene would not do any good. She would just ignore him.

The waiter came back and placed a glass of champagne at her place. She looked at it confused and it took her a minute to frame her objection in French, that she had white wine, not champagne. "Ca, ce n'est pas exact..."

"D'accord," the waiter agreed. "L'homme fous a donne le champagne," the waiter explained.

"Who?" Beth asked, and the waiter nodded towards the far table where she had spotted the watcher. She glanced in that direction as she muttered, "Merci." The watcher was no longer watching her. Instead he was talking to a man standing next to his table with his back towards Beth. As she watched, the watcher picked up his things, left some euro's on the table, got up and left, while the other man turned and walked towards Beth. As he sat down at Beth's table the waiter returned placing an ice bucket with a bottle of champagne in a stand next to the table before deftly moving on to wait on other customers.

Beth's eyes teared up as she reached across the table. "I have missed you so much," she said.

Mark smiled back at her as they held hands across the table. "I told you I would come back."

"But, is it safe?" Beth asked. "Wasn't that one of the NSA agents you were talking to?"

"Yes, it was."

"But," Beth started.

"It's alright. He has a picture of you eating alone and is going back to report that to his superiors."

"But he talked to you," Beth objected.

"He talked to a Frenchman, asking about the food at this restaurant."

Beth paused. "The cube."

"Yes," Mark said simply.

"But, how do we know there are not more watching?" Beth asked, anxiously looking around. "I couldn't stand losing you again."

"Don't worry," Mark said consolingly. "He was the only one. I can sense everyone around us and no one is paying any attention to us, not even the waiter," Mark said with a laugh.

"You are sure? Absolutely sure?"

"Absolutely."

"The cube is that powerful?"

"Now that I know how to use it, yes," Mark said. "I have spent the last several months delving into it and have tested it several times."

"Tested it?"

"Yes. I flew down to a small town and interacted with the locals using the cube. As I got better, I moved up into larger towns and then cities. When I could survive Tokyo, I figured I was ready."

"Survived?"

"Ok. Bad choice of words," Mark conceded. "I meant handled. You wouldn't believe how noisy everything is."

Beth glanced at the traffic going by.

"No, I mean in here," Mark said, pointing to his head.

"So you are telepathic? You can read everyone's mind?" Beth asked.

"Basically, yes. Although there are several levels."

"And you can control them," Beth said, rather than asked.

"Yes."

"And they don't know it at all?"

"Correct."

"Are you controlling me?"

"I told you long ago, I would never touch your mind with the cube. Not without permission," Mark said.

"But how would I know if you did," Beth asked.

"When I start winning our arguments," Mark said with a smile.

Beth laughed, the growing tension gone.

"What do we do now?" Beth asked.

"First, we order dinner," Mark said, and as if on cue the waiter came to their table. After they ordered, Mark turned to Beth. "You still have more questions."

"How do you know?"

"I don't need the cube to know," Mark said. "Over twenty years of marriage tells me that."

Beth smiled. "You don't seem different. Not much. A bit more preoccupied, perhaps."

"That is the cube," Mark said. "As we sit here, I can hear the thoughts of everyone around us, including those people walking down the sidewalk," Mark said while pointing to a couple across the intersection pushing a stroller away from them. "The hardest part is filtering it. Each person has several levels of consciousness with all sorts of conflicting thoughts and emotions. It took me a long time just dealing with one person. Multiply that by tens or hundreds and it is like standing in front of a rock band and trying to pick out one little melody. I finally figured out how to filter it, which is good because otherwise I would have gone crazy. Right now I'm just scanning over the top of everyone, making sure that no one is paying any attention to us. If someone does, like George there," Mark said, pointing back to the empty table where the watcher had been. "Then I delve deeper. In George's case, I convinced him there was no need to watch any longer. You are dining alone. He has his cellphone picture to back it up."

Beth sipped her champagne as she considered what Mark had said.

"Then you can come back here and stay," She finally said.

Mark hesitated. "I can visit. And you can visit me on the mothership. And we can travel. But I cannot stay."

"Why not?"

"Several reasons. First, what I am doing now takes a lot of energy. It is exhausting. I have to go back to the mothership where I am alone, so I can drop all my defenses and rest."

"But maybe with time you could stay longer," Beth said. "Like exercise. The more you do it the longer you can do it."

"That is true," Mark agreed. "And I can already spend longer than I could. That is what took me so long to come here in the first place, I had to work up to it."

"But," Beth said. "There is a but."

"Yes, there is. I can only sense and control those around us. If the NSA, or anyone else for that matter, ever figures out I am back…"

"Then you could control them, like you did George," Beth interjected.

"Once they know I am back and figure out my power," Mark continued, "they would take me out from a distance. I can't stop a sniper. I can't stop a drone attack. If they are far enough away, I am helpless."

"But you controlled so many people in the China sea, and they were not close to you," Beth objected.

"I controlled them because I controlled everyone around me, controlled them and channeled them and leapfrogged to the Captains. Nearly killed me too."

"But couldn't you do that again?"

"I could. But that is why I had to leave," Mark said. "The danger of me controlling everyone is too great. I would become the ultimate dictator. And then what would I do? I have already killed over a hundred people while escaping from China."

"People who were trying to kill you," Beth said.

"People who were following orders. Fathers, husbands, who knew nothing about what was going on, only that terrorists were attacking their countrymen. And I was that terrorist. And they died. How many more deaths could I justify? Just read the news. There are several areas where I would love to go and take out the terrorists. But who am I to play God? Who am I to decide? And even if I did all this, set up a utopian society. Which I don't think I could do. But even if I did, what would happen when I'm gone? It would all fall apart. And the fall would be greater than what I created. History is full of those examples. And what if someone else got control of the cube? Can you imagine Hitler with the cube? Stalin? Name anyone. No. I have to stay away. Mankind is not ready for the cube technology."

"What about us?" Beth asked.

"There will always be us," Mark said.

"We will visit, often. We will travel, anywhere we want."

"The kids?"

"We will visit them, too. We will always be on holiday."

"But then you will have to rest," Beth said. "And when you do, I will be here alone."

"We can always rest at my place," Mark said.

"Your place?"

"The mothership. There is plenty of room, and the view is pretty good."

"What is the view?" Beth asked.

"Right now? The dark side of the moon," Mark answered. "But you should see the rings of Saturn this time of year."

Beth sipped her champagne. Slowly a smile spread across her face. "You always said you wanted a motorhome when you retired."

Mark chuckled. "The ultimate Winnebago. We can go wherever we want."

"Our second honeymoon," Beth said, holding up her champagne glass.

"Our second honeymoon," Mark agreed, tapping her glass with his.

## THE END

Made in the USA
Charleston, SC
19 July 2015